Holiday Romance

ALSO BY CATHERINE WALSH

Snowed In
One Night Only
The Rebound
The Matchmaker

CATHERINE WALSH

Holiday Romance

FOREVER

New York Boston

This book is a work of fiction. Names, characters, places, and incidents are the product of the author's imagination or are used fictitiously. Any resemblance to actual events, locales, or persons, living or dead, is coincidental.

Copyright © 2022 by Catherine Walsh

Cover design by Beth Free, Studio Nic&Lou. Cover illustrations by Shutterstock. Cover copyright © 2025 by Hachette Book Group, Inc.

Hachette Book Group supports the right to free expression and the value of copyright. The purpose of copyright is to encourage writers and artists to produce the creative works that enrich our culture.

The scanning, uploading, and distribution of this book without permission is a theft of the author's intellectual property. If you would like permission to use material from the book (other than for review purposes), please contact permissions@hbgusa.com. Thank you for your support of the author's rights.

Forever
Hachette Book Group
1290 Avenue of the Americas, New York, NY 10104
read-forever.com
@readforeverpub

Originally published in 2022 by Bookouture, an imprint of StoryFire Ltd.

First Forever Edition: October 2025

Forever is an imprint of Grand Central Publishing. The Forever name and logo are registered trademarks of Hachette Book Group, Inc.

The publisher is not responsible for websites (or their content) that are not owned by the publisher.

The Hachette Speakers Bureau provides a wide range of authors for speaking events. To find out more, go to hachettespeakersbureau.com or email HachetteSpeakers@hbgusa.com.

Forever books may be purchased in bulk for business, educational, or promotional use. For information, please contact your local bookseller or the Hachette Book Group Special Markets Department at special.markets@hbgusa.com.

LCCN: 2025939258

ISBN: 9781538772546 (trade paperback)

Printed in the United States of America

LSC-C

Printing 1, 2025

This one's for Áine

Holiday Romance

PROLOGUE
CHRISTMAS EVE, NINE YEARS AGO

Chicago

"Are you sure?"

The sales assistant doesn't even try to hide her frown as she follows my pointing finger to the bottom shelf behind her. There, nestled among the daintier and more expensive perfumes, sits a squat green vial that looks like it was left there by mistake.

"It's calling to me," I say.

The woman, Martha, according to her name tag, hesitates, but when I just smile, she sighs, her snowflake earrings sparkling as she bends down to grab it. "I think the Armani would be a better choice," she says as I push up my sleeve. We've already doused my other arm in five different perfumes and I'm running out of unscented skin. "There's twenty percent off."

"That one was too nice," I say, holding out my wrist. She sprays it dutifully and I lean down to sniff, wrinkling my nose at the faux apple scent. Sickly sweet with a strong chemical undertone. My sister will hate it.

Which means it's perfect.

"I'll take it."

Martha coughs as the fumes reach her. "If you're worried about budget, we have plenty of cheaper options."

"I'm not," I assure her. "This is the one. Really."

She opens her mouth to protest as the next song starts to play over the speakers, something about sleighbells and reindeer and a jolly good time. A visible shudder runs through her, and I wince in sympathy. I can only imagine how many times she's had to listen to it.

"Do they ever switch up the playlist in here?"

"That would be a no." Her eyes flick to the perfume and then to the line of people forming behind me. I see the exact moment she labels me a lost cause. "Gift wrapped?"

"Please."

She hides the bottle in a mound of tissue paper as though it personally offends her and I mentally cross the final item off my to-do list. With Zoe's present sorted, I am officially done and heading home for the holidays. Or, more realistically, for a week in December. My family has never been big into Christmas, but everyone expects me to go back and so back I go. At least it means I get to be the favorite child for a few days. Moving to the States for college grants me a certain air of novelty whenever I return, which basically means no chores. Zoe was livid last year when she had to do the dishes three nights in a row. Mam insisted I was too jet-lagged and, honestly, what kind of daughter would I be to argue with my own mother?

"Are you *sure*?" Martha asks, dropping her customer service smile as she clutches the plastic bag.

I hand over the cash, trying not to laugh at her reluctance. "Positive."

I step away just as my phone begins to ring, my good mood plummeting when Hayley's name flashes up on the screen. For one wild moment, I think about not answering it. I wish I'd carried through with that impulse as soon as I do.

"I need a favor."

I turn, fighting my way through the crowded duty-free of O'Hare airport as her voice sounds in my ear. Hayley was the first friend I made at Northwestern. She lived three rooms down from me in our first year and I'd latched on to her in the way any newbie does when they're searching for a friendly face. And while the first few months didn't raise any red flags, the more I threw myself into my new life, the more I realized that there were other, much nicer people I could spend my time with. People who I had more in common with than the girl I always had to buy coffee for because she left her wallet in her other purse. She'd stuck around, though, clinging to me in a way I found both confusing and flattering even though it was clear our friendship was hard work.

Zoe always said I was a pushover, but it's not like they teach you this stuff in school. I'd been given lots of colorful leaflets about making friends on my first day. Not a whole lot about dumping them.

"I'm kind of busy right now," I say. "I'm at the airport, remember?"

"It's a really urgent favor."

"I doubt that." I try not to sound as grumpy as I feel. "But what's up?"

There's a loud smack of gum as she answers. "Can I borrow your blue dress for a thing tonight? The one with the back straps?"

"I packed that one."

"What about the green one that makes you look like you have breasts?"

"I have breasts," I huff. The girls just need a little accentuation help sometimes. "Anyway, Andrew's not going to care what you're wearing."

"Andrew?"

"Your boyfriend," I remind her, wincing at the thought of her getting it on in my clothes. They've been together for a few months and I've barely seen him without her tongue down his throat. I chatted with him the first time we met, both of us pleased to find another Irish person so far from home, but I don't think Hayley liked the thought of us bonding and she's made a point of keeping us apart ever since. To be honest, I'm starting to think she doesn't like anyone in her life doing something that isn't solely with her. But now that jealous streak is nowhere to be found as she hums down the line.

"What?" I ask, knowing it's exactly what she wants me to do.

"I'm thinking about breaking up with him." She says the words casually like he's an old pair of shoes she's considering throwing out.

"Since when? I thought you liked him?"

"I did." A pause. "He makes a lot of jokes."

I roll my eyes as I start walking again, weaving through the other travelers.

"But I couldn't dump him right before the holidays," she continues. "I'm not a monster."

"No, you're right. Cold, dark January will be much better." Poor guy. He seemed perfectly fine the few times we've talked. Or maybe it's loyalty to a fellow countryman that's making me feel so bad. "Where are you going tonight?"

"Dinner with Rob." She's barely able to hide her glee. "We hooked up last night after he—"

"What?"

"Billy's friend."

"No, I know who Rob is," I say, picturing the muscly frat boy who's been slobbering over her. "What do you mean you hooked up?"

"We went back to his place after Kendra's thing and, Molly, you would not *believe* what he can do with his—"

"So, you ended things with Andrew?" I interrupt, confused.

"I said I'm thinking about that."

. . . Yeah, I need new friends. "You cheated on him?"

"It's not cheating if I'm going to break up with him."

"Yes, it is!"

"Oh my *God*," she groans. "This is not a big deal."

"You need to break up with him if you're seeing someone else, Hayley. It's cruel."

"All right," she huffs. "Fine. I'll do it now."

"No, not *now*. Wait until classes start back."

"But you just said—"

"I know what I said." I tug my suitcase closer to my body as I step onto one of the automatic walkways, catching my reflection in the mirrored wall opposite and schooling the heavy scowl I find there into something more public-friendly. Maybe she was right the first time; who wants to get dumped on Christmas Eve? "How about you don't see Rob from now until you do?"

"But I'm seeing him tonight," she says, like I'm an idiot. "Look, if it's such a big deal to you, I'll message Andrew."

"Hayley, you can't!" I snap, freaking out at the thought of her breaking up with him over text. I don't even know the guy that well, but there's such a thing as common decency.

There's silence on the other end of the line and I think she's finally realized how shitty that would be when she snorts. "Okay, *Mom*."

"Hayley—"

"I've got to go." Her tone changes to one of supreme boredom. "I'll see you when you get back."

"I gave you a key to water my plants, not to borrow my dress so you can cheat on—"

"*Bye!*" she calls down the line and immediately hangs up.

I stumble off the walkway, staring at my phone in outrage. I need new friends. That can be my New Year's resolution. New friends. New, non-terrible friends.

I'm in such a mood after the call that it takes me another five minutes before I realize I've gone in the wrong direction, and by the time I make it to my gate, sweaty and flustered, they're halfway through boarding.

It's a small plane. Two seats on either side and two in the middle, each one packed tight together. Progress down it is frustratingly slow as people hobble along, stuffing bags into overhead compartments and fumbling with heavy winter coats.

I match the shuffling steps of the person in front of me, concentrating so hard on not banging my suitcase on anyone's elbow that it's only when I stop by my row and relax my aching fingers that I glance at the seat next to mine. I like to think I have acceptable standards for traveling. All I want and expect is someone who keeps their shoes on and doesn't steal my food when I go to the restroom. Just a polite, normal stranger who I can ignore for seven hours while I try and get some sleep. So you can imagine my horror when, instead of greeting some unknown frequent flyer, I stare straight into the eyes of Hayley's soon-to-be ex-boyfriend.

Andrew Fitzpatrick looks just as surprised to see me as I am to see him. But instead of the sinking, *you've got to be kidding me* feeling I'm experiencing, he just smiles. It's the kind of smile that Hayley gushed over after their first date. A freaking white-teeth, dimpled, make-you-feel-all-warm-inside smile. And he directs the full force of it right at me.

Crap.

"Molly?"

Crap crap crap.

"Hello!" I chime a little too loudly. Indoor voice, Moll. Or plane voice or whatever.

"Is this you?" He points to the seat next to him and I glance around for another miraculous one to appear. Of course, it doesn't. This flight was booked out days ago. He knows it too, not even waiting for me to respond as he stands, slipping into the aisle. "That's crazy," he continues. "And you've bagged the window seat."

A.k.a. the trapped seat.

I store my suitcase overhead before I do that awkward shuffle past him. Seven hours. I'm going to have to lie for the next seven hours. Seven hours and thirty minutes by the time we take off and land. Maybe I could pretend to be asleep. Maybe I could—

"How's college going?" Andrew drops into the seat next to me as I shove the duty-free bag under the chair in front. He immediately puts his seat belt on, even though people are still boarding the plane. "You're studying business, right?"

Small talk. I don't usually mind small talk. But in these kinds of situations, small talk tends to lead to big talk. "Economics."

He lets out a low whistle. "That sounds even fancier. You're going to be an economist?"

"A lawyer. I think."

"You think?"

"I've got the grades."

He looks at me like I've said something funny. "But do you want to be a lawyer?" he asks when I don't say anything more.

"I haven't decided yet." The words come out more defensive than I mean them to and a moment of silence descends just long enough to make me feel rude. "And what about you?" I ask. "How's your... thing?"

His lips twitch at my hesitation. "Photography. It's going well. Hayley might have told you already, but I'm applying for internships next summer to see if I can stay in Chicago. Might not be the smartest decision seeing as how everything's unpaid. Like *aggressively* unpaid. But I'm crashing with my uncle until he gets sick of me. Free board for a few months if I do the graveyard shifts at his store." Andrew leans my way as a flight attendant slams our overhead compartment shut. "Does it smell like cotton candy to you?"

Great. "That's me. Sorry." I sniff my right arm to make sure. "I was picking out a perfume," I explain as his expression brightens.

"Really? Maybe you can help. I wanted to get Hayley something as a surprise. She didn't want to do Christmas presents but technically it will be January when I see her so... What?"

"Nothing." I smile, tugging out the inflight magazine from its little seat pocket. Why did she tell me about Rob? Why? Why why why why—

"I was thinking this one."

I watch as he opens his own copy and flicks to the gift page, pointing to a small Chanel bottle.

"It says it's a classic," he says, peering at the tiny text beside the picture. "Eighty-nine dollars. What do you think?"

I think I'm going to kill Hayley.

Eighty-nine dollars. Someone doing graveyard shifts for his uncle and sitting coach on a budget Irish flight does not have eighty-nine dollars to spend on a girl who's going to dump him in a week.

"You can't buy her something on a plane," I say as he takes out his wallet. "You should buy it from somewhere special."

"I won't tell her if you won't."

"And that seems like a lot of money."

He reaches for the call button. "I've saved for it."

"But—"

"Excuse me? Mr. Fitzpatrick?" We both turn as another flight attendant approaches us from behind, a teasing look on her face. "Your brother called ahead," she says, and a look of utter confusion crosses Andrew's face.

"A chorus of 'Happy Birthday' was mentioned," she continues, handing him a small square envelope. "But would you settle for a free drink on us?"

"Gladly," he says, sounding relieved as his eyes slide to mine. "Can we make it two?"

"Of course," she says. "What can I get you?"

"Oh..." I glance at Andrew, who just waits. "White wine?"

"I'll have the same," Andrew says, showing her the magazine. "And can I get—"

"We'll begin our boutique shopping as soon as we're in the air," she interrupts with a bright smile. "Seat belt," she adds to me.

I buckle up as requested, waiting for her to disappear

behind the curtain. As if this day could get any worse. "It's your birthday?"

To my surprise, he bursts out laughing. "No. This is my brother's idea of a joke. Christian's just hoping to embarrass me." His smile falters as he glances back at me. "Hey, are you okay? You've gone white as a ghost."

"It's the lighting," I lie. Okay. At least she's not cheating on him on his birthday.

Oh my *God*, that should not be my baseline!

"I knew he'd try something like this," Andrew continues as I try to calm down. "You got any siblings?"

"Just one. My sister."

"Older or younger?"

"Older. By about three minutes."

His brow furrows before he gets it. "You're a twin?"

"An identical one."

"Seriously?"

I nod, fighting back a wince at his enthusiasm.

"Wow, that's . . ."

And here we go.

"Completely normal and unimpressive," he continues, smiling when my eyes slide back to him. "You must be sick of people going nuts when you tell them."

"Just a little," I admit.

"Sorry."

"No, I get it. It's when they start asking if we feel each other's pain that I lose the will to live."

He laughs and I relax a bit. "There are four of us," he says. "Liam's the eldest. Then me, then Christian. And now Hannah, who's six."

"Six?"

"She was a welcome surprise." He slides his finger under

the lip of the envelope, smirking when he opens the card to reveal nothing but a crudely drawn middle finger. "Classy. You get on with your sister?"

"Yeah. For the most part."

"I bet it's hard to be so far away from her."

"I never really thought about it," I say honestly. "I mean, we text all the time so..."

"Still," he prompts. "It will be nice to be together at Christmas."

"Sure."

"Sure?" He smiles again. Big smiler this one.

"We're not really Christmas people," I explain.

He gives me a skeptical look. "You're literally flying home on Christmas Eve."

"Coincidence. I work part-time at a shoe store and was going to work over the holidays, but my boss didn't have the hours and Zoe wanted me to bring stuff over so..." I trail off as he stares at me. "Here I am."

"You're breaking my heart here, Molly."

"It's not like I'm a Scrooge!" I say. "I'm just not really into all the—"

"Love?" he supplies. "Comfort and joy?"

"Toys. Money. The same twelve songs played over and over again."

"Ah, the commercialization argument."

I frown at how quickly he dismisses it. "Unless you're doing it for the kids, Christmas is nothing but several weeks of expensive stress that will inevitably end in disappointment. How can anything live up to that kind of expectation?"

"Wow. So, you're like a grinch?"

"I'm not a—"

"A real-life grinch."

"I'm practical."

"I'm getting that," he says, looking like he's enjoying himself. "But it also sounds like you're doing Christmas wrong."

"It's not the same for you. You just said it yourself, there's a child in your family. That's different."

"Child or no child, you're never too old to hole yourself up in the house for a few days and eat until you puke. Not to mention the fashion." He gestures at his sweater and it's the first time I notice the cheery reindeer embroidered on the front.

"Reindeer don't wave," I tell him.

"Rudolph does. Rudolph loves to wave."

I snort. "I get it now."

"You do?"

"Mm-hmm. You're from one of *those* families."

He only looks amused at my suspicion. "Those families?"

"The ones in the commercials. Matching pajamas. Roaring fire."

"Unashamedly. I'm going to guess you're not?"

"Like I said, not big Christmas people." I frown when he continues to watch me, a new glint in his eye that immediately puts me on edge. "What?"

"Nothing. Just thinking about what I can do to make you a fan of the most wonderful time of the year."

"How about not saying things like that for a start?"

He grins. "I'm going to change your mind about this."

"Confident thing, aren't you?"

"Of course I am. So confident that I bet you I will change your grinch-like mind by the end of this flight."

"An actual bet?" I press my lips together, fighting back a smile. "How much are we talking?"

"One million—"

"*One* dollar," I say, lifting a finger. "And you should know that I'm extremely competitive."

"And you should know that I may look innocent, but I'm not above playing dirty."

"Innocent, huh?"

He gestures vaguely to his face. "I've got the whole boyish thing going on. I know my strengths."

I laugh at that, and he brandishes the fake birthday card between us. "Now," he says. "Do you want to see how much free stuff we can get out of this or what?"

His phone vibrates on his lap before I can respond, making me jump. Sometime during the last few minutes, we've both turned completely toward each other, and my stomach drops like we just hit turbulence when I see who's calling. I'd somehow forgotten all about Hayley as we talked, but now she screams her way back to the front of my mind as Andrew brings the phone to his ear, not noticing my panic.

"It's Hayley," he says as my pulse starts to race. "She's been studying so much; I didn't even get to see her before I left." He turns to the front, smiling broadly. "Hey, babe! You'll never guess who—"

I snatch the phone from his hand before I can think, pressing the button to end the call.

Silence. Awkward, awkward silence for the longest second as Andrew just stares at me. And then: "What the f—"

"You shouldn't answer your phone when we're flying."

"We haven't started moving yet," he says slowly. "The doors are still open."

"It can still affect the system."

His mouth opens and closes, all traces of joking vanished. "Can I have my phone back?" he asks eventually.

I think about saying no. About saving him from what I know is about to happen even at the expense of me acting like a weirdo. He's a nice guy. A nice, festive guy and if this has to happen, I don't want it to happen when he's just spent ten minutes harping on about Christmas. But the unimpressed look on his face tells me he's about to call for security and I would really, *really* like to not get arrested.

"Right. Sorry." I hand it back to him. "I'm a nervous flyer."

"... Okay?" He turns away from me as much as he can in the small space, but I don't let up.

"So that bet, huh? You were going to convince me?"

"Look," he begins, but the phone buzzes again and we both look down to see a message flash up on his screen. I think I'm about to be sick.

Not by text.

Not on Christmas Eve.

She wouldn't.

Beside me, Andrew goes very, very still.

She would.

"White wine?" The oblivious flight attendant reappears beside him, two plastic cups in her hands. "We aren't supposed to open the bar until after takeoff, but—"

"Yes!" I exclaim, half standing as I startle the poor woman. "Yes, please."

Andrew doesn't move as I take the drinks and neither does our new friend, who looks a bit too pleased with herself.

"I know we said we'd let you off easy," she says as he stares down at the text. "But seeing as it's our last flight before Christmas, we couldn't ignore the opportunity to embarrass our passengers."

I glance behind her as two other attendants make their way toward us. Oh no. "I don't think—"

"*Happy Birthday...*"

Oh *no*.

A deep pink flush spreads upward from Andrew's neck

as the cabin crew and then the majority of passengers take up the song.

"Happy Birthday, dear Andrew..."

As they do their rowdy best with the octave leap, Andrew slowly raises his head to look at me.

"Happy Birthday," I say with a weak smile, and down my cup in one gulp.

CHAPTER ONE
DECEMBER 21, NOW

Chicago

I took a quiz the other day. One of those "what should you do with your life, you indecisive idiot" ones. Each question was meaningless (pick a color, choose a salad dressing) and interspersed with memes of celebrities I don't recognize anymore. At the end of it, I was told to become a kindergarten teacher. I didn't like that, so I took it again. It told me to go to medical school. As if that was a thing I could just rock up to one evening.

I've decided to quit my job, you see. No, I've decided to quit my *career*. Three years of law school, four years of law, and five weeks ago, I sat at my desk several hours after I was supposed to have gone home, closed one document, opened another, and realized that not only was I completely miserable, but I had been for a while.

It was like the shower in my first apartment, warm and normal one second, icy cold splinters the next. Don't get me wrong, it was a relief to finally acknowledge it, but ignorance is bliss, and when my next stage of enlightenment didn't come, when I didn't suddenly realize my passion for salsa dancing or my hidden dream to become an accountant, all I was left with was this sick, twisted feeling in my stomach while two little words echoed in my mind, over and over and over again.

Now what?

I still don't have the answer.

When most people decide to change their lives, they usually know what they want to change them *to*. They take over a crumbling chalet in the south of France, they retrain as a social worker, they sell all their belongings and become a nun.

They tend not to talk about things like rent and student loans and health insurance. There's never a four-part YouTube video about all the things I'll still somehow have to pay for. Never a three-thousand-word blog on how to start again in a realistic, not-completely-abandoning-my-old-life way.

"Molly."

Maybe I'll start playing the lottery.

"*Molly.*"

Or I could get a cat.

"Hey!"

I look up at the rapid knocking on the wall to see my friend Gabriela standing in the doorway.

"Didn't you need to leave ten minutes ago?" she asks. "I thought you were done."

"I am done."

I am not done. I am never done.

"It's fine." I turn back to my laptop and the contract within it, blinking as the words swim before me. "I've got a forty-minute window for delays."

"Of course you do." She steps fully into the room, her arms crossed over her chest. You wouldn't know from the look of her that she started work at seven a.m. this morning. Her navy dress is still wrinkle-free, her makeup fresh, her dark curls pulled back into a low ponytail, showing off her heart-shaped face. One of those curls bounces free as she comes closer, peering at the piles of paper before me. "Is it the Freeman contract?"

"Is it ever not the Freeman contract?" I mutter. "Or do we just have one client now?" Because that's what it feels like. It's all I've been working on for the past few weeks. Or maybe it's years. At this stage, I really can't remember. Back and forth on the sale of a company that should have been agreed on months ago. "It's like I'm being paid to waste everyone's time."

"So long as you get paid," she murmurs, dragging one of the folders toward her.

Gabriela also did three years of law school. Three years of law school and five years of law. She showed me around on my first day at Harman & Nord and their swanky skyscraper office on LaSalle Street. The same one we're in right now. Gabriela doesn't want to quit her job. Gabriela, like the rest of our small circle of friends, loves her job and doesn't mind the pressure or the late hours or the ruthlessness that I'm understanding more and more I simply don't possess.

"It's fine," I repeat as she starts to read. "Honestly, I've..." I trail off as she looks at me. "... been reading the same page for the last hour," I admit.

"You need a vacation."

"I'm going on one."

"No, you're going home," she says pointedly. "Home is not a vacation. Especially not during the holidays. Especially not when you hate the holidays."

"I don't hate the holidays," I grumble, snatching my folder back. "I just don't go around with reindeer antlers on my head. There's a middle ground."

"You should just stay here next year."

"I can't," I say, rubbing my tired eyes for exactly two

seconds before I remember I have mascara on. "I have to go back."

"You go back all the time. Make your folks come here. Give them the tour, let them see how impressive you are." She tilts her head, smiling prettily at me. "We can go for dinner and you can tell them how wonderful a mentor I am."

"Is that what you are?"

"Parents love me. I'm very polite."

"You're a suck-up; there's a difference." I close my laptop and start stacking my stacks into one giant stack, but Gabriela just stays where she is, watching me with a thoughtful expression. "What?" I ask.

"Nothing." She runs a finger across the dark wood of the desk before her eyes drop to my stomach. "Are you pregnant?"

"*What?*"

"You can tell me if you are."

"No!"

"No, you're not pregnant or no, you're not going to tell me if you are?"

"Both," I snap.

"Okay."

"I'm not even seeing anyone."

"*Okay.*" Her voice lowers to a whisper. "But is that the problem? Do you need some sex? We can get you some sex."

"Oh my God." I shove my laptop bag at her and gather my papers. "Stop talking. We're no longer friends."

"It's just you've been so distracted lately," she says, hurrying to keep up with me as I stride out of the room. "And I want you to know that if something's going on, you can talk to me. I'm a great listener. A lot of people confide in me."

"Who confides in you?"

"Michael."

"Michael's your husband; he has to confide in you."

"Yes, but I'm also great at it. And as two gals at the boys' club, we need to stick together."

"Two gals at . . . You've been listening to those podcasts again, haven't you?"

"Women supporting women," she insists. "That means we have to talk to each other."

"Not about my womb though, Gab."

We head back to the other side of the floor, down the long corridor lined on either side with glass-walled meeting rooms. For a lawyers' office, we have ironically little privacy. I've always hated it. Especially in my more anxious moments when I feel like I'm in a fishbowl. Like there are eyes on me all the time, waiting for me to slip up. Even now, the floor is busy, most people having already gone out for dinner and come back to work well into the night.

"Have you slept with anyone since Brandon?" Gabriela asks, still clutching my laptop bag as we reach my desk.

"Why does it matter?" I groan, wincing at the mention of my ex. "When's the last time you had sex?"

"This morning."

"That's . . . I didn't need to know that."

"Then why did you ask?"

"Because you—" I exhale sharply, pulling out the folders I need before tugging my coat on. "It's not about that."

"But you admit it's about something."

"I do," I say, placing the documents inside the bag. "But it's nothing serious and I'm fine. Or as fine as I can be after the week I've had." And the weeks I'm about to have. I take out the small suitcase I'd shoved under my desk, thinking about all the work I still have to do. It's not that I never talk to Gabriela about this kind of stuff, but I know she wouldn't understand. Both her parents are lawyers. Her brother is a lawyer, and her grandfather was a lawyer. All her friends are lawyers. It will never have occurred to her to do anything else. It will never have occurred to her that there *is* anything else and I know she'll try to talk me out of whatever this is I'm feeling and, to be honest, she's better at her job than me. She'll win.

"I just want you to know that I'm here," she continues. "And that I am ready to actively listen should you want someone to do so."

Amusement overtakes annoyance at her earnestness. "I know," I say, taking the bag from her and slinging it over my shoulder. "And I appreciate it. You know I do. But I'm fine."

"I just want to help."

"You can help me find my coat."

"You're wearing your coat."

Yes, I am.

"Okay, maybe I'm a *little* distracted." I check the time as I yank my blond hair back into a ponytail. Thirty-minute window for delays. "Don't move." I pull out a white cardboard box from my bottom drawer, grinning when Gabriela gasps in delight.

"I thought we weren't doing presents this year! You said you were going to go to that beginners' samba class with me and not make fun."

"I'll still do that," I promise. Gabriela and I usually trade each other small things for the holidays; favors or strictly budgeted gifts. Two weeks ago, she helped move my new mattress up three flights of stairs. Something that, for two not-so-tall girls, is a lot harder than it sounds. "This is for you and Michael," I explain. "Espresso brownies from that bakery in Little Italy." I pry open the box, presenting the neatly sliced squares of goodness. "Remember I brought them to your birthday party and you ate six?"

"I don't because I'm pretty sure I had a bottle of

champagne alongside them." She reaches for the one closest to her, groaning when she bites into it.

"Put them in an airtight container when you get home," I tell her as she takes the box from me. "And keep them at room temperature. They're best with a bit of cream. And maybe some powdered sugar. Or a little bit of—"

"I love that you think these babies are making it home," she interrupts, licking the crumbs from her lips. "You should have been a chef."

"I don't make food. I eat food."

"None of the work and all of the reward. I respect that." She shoves half the brownie into her mouth, holding up a finger. "*Waif ere*," she says around the slice, which I take to mean "Wait here," and I watch curiously as she opens a drawer in her own desk opposite mine, pulling out a Chicago Cubs teddy bear.

"It's for the baby," she says. "So your sister can raise her child right."

"Gab! You didn't have to do that."

"I know, but I'm nice." She lingers as I tuck it into my suitcase, fitting it in beside all the other food and the few pieces of clothing I'm bringing home with me. "How is that all you're taking?"

"It's just for a few days."

"Yeah, but it's Christmas," she protests. "What about presents?"

"I give most people money as a present. They expect it and they want it."

"That doesn't seem very Christmassy."

"And yet I remain everyone's favorite relative." I straighten, mentally going over the most important things. Clothes, wallet, tickets. Keys, passport, phone.

"You good?" Gabriela asks when I finally look at her.

I nod. "And if I'm not, it's too late. I'll be on my phone if you need me. And I'll be online from tomorrow. And—"

"*Goodbye*, Molly," she says, pushing me out the door.

"Bye," I say automatically. "Happy Christmas, I guess."

"It's good that you sound so miserable when you say that. Really gets me in the festive spirit."

She waits with me until the elevator comes, waving cheerfully as she eats the other half of her brownie. It takes an age to get down, stopping at every other floor before we hit the lobby. Outside, the surrounding skyscrapers tower above me, the streets full of people heading to restaurants and bars and clubs. At least at this time of day, it doesn't take long to catch a cab, and in no time at all I'm speeding west across the city, aiming for the interstate.

The snow falls thickly around us, gathering in a way I'm still not entirely used to even though I've lived here for years. I was still a teenager when I arrived and thought myself incredibly grown-up even though I was scared shitless. I spent that entire flight wondering if I was making a giant, expensive mistake, but any doubts I had vanished as soon as I stepped off the plane. I knew as soon as I did that Chicago was my city. And I was lucky that it was. There's no predicting it sometimes, what calls to you and what doesn't. But in the same way house-hunters can walk through a front door and know instantly whether or not the four walls are for them, I knew as I settled into my life here all those years ago that this was where I belonged.

It's a gut instinct. A feeling.

Or maybe it was fate.

My parents assumed that after college I would move back to Dublin, but it never even occurred to me, the excuses rolling off my tongue whenever they asked. Summers were spent with friends and boyfriends. College was followed by law school. Law school by work. And alongside it all was a life I built from scratch. An apartment to call my own, friends I adore, and a city I now know like the back of my hand. I love the parks and the festivals and the beaches. I love the architecture and the people and how easy it is to get around. I love how I have some of the best food in the world right outside my front door. And I love that it's all mine.

Even now I think my family still expects me to return to Ireland. But how can I? This is my home now. And I can't imagine being anywhere else.

So I've been thinking…

My sister's text comes through as we near the airport, followed by a series of emojis that she likes to punctuate every message with.

Oh no.

Instead of you coming here for Christmas why don't the two of us bail and get the first flight to some Greek island?

I don't think they'll allow you on a plane this far along.

I'll wear a very big coat. They'll never know.

Zoe is eight months pregnant and due in early January. I think my parents are even more excited than she is about it and recently made her move back into their house so they could fuss over her.

A couple of carolers came to the door earlier, she continues now. *Dad tried to be funny and requested Hotel California. Mam gave them some leftover packets of M&Ms like it was Halloween.*

And people wonder where I get it from. I can already picture how the next few days are going to go. The big family reunions (yes, it's hard work, no, I'm not married yet) and the smaller dinners at home where the four of us awkwardly carry out our strange version of Christmas. Mam will go to bed early and Zoe will slip out to meet a friend and Dad will corner me in the living room and ask the same gruff but well-meaning questions about my retirement plan and the insulation in my apartment building and whether or not I took his advice about investing in a good toolbox, because he doesn't really know how to talk to me anymore but still wants to try. Every year it's like the four of us are halfheartedly acting out something we saw on television, and more and more I wonder why we bother to pretend at all.

My phone buzzes as a photograph comes through of my very small, very single childhood bed, made up with blankets that I'm pretty sure my parents had since before I was born.

#Glamour, Zoe writes underneath, and I sigh, mentally apologizing to my poor back muscles. I'll need to book a massage as soon as I get back here.

Traffic slows as we near the airport, but at this time of year, I suppose I should be grateful we get there at all, and I tip the driver as I get out, checking in my suitcase and keeping my laptop bag on me. By the time I make it through security, I have zero time for delays and head straight to duty-free like a woman on a mission.

"Excuse me," I ask, stopping the nearest worker with a lanyard around their neck. "What's the worst-selling perfume you have?"

Five minutes later I leave smelling like an obnoxious concoction of pop-star-branded scents, with one sparkling pink bottle swinging from the bag on my wrist.

Eventually, I get to my gate, weaving through tired, disgruntled families and solo adults staring into space until I spy a dark-haired man sitting hunched over a *National Geographic*. I can't see his face, but I can picture his creased brow as he reads, the way he mouths every other word even though he swears he doesn't.

For a moment, I just watch him, and then I take a step and then another and another, and with each one, I feel the world outside slowly slip away. No more worries, no more planning, no work, no nothing. I'll have to deal with it all when I get back. Hell, I'll probably have to deal with it when I land. But not right now. It's the one time of year when I put my work second.

I'm smiling when I reach him and don't hesitate as I reach forward to pluck the magazine from his hands.

"Excuse me, sir," I say as he rears back, startled. "I think you're in my seat?"

Andrew Fitzpatrick's shocked look disappears as soon as he sees me. He grins up at me with those hazel eyes as if I'm the best thing that's happened to his day. I know he's the best thing that's happened to mine.

"Hey, stranger," he says, leaning back against the chair. "Fancy seeing you here."

CHAPTER TWO
EIGHT YEARS AGO

Flight Two, Chicago

Just don't meet his eye. Don't meet his eye and don't even look his way. Look down! Look down at your phone and pretend to be busy like the coward you are. Look down look down look down.

I look up, watching Andrew joke with a flight attendant as he makes his way slowly toward me.

He's shaved off all his hair and it doesn't suit him. I would say I barely recognize him, except for the fact that I definitely do. I'd know that face anywhere. I've thought about it enough these past few months, putting our flight last year right up there with the time I called my teacher Mam, or when I forgot to lock the restroom door on a train and a poor woman saw a lot more of me than either of us would have liked.

That is to say, it was embarrassing as hell and I've replayed the moment I snatched the phone from his hand at least once a week. After the Hayley incident, we didn't say another word to each other and, when we landed, he vanished up the aisle before they'd even opened the doors. The last time I saw him was in baggage claim at the Dublin airport, where he was yelling down the phone at someone. One guess as to whom.

Hayley, I only hung out with once more, at some random guy's party she dragged me to a week after I got back. I called her out on what happened and she laughed it off, but she stopped texting me soon after and I let her. I made new friends, I settled in, I moved on.

But now? *Now??*

I mean, I know we're both from a small country, but come on.

I slink farther into my seat, pretending to scroll through a news article while I remain extremely aware of the empty seat beside me. Aware because it's one of the few empty ones left.

And Andrew keeps coming.

My heart starts to pound as I watch him approach from the corner of my eye. I mean, this is ridiculous. There's coincidence and then there's just plain old cosmic injustice. He could have booked any seat on any plane on any day, so why does it have to be this one? Why does it have to—

"Excuse me? Do you mind if I move your coat?" Andrew stops right beside me and I have no choice but to glance up, clinging to the vague hope he's forgotten all about me.

He has not.

He stares at me, hands frozen above his head, about to shove his bag into the compartment. As soon as our eyes meet, all that embarrassment increases tenfold, and I flush when he just stands there.

"Hello," I say with the biggest, falsest smile on my face. The word seems to trigger something in him, and his expression wipes blank as he drops his arm, swinging his bag back to his side before he moves on like he didn't even see me.

Okay, not great.

I turn weakly back to the front, pretending not to listen to the polite conversation happening a few rows behind. A minute later a confused woman appears next to me, smiling sympathetically as she slides into the seat.

"Had a fight with your boyfriend?" she asks, and I grit my teeth, risking a glance over my shoulder to find Andrew looking right at me.

I immediately spin around, slumping so he can't even see the back of my head.

But it doesn't matter. I still feel his eyes on me the entire flight.

Now

I toss the magazine back onto Andrew's lap, taking in his sweater, a clashing red-and-green monstrosity, with resigned acceptance.

"What the hell is that?" I ask, gesturing to his face.

"Oh, this?" Andrew strokes his chin. "My manly scruff because I'm a manly man?"

"Are you growing a beard?"

"The fact that you have to ask that question makes me want to lie and say no."

It's going to be a great beard and we both know it. I've just never imagined him with one before. I always thought his face was too open for one, with that stupid dimple in his left cheek and those ridiculous eyes that seem to change color whenever they want to.

"What happens in the summer when you tan but then decide to shave and your face is two different colors?"

"Would you believe I haven't thought about that?"

I smile but can't keep it up for long. "I'm sorry I'm late. I had some things I needed to finish up at work."

"Pretty sure late is me in the air and you on the ground. The plane's still there, in case you missed the big tube thing outside."

"I wanted to surprise you." I drop into the seat next to him and hand over the envelope I'd kept in my pocket for the last few days.

"This doesn't *feel* like diamonds," he jokes, pretending to weigh it.

"It's a first-class upgrade."

His amusement fades as he stares at me. "Come again?"

"I think the lounge will be manic, but we can check—"

"How much did this cost?" He sounds horrified as he opens it, drawing out the tickets like they're from Willy Wonka himself.

"Don't worry about it. Less than you think."

"Moll, Christmas prices are bad enough—"

"I said don't worry about it," I interrupt. "Do you know how many unused air miles I had? I had to spend them on something. Besides, it's our ten-year anniversary."

"Ten?" He frowns as I start to feel a little hurt. "Are you sure?"

"Yes! Our first flight was ten years ago. That's an anniversary."

"Can't be more than seven."

"It's ten! It's—" My mouth clamps shut as he holds up his fist between us, a gold chain dangling from his clenched fingers. At the bottom of it, glinting in the fluorescent light, is a small blue pendant.

"Happy ten-year anniversary," he says as I take it.

"You're a jerk," I mutter, but there's no heat to the words as I admire my present. Simple and small and perfect for me.

"Careful," he says as I undo the clasp. "The elderly, heavily accented man at the antique shop told me it was cursed."

"Oh, he did, did he?"

"Something about three ghosts on Christmas Eve? Or maybe it was a golem. I went back the next day to check but the place had mysteriously disappeared." He helps gather my hair from the nape of my neck as I put it on. "I can guarantee you it didn't cost as much as these tickets did," he adds. "Or much at all to be honest. But it's only the first part."

Now that gets my interest. "I get a two-part present?"

"Anniversary present and a Christmas present."

"We don't do Christmas presents."

"I'm a bad boy, Molly. I do what I want. I'll give it to you when we land; it's in my suitcase." He scratches the side of his jaw as I twist the chain into place, positioning it against my throat to show him. "It looked bigger at the store," he says as if I'd care about something like that.

"It's beautiful, thank you."

"You're very welcome." His eyes flick up to meet mine, a smile spreading across his face. "Merry Christmas, Moll."

And just like that, I'm the happiest I've been in weeks. "Merry Christmas, Andrew."

"So, any new women in your life I should know about?"

I adjust myself on the stool as I shed another layer. Our flight's delayed forty minutes so we're sitting at one of the small bars dotted around the gate. Me with a glass of sparkling water in front of me, Andrew with ginger ale. We tried the first-class lounge, but it was predictably full due to the number of planes struggling to get on the runway. The snow is particularly heavy this year, but I'm not worried about it. Whereas an inch of the stuff would throw Ireland into chaos, Chicago knows how to handle itself.

"Just one," he says, reaching for the small bowl of tortilla chips between us. "Her name's Penny."

I try not to show my surprise as I take a sip of my drink, the bubbles burning my tongue. He conveniently left *that* out of his last few emails.

Zoe once said that Andrew and I had the strangest friendship she'd ever heard of. But I didn't think it was that bad. We lived on opposite sides of the city and he was often traveling for work while I was simply *at* work all hours of the day. We rarely saw each other outside of these flights. And while I firmly believe that an online-based friendship can be just as real as an in-person one, because of my workload, if it weren't for this little tradition, we probably would have lost touch by now.

But just because we didn't see each other didn't mean we didn't talk. Texts, emails, phone calls. He was the first person I told when I found out Zoe was pregnant. When I got my apartment, my job. He seemed mostly concerned with sending me memes and photos of suspiciously stained furniture he'd found abandoned on the sidewalk. (*Found you a futon*, he'd write. Or his favorite, *Let's play is that blood or ketchup*.) But he usually kept me updated on his girlfriends. In fact, he went so far as to introduce them to me the rare times we met up between Christmases, probably so they didn't get concerned that their new boyfriend was constantly sending pictures of disease-ridden armchairs to another woman.

"When did this happen?" I ask, trying not to sound hurt that I didn't know already.

"About two months ago," he says casually. "She's cute but a snorer. And a very early riser."

"You met her two months ago and she's moved in already?"

"Well, it feels cruel to keep her outside at this time of year."

I stare at him as he spins his phone on the counter, waiting until I get it. It takes me at least five seconds longer than I'd like to admit.

"You got a *dog*?"

"My roommate got a dog," he corrects, pulling up a photo.

"You got a dog!" I coo over the little sausage. "Penny?"

He nods. "We're very happy together."

"And I'm happy for you. I know you wanted one."

"So long as the neighbors don't complain we should be okay. Not sure about the guy across the hall though. Looks like a snitch."

I hand his phone back, hesitating as I try to gauge his mood. "So, Marissa's gone?"

"Who?"

I wince and he shrugs. A petite, raven-haired marketing executive he'd met online, they'd been on and off for the past year.

"We tried," he says. "But that didn't seem to matter in the end."

"I'm sorry. She was sweet."

He scoffs. "You only met her once and you didn't even like her."

"That's not true!"

"You never like anyone I date."

"I liked that teacher."

"That teacher," he repeats flatly. "You can't even remember her name."

Like it's my fault his exes are so forgettable. "Soph—"

"Emil—"

"Emily!" I slam my hand against the bar in victory. "Emily. Emily the teacher. With the incredibly quiet voice."

He gives me a fond look. "You're such a bitch."

"Emily was years ago," I remind him. "And didn't she dump you for that married guy? I'm not even supposed to like her."

"Alison dumped me for the married guy. Emily ghosted me."

"You have terrible taste in women."

"Hey," he says, one hand going to his heart. "Words hurt, Molly. Maybe terrible women just have a taste in me. Anyway, look who's talking. What happened to Brandon? You never told me why you broke up with him."

"He chewed with his mouth open."

"Seems fair."

I force a smirk as I gaze down at my drink, twisting one of the rings from my finger. "He got a new job in Seattle," I explain. "Moved away."

"And you called it quits?"

"It was a good job," I say lightly. "But I have no interest in long-distance and I wasn't about to move there with him. We'd only been together for a few months. I mean, I was still scared to go number two when he was in the apartment."

"The real second base."

I kick his leg under the counter and take another sip. "I asked him to stay," I say after a moment.

The humor fades instantly from his face. "Ah, Moll."

"I'm fine. Honestly, I'm so used to being alone now I don't know if I'll even like it when I find someone I *do* want to be with. I'm not sure I know how to bend like that anymore."

"I don't want to hear about your sex life."

"I mean in terms of compromise, asshat." I glance over his shoulder as the departure board flickers. Our flight status remains unchanged. *Delayed*. It's not that I mind the extra time with Andrew, but I would have much preferred to have it while sitting in first-class seats. "How long until they legally have to order us a pizza?"

"You're the lawyer."

"Not a pizza lawyer."

"True. How's it going anyway?" he asks. "Make anyone rich this month?"

"Three, I'll have you know."

"Did they deserve it?"

"All my clients deserve it." I drain my water, eager to change the subject. "How much time off do you have this year?"

"Just two weeks. I'm fully booked up then."

"And you only sound a little smug."

He grins. "I've been working on a more humble persona."

"Uh-huh. And how's that going for you?"

"Not as fun," he says, and I laugh.

When we first met, Andrew dreamed of traveling the world as a photojournalist. Of far-flung places and images of life in all its forms. And he tried. For years he tried. But the assignments were few and far between and, like it does for most people, practicality won out over wishful thinking. Weddings paid his bills, graduations and bar mitzvahs brought in a steady income. He never resented it. He told me once that he found a lot of joy in the ordinary, that he loved his work and the people he met. I believed him. And if I didn't, all I'd need to do is look at his photographs to see it.

"I'm thinking about getting a new website," he continues. "There's a guy I know who—"

"*Shit.*"

We both glance at the exhausted businessman beside us. "Sorry," he says when he sees our attention. "Excuse me, sorry. My flight just got canceled." He slides off the stool without another word, bringing his phone to his ear.

"That sucks," Andrew mutters, and I nod, suddenly worried as I check the time.

"It'll be fine," Andrew says, guessing my thoughts. "It's a busy night. We've been through this before."

We have. Last year we were delayed five hours, not long enough to go home but enough that everyone was *very* annoyed. It was the closest we ever came to a real argument until eventually, just to waste some time, we decided to get some food. I ordered cheese fries, but they were out of cheese fries, and I was so tired and so hungry that I burst into tears, and then Andrew wasn't mad at me anymore. He looked like he was about to march into the kitchen and make them himself.

"What?" he asks now, and I realize I'm smiling at the memory.

"You're a good friend, you know that?"

He eyes me suspiciously. "You need a kidney or something?"

"I mean it," I say with a laugh. "Come on, let's have a proper drink. We might as well if we're stuck here."

"I'm okay."

"I insist. What do you want?"

He takes so long to answer that I stop trying to get the barman's attention and turn to him.

"My treat," I say.

"I've actually stopped."

"Stopped what? Oh!" I make a face. "Like a pre-Christmas cleanse?"

Another pause. "No."

Awkwardness settles over us, straining the silence as, once again, it takes me way too long to put two and two together.

"*Oh*," I say slowly. "Like . . . forever?"

"That's the plan. I'm two months sober as of yesterday."

I relax a little at that. Sober sounds like such a serious word. Sober is a word for addicts and alcoholics and . . .

I stare at him as he watches me, looking tense. Oh my God. "Why didn't you say anything?"

"It's not a big deal."

"Yes, it is," I say, flustered now. "That's . . . that's great, Andrew. Congratulations."

He smiles slightly. "Stop panicking."

"I'm not! I'm fine." I tip my water glass to my lips only to realize too late it doesn't have any water left. "So, is it like a sponsorship thing or what?"

"I'm following a program, but it's mainly just me. It was getting a bit . . ." He shakes his head. "Anyway. It's all good. I'm seeing how it goes. But you? You deserve some champagne."

"No, I can just—"

"It's Christmas," he interrupts firmly. "And I promise that as tempting as you are, you knocking back some bubbles is not going to trip me up."

"I'm really ok—"

"This is why I didn't tell you," he says gently. "Please don't make it a thing. Have a drink, Moll."

I hesitate at the sincerity in his voice. "Well, now it's

awkward if I do and awkward if I don't," I grumble, and he grins.

"Then my job here is done." He holds up a hand, instantly making eye contact with the barman. "Besides," he adds, glancing over his shoulder as snow continues to fall on the runway. "Looks like we're going to be here awhile."

CHAPTER THREE

One glass slowly turns to two as our flight is pushed back and back and back. Too hungry to wait for food on the plane, we end up ordering burgers and Andrew shows me so many videos of Penny that I don't notice how crowded our terminal has gotten until I get up to use the restroom and find the line snaking past the vending machines. The place is packed with people, other passengers finding space where they can along walls and windows, distracting sulking children with books and iPads and whatever they can get their hands on. By the time I make it back to the bar, there's even more, but they don't look as annoyed as you'd expect for a delayed flight this close to Christmas. They've gone past that. They look *worried*. And for the first time since I arrived, I start to feel the same.

I gaze up at the departure board by the bar and the long *Delayed* column beside each flight. God. If this turns into an all-night thing, I'll end up falling asleep on the plane and the upgrades will have been for nothing. It wasn't the little luxuries I was looking forward to, though they were certainly a perk, but Andrew was such a nerd about this part of our tradition and I selfishly wanted to see his reaction to everything. I wanted to make him happy.

Sober. I frown as I think back to the last few times I've been with him. Since when has he not been sober? Yes, alcohol was usually involved, but it was only ever a glass or two in restaurants and bars. No warning signs. I don't think I've ever even seen him drunk. I've seen Gabriela drunk lots of times. *I've* been drunk lots of times. But Andrew?

Once? Maybe twice? And he wasn't even that bad. I mean, it *was* Christmas. It's to be expected.

A short whistle drags my attention back to the man himself and I turn to find him sitting with his back against the bar, watching me.

"You all right there, Moll?"

"I like your sweater."

"You hate my sweater."

I do hate his sweater. I always hate his sweaters. He's big into the novelty Christmas outfits and this one is no different, bright green and dotted with red-and-white candy canes. Every year he wears something new, and the gaudier it looks, the happier it seems to make him.

"I like that you like your sweater," I explain.

He smiles faintly but doesn't move from his spot. "Can I talk to you for a sec?"

"Depends," I tease, sauntering over to him.

"Depends?"

"On what you want to talk about." I lean against the counter and turn my phone over. The screen is full of notifications, which doesn't immediately worry me because I choose to live chaotically when it comes to app alerts, but instead of the usual group chat updates and newsletters from a nail salon I went to once five years ago, I see a dozen very urgent-looking notices.

"... and you're not listening to me."

"Huh?" I glance up to see Andrew staring at me with an exasperated look. I'd completely zoned out. "Sorry!" I grimace. "Sorry. It's just . . . are you seeing this?"

He frowns as I show him my phone before taking his own out from his pocket.

"A storm?" he asks, skimming the news.

"But, like, a *storm* storm." Right over the Atlantic. "Do you think we'll get out okay?" I look over at the rest of the passengers to see the news is starting to spread. Every second person is now on their phone, their expressions tight. "Surely they can just go *around* the storm, right?"

Andrew looks deadly serious. "Do you think we should tell the pilots that plan?"

I punch him in the thigh. "Well, we can wait, can't we? It's not like we have anything else to do and the lounge will empty soon and some spots will open up and—"

"Another glass of champagne please," Andrew calls to the barman. "For the lady freaking out?"

"I'm not freaking out." I'm just . . . *perturbed*. Perturbed feels right. We've never not gotten home for Christmas before.

"Drink your juice," Andrew says, interrupting my panic as he slides a full glass toward me. "And calm down. You're making me nervous just being near you."

I stick my tongue out at him but take a sip. "What did you want to talk about?" I ask, distracted as more and more people start to move. Do they know something we don't? Some of them are in a line. Should I be in a line?

"It can wait," Andrew says.

"What can?"

"Jesus Christ." I glance back as he starts to laugh. "You've completely lost it."

"I'm sorry! I'm *tired*."

He shakes his head, but he's smiling. "Come on, chug that back and we'll see if there's any more space in the lounge. Maybe you're just feeling rattled being amongst the plebs."

I don't respond as an ominous hush falls over the terminal. There's a flash of color by the gate as the doors to the tunnel open and we both turn as the cabin crew, *our* crew, strides out. Hundreds of heads whip their way as they manage to professionally avoid every desperate eye, as though knowing if they meet any they'll be immediately surrounded.

A grim-looking man in a yellow vest heads to the check-in counter, reaching for the microphone, but whatever he was going to say is quickly drowned out by the huge groan that spreads throughout the crowd as the departure board flickers to life one final time.

Canceled.

Canceled. Canceled. Canceled.

The place erupts.

Gate by gate, the would-be passengers grab their bags and their companions until the place is a hive of anxiety. Flight after flight changes on the board, all saying the same thing.

Oh my God.

"Okay," Andrew says, his voice ridiculously calm. "Plan B."

"You have a plan B?"

"I will in about two minutes," he says, unlocking his phone.

I slide off my stool, downing my drink as the steward tries to calm the sudden mob in front of him. I'm two seconds away from joining them myself.

What do we do? If every flight is canceled, we can... what? Get to another city and try to catch a flight there? A flight at this time of year? And even then, the storm is over the Atlantic, meaning every plane going that way will be affected. And everything else... We're four days out from Christmas. It's not like they're desperate to fill seats.

"We're not going to get another flight," I tell him.

"You don't know that."

"We're not, Andrew."

When he doesn't answer, I turn back to find his brow furrowed as he swipes through his phone. And I know why. Family is number one for Andrew. Not that I don't also love mine, but my sister and my parents and I are the kind of unit that is perfectly fine not speaking to each other for a few months beyond the occasional *I'm still alive* message. Andrew couldn't be more different. Christmas is a big deal in his household. I know it is because he won't shut up about it. He says it's for Hannah, the baby of the family, but by my calculations, the girl is sixteen now and yet they still go full throttle. He doesn't even pretend to be embarrassed about it. He loves it. I know he does. And he's *always* home for Christmas.

For a moment, the only thing I can do is watch him, my heart breaking at the frustration starting to creep into his expression. With all my planning, this was something I'd never factored in, and I have no idea what to do.

"We should book onto something in the morning," he says, still scrolling. "The storm will have passed by then. We can..." He trails off as his screen goes blank before a call comes through.

"It's Mam," he says, staring at it. "She usually stays awake until I'm on the plane."

We both wait until it stops ringing, only for it to immediately start again. Andrew's chest moves up and down with a heavy sigh before he clicks accept, moving a few paces away.

"Hiya!" he answers with false cheer. "Yeah, I'm... Yeah, it's not looking good, I'm afraid. No, we'll figure something out. With Molly, yeah."

I put my glass down, starting to feel ill as I gather my coat and purse. I need to join one of these lines and I'm halfway to doing just that when my own phone rings.

Relief trickles through me when I see the name on the screen.

Zoe. My sister will know what to do. My sister always knows what to do.

"Your flight's canceled."

"You don't say," I huff, remaining by the relative safety of the bar. All around me people are moving, ushering children and friends toward anyone who looks in charge. "Why are you even awake?"

"Oh, I don't know, Molly, maybe it's because I have a human being growing inside me and I have to pee every thirty minutes. What are you going to do?"

"About the flight or the peeing?"

"You're not funny. I'm the funny one."

"Debatable," I mutter. "And I don't know yet. It's a nightmare here."

"The BBC says seventy percent of planes due to fly over the North Atlantic tonight are grounded and the other thirty percent will probably follow."

"And you're calling me with a solution, right?"

"I'm calling to remind you that if you don't get your ass back here, I'll kill you. You can't leave me alone with Mam and Dad. This is the one time of the year all the pressure is off me because everyone's fawning over you and you are *not* taking that away from me. Surely they have connecting flights from Canada or something."

"We'll still have to cross the ocean." I glance over my shoulder to find Andrew rubbing a slow circle into his forehead. He's told me a lot about his mother, an energetic, well-meaning force of a woman who's always struggled with him being so far from home. I can only imagine the conversation he's having. "I think we're just going to have to wait for the storm to pass."

"They're saying it's going to be another day or two at least."

"Who's they?"

"The weather guy," she says defensively. "The one with the tie."

"They all wear ties!"

"Molly?"

Andrew walks toward me, his hair sticking up at various angles where he's been pulling it. "We'll figure something out," I say to Zoe. "Break the news to Mam when she wakes, will you?"

"Oh sure, leave it to me to ruin Christmas."

"Would you just—"

"Love you!"

I focus on Andrew as she hangs up. "Everything okay?"

"Mam's panicking," he says, grabbing his coat. "I'm going to go get in line and see what our options are. You okay to mind our stuff?"

"Of course."

"And maybe you could look up some—"

"I'm already on it," I say confidently. "Don't worry. We'll get something."

He nods, his attention already on the other side of the terminal where people are beginning to gather. "Not like it's a busy time of year," he says, trying to joke.

My answering smile fools no one, but I manage to keep it up until he goes and I take a seat at the bar to call Gabriela.

"Okay," she says when she answers. "So, when you said you'd be on your phone, I didn't think you actually meant—"

"My flight's canceled."

"*Noooo*," she says softly. "You're kidding. Because of the storm? I didn't think it was going to get that bad."

"I don't think anyone did."

"Are you okay?"

"I think so. I mean, yeah, I'm annoyed, but I'm fine. It's Andrew I'm worried about. He's big on Christmas. I've never seen him in panic mode before."

"Andrew?"

"My friend?" I hold the phone between my shoulder and my ear as I open my laptop and log in to the Wi-Fi. "My plane friend?" I add reluctantly.

"*Oh*. The man you fly economy for?"

"That's the one."

"That's cute that you guys still do that," Gabriela continues, and I grimace as my email blinks to life before me, updating by the dozens in the few hours since I last looked at it.

"I just wanted to call and let you know that I might be offline tomorrow," I say. Neither of us bats an eye about the fact that tomorrow is a Saturday. "We might not get out of here until the morning. But I'll keep you updated."

"I'm so sorry, Molly. Let me know if there's anything I can do."

"Can you fly a plane?"

"No, but I love a challenge."

We say goodbye, Gabriela's voice full of sympathy as I start a fresh spreadsheet and start Googling.

CHAPTER FOUR
SEVEN YEARS AGO

Flight Three, Chicago

I pick at my cheese fries, pushing them around the plate as I try to drum up the appetite to eat another one. I don't know why I agreed to this. Well, I do know why. I panicked. But what's a girl supposed to do when Andrew Fitzpatrick comes striding toward you like you're the final boss in a video game he just can't beat? Like he's been expecting you.

I certainly wasn't expecting him. So all I could do was sit there in the middle of the terminal and freak out as he approached, wondering what I'd done to make the universe hate me so much.

"11C," is all he said, thrusting his ticket at me.

I was completely lost for a solid five seconds before I realized what he'd meant. "34B," I responded, showing him my own seat number.

He was surprised at that. Maybe even annoyed. And then, like he'd decided to simply stop feeling both of those things, he sat down next to me, hugging his backpack to his chest.

"You want to get something to eat?" he asked.

I wasn't hungry, but I said yes.

And now here we are.

I peek up at him from under my lashes, watching him studiously ignore me like I am him. He looks different up close. Older. Granted, I'm older too, but some days I still think I look like a teenager. So does every bouncer and barman in Chicago apparently. The round face and doe eyes don't help, and if I'm not in my heels, I get mistaken for a high schooler more often than I'd like. But Andrew looks like he's grown up. He's lost a bit of the puppy fat from around his jaw and his brown hair is longer, swept back in a messy, almost stylish way. I say almost because he still dresses atrociously, tonight wearing a blue T-shirt with a cartoon elf on the front that is extremely hard not to keep looking at.

"So, are you some hotshot lawyer now?"

My eyes snap up from his chest as he finally speaks. "What?"

"You said you wanted to go to law school."

"I'm still studying," I say, surprised that he remembers. "What about you? Photography, right?"

He nods. "I've got a job with a portrait studio on Michigan Avenue. Babies. Families. That kind of thing."

"You like it?"

"I love it," he says, and I blink at the simple way he says the words. "The kids especially. I'm like a kid whisperer. You've never seen a four-year-old sit so still." He wipes his mouth with a napkin, his burger demolished. "You should pop by. I'll get you a discount."

"Oh, no," I say quickly. "I hate having my picture taken."

"We get that a lot. But it's never as scary as people think."

I shake my head, taking a sip of my beer. Andrew got both of us a drink, despite my weak protests. He's already finished his and the rules of buying a round dictate that I need to catch up.

"My boyfriend's sister just got engaged," I say, feeling rude to shut him down. "I'll put her on to you guys."

"Your boyfriend?"

"Daniel." I feel a burst of happiness just saying his name. I met him via an app this summer and I'm mildly (extremely) obsessed with him. He lives in an apartment near Lincoln Park and wants to work with animals. I am trying to be chill, but no. There is no chill right now when it comes to Daniel.

"We've been together a few months," I say, taking another sip. "He's... What?"

Andrew laughs as I fidget. "You're doing that I'm-in-love smile."

"No, I'm not!"

"Hey, own it. Law school, lover. You're living the American dream."

I huff, finishing the bottle before placing it down with a thump as silence descends again. Our eyes meet over the table, both of us acknowledging that this is weird, but also not as weird as it could be. Probably because of him. He was always easy to talk to and certainly seems to have forgiven me for whatever indirect role I played in him dating a shitty person.

An announcement crackles above our heads, calling our flight, and I glance around as a few other diners start to move, wondering what the polite thing to do is.

"You want to see if we can swap seats?"

"Huh?" I twist back to find Andrew watching me, a hesitant smile on his face.

"I'll sweet-talk the person next to you. You don't have to talk to me or anything," he adds with a shrug. "I mean, I'll talk to you so it *would* be weird if you—"

"Yeah, yeah." I smirk, thinking it over. It's an overnight flight, but I'm wide awake, and a bit of company doesn't sound like the worst thing in the world. "Sure," I say. "Let's see you turn on the charm."

"Oh, I don't need to turn it on," he dismisses me as we gather our things. "It's always on."

"Hmm."

"I'm very charming," he argues. "Five bucks says it takes me less than thirty seconds."

"Ten says it takes you more. And I'm pretty sure you still owe me a dollar from our last wager."

"Oh, so you want to go there, do you?" He takes a step in front of me, spinning around so he's facing my way as we walk toward the gate. I'd spoken without thinking, but there's no annoyance in his expression. If anything, he looks like he's teasing me.

"You're the one who said you'd change my mind about Christmas," I point out.

"Yes, I did." He sounds delighted that I'm playing along. "Okay. Let me play for my losses. Add on a dollar and throw in a movie choice."

"A movie? I thought you wanted to talk?"

"I'll talk during the movie. People love that."

He smiles when I laugh, his hands sliding into the pockets of his jeans.

"It's a seven-hour flight," he continues. "You've got to break it up."

Seven hours. The last time I had to sit next to him for that long the very idea of it had filled me with horror. Now I was weirdly looking forward to it.

"So, do we have a deal?" He holds out his hand and I don't hesitate to clasp it. We shake.

"Deal," I say, and a smug look crosses his face.

"Thirty seconds," he reminds me, taking out his passport. He does it in fifteen.

Now

I'm starting to think we're not getting out of Chicago tonight. We might not even get out tomorrow. Andrew's still waiting in line with at least twenty people in front of him and I'm surrounded by twenty more as I sit by the bar, watching news of the storm as I periodically refresh my phone for flights in the morning.

Nada.

I move back to my work email, refreshing that too, but the damn contract I'm waiting on still hasn't come back, which means someone's getting a very early phone call from me tomorrow. I usually don't like working when I'm with Andrew. He's pretty understanding about it, encouraging even, but we almost came to metaphorical blows over it the last time we were delayed like this and I don't want to make tonight any worse than it is.

Another refresh of flights and I shoot off a few emails, fruitlessly trying to catch up. I'm not usually so behind, but Spencer got mono like it's 1952 and Caleb thinks he's too important to be working on anything he's actually assigned to. Gabriela already helps me too much as it is, so I'm not going to go running to her. Which leaves me by myself.

Send email. Refresh flights.

Google career options for tired girls who still want to afford their nice apartment.

"My boyfriend flew out yesterday."

The man next to me speaks at a normal volume, but he's

not looking at me. His gaze is absent, almost mournful, as he stares unseeing at the row of beer bottles across from us.

"It's his first time meeting my family," he continues. "But I had to work last minute so he flew out by himself and now I'm here and he'll be there. With my parents. Alone. For Christmas." He takes a shallow breath, finally looking at me. "Do you think I did something in my past life? Is this my punishment?"

"I'm sure they'll get on great," I say awkwardly, but he shakes his head.

"They don't know about him. I mean they know *of* him, but not that he's ... that we're ..." He trails off, that mournful look coming back.

I reach out to pat his back. "Gay?"

"What?" He shakes his head. "No. They know that. We're vegan."

Oh.

He groans, dropping his head against the counter. "I had a whole speech prepared. We were going to sit down and discuss it. Steven's too polite for them. He'll end up with second helpings of turkey and ham without me there. He's a skinny guy, you know? My mother's going to think we can't afford to eat if he refuses."

I continue to pat his back until Andrew appears at my shoulder a moment later, looking in concern at my new friend.

"Is he okay?" he asks.

"He's vegan," I explain as the man proceeds to bang his head lightly against the bar.

"Ah." His eyes slide from the stranger to me. "Can I talk to you? Privately?"

We move a few paces away to a closed kiosk. The airport is quieter now, but still busy with other desperate souls like us. "Anything?" I feel ridiculous as soon as I ask it.

He shakes his head. "We'll figure it out," he says, as though he's the one about to comfort me.

I stare up at him, hating the resignation on his face. It's a look I'm not used to seeing on him. I've always been the pessimist in this friendship and I'm free to be because he is so resolutely not. So this? This right here? No.

"It'll be okay," he continues, and he doesn't even try and sound like he means it.

"It will be," I say, and I must sound as determined as I pretend to be, because some of the tightness leaves his expression. I swear to God he almost smiles.

"I know that look."

"Is it my 'I've got this' look? Because I do. I'm going to sort it out."

"You can't control the weather."

"No, but I can circumvent it. Not every flight is canceled. We'll find something. Just let me . . . let me think. Okay? I'll get you home."

"Molly—"

"Ten-year anniversary," I remind him, taking out my phone. There must be *something*. "I've already ruined the first-class lounge. I am not about to ruin Christmas."

"And there you go acting like you're in charge of US airspace again. Put the phone down," he adds, but I shake my head.

"We're getting on a plane tonight," I tell him. "We're doing this. Christmas miracle time. Happy, jolly Christmas mir—"

He moves so fast I don't have time to react. One second, he's standing at the end of the bar, the next he's right in front of me, plucking the phone from my hand.

"Hey!"

He ignores me, shoving it into my pocket before clasping

my shoulders. I suck in a surprised breath as he dips his head to stare straight into my eyes.

"It's okay," he says firmly. "It's out of our control. The airlines don't know anything more than we do. But no one's going anywhere tonight. The best they can do is find us a room and, to be honest, I don't want to spend the night in some anonymous roadside hotel. I've discussed it with my folks and they agree."

"About what?"

"About staying here." He takes a steadying breath and releases me, his smile tight. "A lot of people spend a lot of money to stay in cities like Chicago over the holidays. Plus all our stuff is here. It wouldn't be so bad."

"You want to stay here for Christmas?" I ask, trying to understand. It's the last thing I expected. "But your family—"

"I know." He doesn't try and hide the disappointment that flashes across his face. "And if a flight becomes available, I'll be the first person on it. But right now, there's nothing we can do except waste our time. They can last one Christmas without me."

The man is a liar. At least, going by what he's been telling me about his family for the last ten years. And he knows it, switching tactics when I remain unconvinced.

"I don't want to spend the next few days refreshing my screen and getting angry at overworked call agents. The storm won't last forever, they'll clear the backlog, and we'll get something. If that's a few days from now, then so be it."

"But you—"

"It will be fun," he insists. "We can order way too much food, watch a bunch of movies. We can make it work."

"You can't just . . ." Wait. "We?"

"Yes, *we*." He looks at me like I'm an idiot. "Unless you want to spend Christmas alone?"

That isn't something that necessarily terrifies me, but this new alternative sounds a lot better. Christmas in Chicago? Christmas in Chicago with *Andrew*?

"Well?" He looks nervous. Almost as if he thinks I'll say no.

"You really want to do this?" I ask.

"It's not bad for a plan B."

It's not bad for any plan.

"We could get cheese," I tell him, almost breathless at the thought.

"I'd say that's a definite possibility."

"And stollen from Dinkel's bakery. And more cheese. We can go ice skating!"

"*You* can go ice skating," he corrects. "I will stand for approximately thirty seconds before falling on my ass and then abandon you for hot chocolate."

I try not to look too happy, aware that this is very much not his first choice, and yet incredibly okay with the turn of events. And maybe I was wrong. Maybe he's not so heartbroken about the storm, because he's looking pretty pleased with our new plan as well.

"All right, then," he says, running a hand through his hair. "Now, how the hell do we get out of here?"

CHAPTER FIVE

It's harder than you might think. It's another thirty minutes before we're finally brought landside and another twenty after that while we wait for Andrew's ridiculously large luggage to be released.

"You hiding a body in there?" I ask as he unpacks his coat. His suitcase is at least three times the size of mine.

"Just clothes, presents, and all manner of American contraband to be swapped for Irish contraband on the way back."

"You should start a little black market," I say, eyeing the dozens of people settling in for a night on the airport floor. I feel a twinge of guilt just looking at them. Should we be doing that? Maybe we could—

"Stop it," Andrew says.

"Stop what?"

"Whatever you're thinking about."

"I'm not—"

"You are. I can always tell." He straightens, zipping up his coat. "They'll put on more flights in the morning and we can check then. In the meantime, do you know what we should do?"

"Book a massage?"

"We should get a charcuterie board."

I snort at the seriousness of his expression. "We can get whatever we want," I tell him.

"I want a panettone," he says. "And some cheesecake. What do you want?"

"Mince pies. Though I've never been able to find them here."

He makes a face. "Because no one actually likes mince pies."

"I like mince pies."

"And you are wrong."

I ignore him as we wind our way slowly around the other passengers, heading for the exit. I'm feeling much calmer now that we have a plan. I'm great with plans. "Where are we going to do this?" I ask, trying not to step on anyone. "My place or yours?"

"Yours," he says immediately. "Not just because it's nicer, even though it is. But my roommate's inviting his girlfriend over for the week and I'd rather not listen to them having sex while we're watching *Miracle on 34th Street*."

I nod, secretly relieved. My place *is* nicer. I've lived for the past three years in a pretty decent two-bed apartment in Uptown. I sometimes rent out the spare room to friends of friends or offer it up to visiting relatives, but I've had the place to myself for the past few weeks and even deep-cleaned it last night so there's no dirty dishes or underwear lying around.

At least I hope there isn't.

"We'll have to get normal food," I say as we stop just inside the doors. Andrew pulls a thick green scarf from his bag and winds it around his neck. "Alongside fun food. I cleared out the freezer last night so do you want to stop somewhere on the way back, or I know a few places we can—"

"Hey, lovebirds!"

I turn, startled, to see a red-faced man on the other side of the doors, sitting on a sturdy suitcase. He's smiling at us and looks far too cheery for someone whose flight has probably just been canceled.

"Can I help you?" I ask, but he just points to the ceiling. I glance back at Andrew with an is-this-man-going-to-kill-us eyebrow raise, but he's not looking at me. He's looking up with a smile and I follow his gaze to a bundle of green leaves directly overhead.

"What's that?" I ask, confused.

Andrew's eyes drop to mine. "It's mistletoe, you idiot."

"*That*'s mistletoe?" No way. "It looks like spinach. Like a sprig of spinach."

"How do you not know what—"

"I know what it *is*. I just haven't seen it before. It's not like I spend December looking up the whole time, is it?"

"You're five foot nothing; you spend most of your life looking up."

"I am five foot *three*, thank you very much. And I can see the world just fine from—"

"Don't be such a grinch!" the man interrupts. "It's tradition!"

"Keep your pants on!" I yell back. Andrew only laughs, but a couple of other people have stopped at the commotion and now suddenly we have an audience.

"These things are so dumb," I mutter, trying not to meet anyone's eye as Andrew pulls a matching beanie on over his hair. "And kind of creepy, don't you think?"

"I plead the Fourth."

"Fifth."

"Whatever."

Another couple moves past as we dawdle, glancing up

as they see the mistletoe. Without even breaking their stride, they turn to each other and kiss, provoking a small cheer from the onlookers.

My mouth drops open as they move on as if nothing happened.

"Bad luck not to kiss," the cheery man yells, turning his attention back to us.

"No, it's not!" I exclaim. "You just made that up!"

Andrew shifts beside me, still looking amused. "Molly—"

"He made that up."

"Just ignore him."

"I can't ignore him. He called me a grinch. Why does everybody always call me that?" I watch with increasing annoyance as an older duo raise another round of applause by locking lips right beside us. "That's it. You have to kiss me."

"You're too competitive, you know that? Let's just find our driver."

I grab hold of his sleeve, that familiar need to prove myself to complete strangers giving me a blissful focus I haven't had all day, and before I can think twice about what I'm doing, I slide a hand around the back of his neck and lift my face to his.

I wasn't lying when I told Gabriela I hadn't been with anyone since Brandon. But the thing is, I also hadn't really *been* with Brandon either. Not for our last few weeks anyway. It had been one of those slow breakups, awkward and unsure, where every kiss became a question, where every touch could be our last. Until we stopped doing both altogether.

So, it might be because I've been so starved of human contact that the moment Andrew and I come together, things start to get . . . different.

It's the heat of him that hits me first, so at odds with the sharp bite of cold air swirling through the doors. The gentle rasp of his beard is a surprise against my skin, especially when compared with the softness of his lips. Men don't have soft lips in winter. Men have chapped lips in winter because they don't know how to use lip balm. But Andrew's are soft. Soft and warm as they cling to mine. Cling because he's kissing me back. This is no peck on the cheek, no joke between friends under the mistletoe. He's standing there and he's kissing me back and I suddenly can't get close enough.

There's a swooping sensation in my stomach that must be from the champagne and it takes more effort than it should to let him go. I force myself to pull away, but Andrew chases me, closing the inch of space I put between us to brush against me once more before he draws back completely.

My stupid heart is pounding when I open my eyes and I find myself staring at his shoulder as he turns back to the now clapping man as if to say, *There you go, buddy. Merry Christmas.*

"Happy now?" Andrew asks me after taking a short bow. "Going to start eating candy canes and join the novelty sweater club?"

I clear my throat, knowing it's my turn for some quip about the taste of his onion rings or how I need to wash my tongue with soap, but my mouth is suddenly dry and I can't seem to force the words out.

"Moll?"

My phone buzzes with a text and I use the excuse to break away from his questioning gaze. "Ride's here," I mutter, barely glancing at the screen, and I walk outside without waiting for him, eager for some fresh air, no matter how cold it is. And it is freaking *cold*. Still, I breathe it in, inhaling until my lungs hurt.

Well, that was weird.

Andrew bumps my arm a moment later and I cast my eye

around the drop-off point for our car. "Blew your mind with that kiss, huh?"

I glance sharply at him, but he's smiling. He's *joking*. "Because I'm just saying, if this is you finally getting into the festive spirit—"

"Okay," I interrupt, and he laughs. The sound of it makes me feel better.

"I think I'm getting hungry again," I tell him. It's not a lie. All that panic takes up a lot of energy.

"We'll get a really big panettone," he promises as I concentrate on locating Trevor and his white Toyota. Not going to lie, it's mainly the *white* bit of that description I'm focusing on. "The biggest panettone in all the land."

"Stop saying panettone," I grumble as his phone rings.

"Must be my panettone guy." He dodges my hit as he retrieves it from his pocket, his smile fading when he checks the screen. "It's Christian. Trust him to be up at this hour."

"Doesn't he live in London?" I ask, tucking my chin into my coat as I shiver. Andrew's younger brother had moved there a few years ago to work.

"He's not a good sleeper."

"Ten bucks says he's calling to yell at you."

Andrew only gives me a look as he accepts the call. "Hey," he says as I shudder again. "Yeah, we're completely grounded." He tugs the scarf from around his neck, holding it out to me and then throwing it at my head when I don't take it.

Put it on, he mouths, and I roll my eyes, secretly grateful as I do just that. I'm wearing my traveling Irish coat, not my Chicago one, and boy oh boy, do I feel the difference.

Andrew scowls at whatever his brother is saying, but he keeps one eye on me until I have the scarf wrapped tight. "It's not like we didn't try to... I *know* Mam's upset, but what am I supposed to do? Yeah, she's here. No, I'm..." His voice drops as he turns his back to me, walking a few steps away. "That's not why I . . . Oh, *real* mature."

I turn away, pretending I can't hear him as I tug the scarf up over my chin.

It smells like him. No, not him. His soap. His *soap*, Molly. Jesus. I glare at the line of cars, annoyed with myself, even as I breathe in the scent.

Seriously though, what is that? Sandalwood? *Pine?* Is pine soap a thing?

"You Molly?"

I jump at the shout across the road as a large scowling man gestures at me from the driver's seat of his white Toyota.

"You going to get in or what?" he asks gruffly when I nod.

I grab a tense-looking Andrew, who hangs up as we hurry to our ride. Whatever Christian said to him has destroyed his good mood and, by extension, mine, and he's silent as we get into the back, head bent as they continue their conversation through text.

We're on the interstate when he finally snaps, shoving his phone away with a noise of frustration as he sits back, gazing out the window. The urge to comfort him is overwhelming, and, as if to prove to myself that nothing's wrong, I slip my hand into his free one and squeeze.

"We can video call your family," I say. "The whole day if we have to. We'll live stream my apartment. Everything but the bathroom."

He sighs dramatically. "But is it really Christmas without one of my siblings barging in on me showering?"

"You guys have strange traditions."

He gives me a halfhearted smile before returning my squeeze and letting me go. "What about your family?" he asks as I bring my hand awkwardly to my lap. "Are they going to be okay with this?"

"They'll understand," I say automatically. To be honest, I've been so focused on him, I haven't even thought about them. "I'll give them a call in a few hours when my parents are up, but it's Zoe they'll be concerned about."

"She's due soon, isn't she?"

"A couple more weeks."

"And then you'll be an auntie." He seems cheered by that. "I'll have to give you all my godparent tips."

"I don't need them. She picked one of her friends as the godmother. I sulked for a whole day."

"As is your right. It's a grave injustice."

"That's what I said. And she just—" I break off as my screen lights up on the seat between us, Gabriela's name flashing in the darkness.

"Work stuff," I explain before he can ask. I sigh, bringing the phone to my ear. "If this is about—"

"I just want you to know that I accept," Gabriela interrupts in a rush.

"Accept what?"

"Position as best person in the whole freaking world."

"Not following."

"Michael's friend's partner works for Delta."

I blink at the back of our driver's head. "Okay?"

"Michael's friend owes us a massive favor because Michael introduced said friend *to* said partner."

"I'm really not—"

"I've traded in that favor for two standbys tonight."

My breath catches as I realize what she's saying. "You got us tickets home?"

Andrew's head snaps my way just as Gabriela speaks again.

"Well, no," she says. "I got you tickets to Buenos Aires."

"*Buenos Aires?*"

"Where you get a connecting flight to Paris," she continues, and I groan, knocking my head back against the seat. "Completely bypassing the storm on the East Coast."

"Gabriela—"

"No, it works out," she says excitedly. "Overnight tonight to Argentina. You've got one stop in Atlanta. Then tomorrow at seven their time another overnight to Paris."

"Paris isn't in Ireland."

"I know that, dummy, but it's nearer, isn't it? You'll be there on the twenty-third. Granted you'll both be zombies, but you'll be a lot closer there than you are now. Come on," she adds when I don't say anything. "I did it! You've got the air miles and you'll get your refund for your first flight anyway."

I will. And I do have the air miles. I have lots of air miles. I've been hoarding them for years, on some wild idea I'll get a sudden impulse to go traveling. And heading south to bypass the storm that shows no sign of letting up is the only option right now. But that's two to three days of solid traveling and all just to see my family for a holiday we don't even care that much about. All just to . . .

My eyes flick to Andrew to find him staring at me. He's not moving, he's barely even *breathing*, a hopeful look on his face that makes my chest hurt.

Ah crap.

"I know it's a lot, but you've got to decide soon," Gabriela says in my ear. "Plane goes in just under two hours and we'll need to book you in. Are you still at the airport?"

"Tonight?" Andrew whispers, and I nod jerkily.

"We just left," I tell her, not able to look away from him. "But we can get back?"

Andrew grins at me and a bizarre kind of disappointment mingles with renewed determination as I pull my gaze away.

"Do it," I say. "Book us in. I've got our details on my desktop. The folder's named—"

"Christmas Flights/Completed," Gabriela finishes. "Because of course they are."

"You know my computer password?"

"It's your sandwich order from that deli down the street," she says casually as I sputter at this blatant invasion of privacy. "You're kind of predictable, you know that?"

"Just book us in."

"Yes, ma'am," she says, and I can hear the smile in her voice. "This makes me feel great. This is my good deed for the year."

"Best person in the whole freaking world," I agree as Andrew starts texting again, his thumbs flying across the screen. "I'll let you know when we're at the airport."

She bids me a delighted "Bon voyage" as we hang up and I lean forward to the driver.

"I don't know if you heard that, but—"

"We're ten minutes away from your destination," he says, not looking at me.

"Right," I agree. "But see the thing is, we really need to get back to the airport."

"And I need to get home," he says. "I'm finishing up for the night."

"But I—"

"For the year," he adds. "My wife bought steaks."

"Trevor—"

"Big ones."

I stare at the back of his head as he stares stubbornly in front.

Fine.

Fine!

I grab my purse from the floor of the cab, reaching for the money that was to make up the vast majority of my relatives' Christmas presents.

"What are you doing?" Andrew whispers.

"Getting you home." I count what I have before leaning forward again. "I will give you one hundred dollars if you turn this cab around right now."

Trevor's eyes snap to mine in the rearview mirror. "Two hundred," he says when he sees I'm being serious. "Cash."

Andrew scoffs and I nod.

"Sold."

"*What?*" Andrew glances between the two of us, shocked. "No!"

"It's fine," I say, handing over the bills. "What's the point of earning all this money if I'm not going to spend it?"

He keeps protesting as Trevor swiftly, and probably illegally, turns the car around, earning a few annoyed honks in the process.

I put a hand against the door to steady myself until we're in the right direction.

"Molly—"

"Too late now," I interrupt cheerfully.

Andrew huffs, but I can already see his mood lifting. "I'll pay you back," he promises as Trevor speeds up.

"Yes, you will."

"Buenos Aires?" he asks, looking dazed.

"I hear their airport is just lovely this time of year."

"And then Paris." A smile spreads across his face. "We'll be able to get back from Paris," he says confidently.

He starts talking about connecting flights, bringing up the clock on his phone to work out the time differences, and it only takes a few seconds before his excitement amps up my excitement. This is an adventure, right? This is either a fun little adventure or possibly the stupidest thing I've ever done. And I once tried to wax my own eyebrows.

By the time we get back to the airport, we're practically jumping out of our seats and Andrew throws open the passenger door before we've even parked.

"Pleasure doing business with you," Trevor calls as I follow him out.

Andrew hurries around to the trunk as I glance toward the entrance, mentally calculating the time it will take us to check the bags and get through security. Thanks to Trevor's driving, we should make it with a good thirty minutes to spare if the lines aren't too long.

"Hey, Molly?"

I turn to find Andrew right behind me and, before I can react, he brings his hands to my cheeks, holding me steady as he kisses me hard on the forehead. It barely lasts a second, but my pulse skyrockets like the overdramatic traitor it is.

Andrew pulls back to grin at me. "You've just saved Christmas."

Technically Gabriela saved Christmas, but I'm not about to correct him. Not while he's still cupping my face. Not when he's looking at me like that.

"Let's wait until we're on the plane," I say as he turns to grab our bags. "Better yet. Let's wait until we're on the right continent."

We walk quickly back through the entrance, right past the mistletoe without even seeing it. Well, I see it. I am extremely aware of it, but Andrew doesn't seem to be so I pretend I'm not and follow him through the crowd.

"Excuse me. Sorry. Pardon me. I'm so— *Watch it*," I snap as a businessman almost runs into me.

I join Andrew at the departure board, both of us gazing up at the handful of flights still scheduled.

"I can't see it," he says, breathless. "Can you see it?"

I scan column after column, but can't see anything heading to Atlanta. "Maybe it just needs to refresh," I say with more confidence than I feel, but it stays exactly the same.

Andrew's expression tightens and I take out my phone, trying not panic as I call Gabriela back.

She picks up on the third ring. "Did you make it?"

"We did. But are you sure you booked the right flight?"

"I'm positive. I checked it twice."

"I don't see anything," I say as Andrew stares at the board so hard it's a miracle he's not giving himself a headache.

"I swear, Molly. I'm looking at the website right now."

"Read out the flight number."

"It's definitely going," she insists. "Delta DL676. Chicago Midway to—"

"*Midway?*" I screech the word so loud that a baby nearby bursts into tears. "We're at O'Hare!"

There's a long pause on the other end of line. "Oh."

I deflate instantly, my adrenaline spike crashing as I turn fully away from Andrew. I can't even bear to look at him.

"I should have checked," Gabriela says, sounding miserable.

"*I* should have told you," I say quickly. "This isn't on you."

"Let me keep looking."

"Gab—"

"There's got to be something. If not tonight, then in the morning." She keeps talking, but at a tug on my coat, I twist around to a grim-looking Andrew.

"I'll call you back," I say when he motions for me to hang up. "She's going to see if we can—"

"How long do we have before the gate closes?" he interrupts, and I check the time on my phone.

"An hour, but..." I trail off, realizing what he means. "That's not enough time."

"It might be. It's what? Forty minutes to Midway?"

"Not in this traffic. And even if it's delayed, there's security and luggage and—"

"I'm not saying we wouldn't need a bit of a miracle," he says. "But we could try. I've got to try."

I don't want to. I *really* don't want to. It was stressful enough getting back here. I don't want to rush across the city just so we can prolong our disappointment.

But he's looking back at me with those goddamn puppy dog eyes and his hair is all mussed up from where he's been pulling at it, and I'm reminded of every single time he's lit up at the mere mention of his family.

When this man became my weakness, I do not know. But tonight, it's like he's got me wrapped around his little finger.

I take a breath, hand clenching around the handle of my suitcase as I already regret my decision. "Okay," I say. "Let's go."

CHAPTER SIX

It's travel chaos outside the airport, with people still arriving for canceled flights. The confusion and frustration in the air is palpable and it doesn't help that the line for cabs is several people deep. Andrew and I don't even bother to join it, both of us glancing about as though for a miracle.

"Will we do that thing where we just shove in front of someone?" I ask, watching a woman climb into a taxi. "Like in the movies?"

Andrew grimaces but doesn't say no and that's when I spot a semi-familiar face walking past us with his cap down low.

"Trevor?"

Our driver glances back automatically at his name, scowling suspiciously when he sees me. "Thought you had a plane to catch?"

"I did. We do! You're still here?" I follow him as he turns away, almost tripping in my haste.

"Just had to use the men's room."

"Needs must!" I chime in a cheerful voice I don't recognize. "And what an incredible stroke of luck for us," I add.

"Because as it turns out, we've gone to the wrong airport and we'll be needing your services again."

He doesn't even turn around. "No."

My mouth drops open and I glance back at Andrew, who's struggling with both our bags.

"I just gave you two hundred bucks," I remind him.

"For a transaction that was agreed upon and completed."

"Oh, come on," I plead. Not the best argument of my career, but it's all I'm really capable of at the moment. We have five minutes max to get into a cab or else there's no point in even trying. "We just want to get home."

"So do I," he huffs. "And you've already delayed me by an hour."

"And paid you handsomely for it. We're from Ireland," I try again, exaggerating my accent in a way that would probably make everyone back home wince. But sometimes you've got to play the leprechaun card. "Do you have any family from there?"

"Nope," Trevor says flatly. "Though an Irish guy pissed in my cab once."

"Okay. So, I agree that's not a great—"

"Goodbye."

"Wait!" I whirl around, almost colliding with Andrew as Trevor stops by his car. I grab my bag and open it up right there in the middle of the road, the stuffed Cubs bear falling to the wet concrete as I retrieve a small pink box I'd placed carefully inside. "Let me bribe you," I say, holding it out to him.

Andrew shifts beside me, picking up the bear. "I don't think you're actually meant to say when something's a bribe."

I ignore him, opening the lid. Trevor peers inside, curious despite his best efforts.

"What the hell are those?" he asks, and I know I've got him.

What are they? They're handmade truffles from my favorite chocolate shop in the city. A.k.a., they're expensive as hell. A sumptuous variety of caramel latte, passionfruit and ginger, toasted coconut rum, and a dozen other practically perfect small dollops of joy. I was going to share them with Andrew once we got to our first-class seats. We were going to eat them with our free champagne. We were going to toast our tenth Christmas flight.

But Trevor doesn't need to know all that.

"Chocolates," I say, bringing the box closer to him. He looks down at them suspiciously, but his expression softens when he sees them. And why wouldn't it? These are good-looking chocolates. I would know. I picked them out myself.

"My wife loves chocolate," he admits gruffly, dragging his gaze reluctantly away from them and back to me. "My daughter too. She's about your age."

"I'm sure you must love her very—"

"She's a pain in my side."

"All right, well—"

"Just get in the car."

I blink in surprise as he takes the box from me. "Really?"

"Don't question the man," Andrew mutters as I hurriedly zip my bag back up. We've caused a *minor* traffic jam behind us and I raise an apologetic hand as we follow Trevor back to the car.

"Should have retired years ago," he grumbles as we get into the back. "You sure you know where you're going this time?"

"Midway," I say as Andrew drags a hand down his face. "And I'm happy to pay any speeding ticket you get."

"I bet you are," Trevor mutters as he pulls out of his space, but there's no heat to the words and, when he glances back at us, he looks almost determined. "Buckle up," he says. "I'll do my best."

The ride south to Chicago's second airport is fast but tense. Neither Andrew nor I speak as Trevor navigates the weather and the traffic, breaking the law only *slightly* as he fully earns those chocolates.

By the time he screeches to a halt at the drop-off point, we have a three-minute window for delays and Andrew scrambles out immediately to the trunk as I lean forward to Trevor.

"If you wouldn't mind waiting for ten minutes just in case we miss—"

"Out."

"Right. Yep. Happy Christmas!"

With our bags in hand, we race inside, pausing only briefly to check the departure board before going to check our luggage in.

Our first hurdle.

"I'm sorry," the woman says as soon as I show her my boarding card. "But the bag drop closed twenty minutes ago for this flight. They're about to start boarding," she adds as if that's a thing we're not *completely aware of.*

"I understand," I say, using my most professional voice. "But the plane is still here and I don't think my companion's giant suitcase is going to fit in the overhead compartment."

"They'll already be loaded onto the airplane."

"The plane that hasn't left yet!" I stress, slapping my hands on the counter with every word. "Please."

"We're just trying to get back for Christmas," Andrew says. "Her sister is about to give birth and I'm the only person who likes my mother's brussels sprouts. It's really important we get home."

The woman looks genuinely sympathetic, but just shakes her head as I resist the urge to slump to the floor and pretend none of this is happening.

"Let's leave them," Andrew says to me, looking desperate. "We'll just dump our stuff here."

"But all your presents," I protest. "And my Tabasco sauce."

"Your what?"

"We can't leave our luggage here," I continue, ignoring him. "That's insane."

"Do you have a better suggestion?"

"Obviously not, but—"

"We're going to miss the plane."

"And they'll destroy our stuff if we—"

"Just go."

We turn back to the counter as the attendant picks up a desk phone with one hand and motions for me to pass my suitcase with the other.

"Go," she says again. "I'll get these on and ring the gate."

Oh my God. "Really?"

"My dad was in the military," she says. "The years he didn't make it home for Christmas?" She shakes her head, tapping a number onto the keypad. "Go. Be with your families. But I can't promise anything."

Andrew jerks toward her, looking like he's about to hug her, but he thankfully turns instead and starts running toward security.

I linger for a second longer, slipping out a small piece of black cardboard from my wallet. "There's this amazing Thai place in Ravenswood," I babble. "They made me this special fifty-percent-off card because I ate there every night for two weeks once. I want you to have it."

The attendant just stares at me. "... Okay."

"Because it's Christmas."

"Molly!"

"Try the papaya salad," I tell her as Andrew's frustrated shout calls from across the concourse. "And thank you!"

I reach his side in record time as we round the corner, my heart pounding with each step.

This is it. We just need to get through security. We just need to get through security and ...

Shit.

Andrew and I come to an abrupt stop as we almost run into the wall of people waiting for passport control. A screen overhead says the wait to get through is forty-five minutes and even the preclearance line is jammed. Despite our rush, for a few seconds the two of us simply stare at the orderly, tired lines in front of us, and I feel my last bit of hope slip away. The gate is supposed to close in another few minutes and I doubt they'll keep it open for much longer.

Andrew exhales sharply, his body tense as he scans each column as though looking for the shortest one.

"I'm going to ask them to let us through," he mutters, and I follow numbly as he approaches a TSA agent standing to one side and starts to plead our case. I don't have the heart to tell him that there's no point. I'm sure they get asked the same thing by a dozen people every minute.

I swallow thickly, adrenaline warring with fresh disappointment as more and more travelers keep joining the lines.

There's a burning in my chest that moves to my throat and my breathing grows shallow as each second passes. We're going to miss the flight. We made it to the airport and now we're going to miss the flight.

"Andrew," I mumble, but he's not listening. To be honest, I'm not even sure if I spoke out loud or in my head.

God, it's warm in here.

"You're going to need to wait just like everyone else," the agent says, sounding like he's reading from a script.

"They're keeping the gate open for us," Andrew says. "If you could just—"

"Andrew," I say.

"Sir, everyone's in the same—"

I burst into tears.

I've always been a bit of a crier. Sad tears, happy tears, angry tears. It's my body's go-to reaction no matter the situation or the time of the month. And usually, it's not so bad. A couple seconds' pause, a tissue under the eyes. I get it out, I fix my makeup, and I move on.

These tears are not those tears.

These are loud, sloppy, sobbing tears that make everyone in our immediate circle stare at us. At *me*.

"We're going... to miss... our *flight*," I wail as the security agent rears back in horror. Even Andrew looks alarmed, and he's definitely seen me cry before.

The agent shifts uncomfortably, one hand raised between us as though he doesn't know whether to comfort or corral me into the corner. "Ma'am—"

"My sister's... having... a baby," I gasp, almost choking myself as I force the words out.

"Just let her through," someone calls from up ahead, and they're immediately backed up by others.

"It's Christmas!"

"She's pregnant!"

"She's not..." The agent's face tightens. "It's her sister who's—"

But he's drowned out by even more voices supporting little old highly hysterical me. A particularly violent hiccup has him wincing as Andrew rubs slow circles into my back.

"All right, all right," the man mutters, hurrying us to the front of the line. "Just make it quick."

It's like he doesn't even know who he's talking to. We rush through passport control and practically fling our stuff through the scanners. By some miracle our bags aren't picked up for extra checks and then we're off, sprinting through the terminal as fast as we can and garnering several annoyed protests in our wake as we dodge wheeled suitcases and roaming shoppers.

"Run," Andrew says, sounding only a little panicked as we careen around a corner. "Run, run, run."

Somewhere above me I hear what sounds like my name being called over the announcement system, and I pick up the pace, my laptop bag banging uncomfortably against my hip as it slides down my shoulder with each step. They made this look *much* easier in *Home Alone*.

"We're here," I yell as we approach our gate. There's no one else waiting but the doors are open, the desk still manned. "We're here!"

An annoyed-looking attendant speaks briefly into a walkie-talkie before rounding the counter. "Ms. Kinsel—"

"Yes! Hi. That's me." We stumble to a stop in front of her as I bring up the tickets on my phone.

"We've been calling you," she says sternly.

"And we came running," Andrew says, grinning at

her. Her glare softens as she takes him in because of course it does, but it's me her attention returns to as she checks our passports.

"Is everything all right, ma'am?"

Andrew's relieved smile fades as he glances at me. It's only then that I realize I'm still crying.

"I'm fine," I say shakily, snatching my passport back in embarrassment.

She doesn't look convinced, but waves us through anyway, shutting the door behind us.

"I didn't know you were serious," Andrew mutters, sounding concerned as we hurry down the tunnel.

"I wasn't," I whisper back. "I'm honestly okay." Only now that I've opened the floodgates, hell if I know how to close them again. Oh God, did I break something inside? Is this just who I am now?

I'm going to be so dehydrated.

We've clearly held up the already delayed flight and get glares from the other passengers, but I don't think either of us care as we head down the aisle to two seats right by the toilets. Not that I'm about to complain, collapsing down as Andrew stores our carry-on bags away. He takes the seat next to me as the attendants begin final checks and close the doors, and I blow out a shaky breath, the sweat cooling uncomfortably on my body from the sudden burst of activity.

"So," Andrew says, opening the plastic bag of airplane freebies. He finds a tissue and hands it to me as the tears continue to stream down my face. "You bring your own bottle of Tabasco sauce home with you?"

"I grew up in a house where the only flavors were salt and pepper." I sniff, dabbing my eyes. "What do you think?"

"I think that if you can keep up this crying trick, we'll never have to queue for anything ever again."

I start to laugh, which somehow only makes me cry harder, but I give in to it, letting my adrenaline tip into hysteria until an attendant politely lets me know that I'm scaring the other passengers.

CHAPTER SEVEN
SIX YEARS AGO

Flight Four, Chicago

"I want you to stop sending me pictures of lamps."

"Now, see..." Andrew shoves my bag into the overhead compartment before sliding into the seat next to me. "Now that you've said that, I'm never going to stop. You've just shown your hand, Kinsella."

"Does your girlfriend know you're sending me pictures of lamps you find on the street?"

"Not only does Emily know, but she actively encourages it so I don't take them home to show her."

I laugh as I bend down to grab my water bottle, my body protesting the movement. I was up half the night with research and ended up falling asleep in an awkward position that every muscle in my body is now punishing me for.

"You all right there, champ?" Andrew asks when I groan.

I sit back up, trying to get comfortable. "I need a massage."

"I have a girlfriend, Molly."

"Shut *up*."

Andrew just grins at me.

He's been hyper ever since we met up at security. At first, I thought it was because of his new relationship, but then I caught the whiff of alcohol on him when he leaned in for a hug and he confessed he'd come straight from a party.

"You're not going to fall asleep on me, are you?" I ask now as he puts his seat belt on. "You look like you turn into a sleepy drunk."

"I can handle myself." He watches some of the other passengers shuffle down the aisle before turning his attention back to me. "You can meet her, you know. Emily. I don't want you thinking you can't."

"Why would I think that?"

He shrugs. "Just don't talk to her or look her in the eye. She gets funny about things like that."

"Sure, sure." I sip my water, watching him curiously. "Introducing her around, are we? Things must be getting serious."

"Yeah, well..." He trails off, looking awkward, and I try to ignore the shallow pang in my heart. They *are* getting serious. It's only been two months since he told me about her. As far as I know, there'd been no one long-term between her and Hayley and I was kind of used to him being single. Or maybe that's just because now I am. Daniel broke up with me in the fall, a real "it's not you, it's me" situation, and I've been moping about it ever since. And that's allowed! Sometimes you need a good mope. But when that moping gets in the way of being happy for others, I know I have to start digging myself out of my broody little hole.

So, I do the first thing that comes to mind, which, as it turns out, is kicking Andrew's foot with mine.

"*Ow*," he says pointedly.

"I'm happy for you."

"And you have a weird way of showing it."

"I mean it, Andrew. This is great. I can't wait to meet her."

He smiles at that. "It *is* great."

"Yes."

"Because I deserve good things."

"You do. The best."

"Including . . ." He waggles his eyebrows as he presses the call button. "Some champagne?"

I laugh. "They're not going to serve you."

"They will. It's Christmas."

"And you're drunk."

"Tipsy. Trust me. I can handle this."

He makes eye contact with a flight attendant squeezing down the aisle and smiles so widely that she falters in her step.

"Smooth," I mutter, but he just hushes me and, as promised, gets us our champagne.

Now

Buenos Aires is a beautiful city. Cosmopolitan, passionate, full of food and dance and *life*. Or at least, so the giant posters surrounding us make it look. I wouldn't actually know, seeing as, without a visa, we're not allowed to leave the airport.

"God, you know what I'd love right now?" Andrew says from where he's sprawled on the chair beside me. "Some of those little truffles from—"

"I will punch you in the face," I tell him. "In your big stupid face."

"I mean the money, I can understand. But the chocolate?" He brings one hand to his heart, looking at me with a wounded expression. "I love chocolate."

"I know you do," I grumble, staring at an image of a red-lipped tango dancer on the opposite wall. "That's why I bought them."

I peer at the overhead lights, trying to decide if I'm hungry or tired or both. We flew to Atlanta, where we waited four hours to fly the ten hours to Argentina, where we're currently waiting for our connection to Paris, which will take another seven hundred and eighty minutes. Thirteen more hours.

Yeah. So much better than staying in Chicago with my bed and my shower and my food and my—

I groan, slumping down in my chair. All my clothes are in my checked luggage, which was something I hadn't been particularly concerned about but is all I can think about now with no change of clothes on me. I probably stink, even with the cheap body spray I bought in the drugstore here.

"We made the right choice," Andrew says, correctly interpreting my annoyance as he scrolls through his phone. "That storm isn't going anywhere. We would never have gotten a direct flight."

"Would staying in Chicago really have been so bad?" I sigh, only half-joking. "I mean, I know you love your family and everything, but..."

Andrew smirks. "I'm never going to stop thanking you for this. You know that, right? I can't think of anyone else who would put themselves through this for me."

"All right," I mutter, embarrassed. "No need to be all sincere about it."

He laughs, mimicking my pose as he slides down his seat, legs spreading in that way men do. I don't call him out on it though. There's no one else in our row and I like the way his knee brushes against mine. I like it even more when he doesn't move it away.

I take a slow breath at the sensation, holding it in as I

try to stay relaxed. We barely spoke once we were in the air, both of us too exhausted to say more than a few words to each other. But I remained constantly aware of him. As aware as I am now as he stares blankly ahead and I stare at him. Discreetly, of course. Face tilted away, corner of my eye, stealthwise. I can't help it. I'm kind of hoping that if I keep looking, I'll eventually see it, whatever had me so confused back in Chicago. Confused now.

"We should try and sleep on this one," he says. "We'll only have an hour to catch the flight on to Dublin." He pauses. "If there aren't any delays."

"There won't be. We'll make it. Maybe we'll even get on the news."

"So that's your plan. Brief, local fame."

"We'll make it," I repeat, and he shoots me a half-smile.

"I know. I think I'll be better once we're . . . I don't know, in Europe?" He laughs at how ridiculous it sounds. "At least it will be a fun story to tell the family. We'll take a break between movies to stretch our legs and I'll say, hey, remember that time I flew twenty-four hours out of my way just to get home for Christmas?"

"Stretch your legs? How many movies do you guys watch in the Fitzpatrick household?"

He grins. "It depends on the year. Dad usually chooses the main one, but he can be unpredictable. If it doesn't scratch the itch, we can go all night, though my parents usually head to bed around midnight." Andrew shifts, twisting his body to face me. "I was going to suggest a movie marathon at yours if we'd stayed. Just Christmas films all day."

I force a smile. "That sounds nice." It sounds very nice. But I don't want to think about all the things he was going to suggest. It had only been for an hour or so, but I'd gotten very attached to the idea of spending Christmas with Andrew.

"We should go to the Music Box next Halloween," he continues, and I raise a brow. The Music Box is the kind of pretentious movie theater that I love and he tolerates. "They do horror marathons," he adds at my look.

"I can't sit still for that long; I'll need to pee."

"I'll get you an aisle seat. Quick escape. Or one of those adult diapers."

"Well, how can a girl say no to that?"

"It's a date then."

My smile freezes on my face as I force myself to turn back and face the tango lady.

Not a date. Not a date! So why—

I flinch at the tickling sensation by my ear and whip my head around to see Andrew drawing back, eyes wide at my exaggerated response. His hand hovers uncertainly between us.

"Your earring," he explains, showing me the small silver crescent. "It was caught in your hair."

My hand flies up to my bare lobe. "I must have lost the backer."

He drops it into my open palm with a frown. "Are you okay?"

"Just tired," I lie. I take out the other one and slip them both into my pocket. Andrew doesn't look convinced, but he lets it go. "Bet you're excited to see the kids," I say, changing the subject. His older brother, Liam, has a boy and a girl. "You must miss them."

"I do," he says. "I swear it's like every time I get back they're whole new people. It was the same with Hannah. Although, the way Liam and Christian used to talk about her growing up, I gather she was very annoying."

I laugh. "Seriously?"

"Nah. I suppose every six-year-old is annoying when

you're eighteen and just want to get on with things. We're close though. She's a good kid. Real smart. Smarter than any of us."

"We should do something next time they come to visit."

"She'd love that," he says, perking up. "She knows all about you."

"She does?"

"Oh yeah. Irish girl making it big in the world? She thinks you're pretty cool."

I stare at him, delighted. "No one's ever called me cool before."

"Hard to believe," he deadpans.

We fall into silence and after a moment he takes off his sweater, using it as a cushion between his body and the chair.

He's wearing a holiday T-shirt underneath because of course he is. Though this one isn't that bad, navy with a gingerbread man on the front. I examine it for a second before Andrew picks a loose thread from his sleeve and then I'm staring at his bicep, and the curve of muscle that disappears beneath the fabric. There's a tiny scar by his elbow, a sliver of raised pink skin from some childhood fall that I'm immediately fascinated by.

"Why didn't you move to Seattle?"

"What?" I jerk my gaze up to find him watching me and try not to look as guilty as I bizarrely feel.

"With Brandon," he says. "You said you asked him to stay, but why didn't you want to move?"

"Because of my job."

"They don't have lawyers in Seattle?"

I frown. "Don't simplify it like that."

"I'm not. I'm just..." He trails off with a shrug. "You're right, never mind."

I can't read the expression on his face. He almost looks frustrated, though that could be the exhaustion. To be honest, I'm kind of surprised we haven't started snapping at each other yet.

"I didn't want to leave," I say. "And I'd have to take the bar exam again. It would have been a whole big thing."

"You'd have to do that to practice in Ireland too," he points out, and I give him a funny look.

"Yeah, but I'm not moving to Ireland, am I?"

"You might someday."

I huff. "You sound like my parents. I have no intention of moving back to Dublin. Chicago's my home now." An uncomfortable thought strikes me. "It isn't for you?" He's lived there even longer than I have.

"Sure it is," he says. "But so is Ireland. If you can have a home in two places."

"Of course you can. But I'd only been with Brandon a few months," I add, feeling the need to point that out again. "Definitely not enough to move halfway across the country."

"So, if you'd been with him longer, you might have gone?"

"I don't know." The words are curt, sounding as annoyed as I feel. "That's way too much of a hypothetical."

We stare at each other for a beat before he nods. "Okay."

"Yeah? So can we change the subject?"

"Sure. Are you seeing anyone else? I don't think I asked."

"That's not changing the subject."

"Never mind then."

"I've been concentrating on myself," I tell him.

"Have you now?" He smiles slightly. "And what does that look like?"

"I do hot yoga on Sunday mornings. And I get a massage every second Tuesday."

"Swedish?"

"Deep muscle." I grimace. "Usually because I've strained something in hot yoga."

He smirks. "Well, I'm glad you're not dating anyone. It means I get you all to myself." He sits up as he speaks, stretching his arms over his head. The movement lifts his T-shirt, revealing a thin band of skin just above his jeans that suddenly has me furious.

I snap my gaze away, my jaw clenching in a way my dentist would *not* be happy about. "So, you want me to be alone then, is that it?"

He pauses. "I didn't mean it like that."

"It sounds like you did."

Andrew goes quiet beside me, but I can't bring myself to look at him. My anger disappears as quickly as it came, leaving me tired and embarrassed and still so very, very confused.

"Sorry," I say after a long moment.

"Me too. I really didn't mean it the way it sounded."

"I know. I just . . ." Need to get away from him. "I'm going to go stretch my legs and text Zoe."

"Molly—"

"I'll be right back." I stand so fast my vision swims, but I ignore it as I stride off, limping slightly from a dead leg. I focus on the pins and needles so I don't focus on him and march down the terminal before taking an abrupt left at a restroom sign.

The hallway is empty and thankfully so is the ladies' room. So, as millions of equally confused women have done before me, I lock myself in the first stall, sit with a huff on the toilet lid, and just . . . ugh.

Maybe I drank too much. Maybe I'm tired and I'm stressed and I had one too many glasses of champagne. That can be the only explanation for why I feel like I'm losing my goddamn mind. Because Andrew and I...

Sometimes I feel like he's been the one constant in my life since I moved to this city. Through the chaos of my early twenties, of finding my way, finding myself, he's always been with me. Maybe not physically. There were years I only saw him a handful of times, but he was always there. I could always talk to him. Could always moan to him. Could always celebrate and commiserate. And now I'm hiding from him in an airport bathroom.

I shouldn't have kissed him.

Why did I kiss him?

I close my eyes, dropping my head to my knees as I feel the beginnings of a headache forming at my temples.

I'm just not going to think about it. That's what I'm not going to do. Instead, I'm going to compartmentalize and focus on getting us back to Ireland and then, *then*, I am going to quit my job and book a vacation and on that vacation I will eat a lot of food and I will fall in love. I will fall in love with a masseuse and he will be very handsome and have an impeccable dress sense and won't be confusing at all.

But for now, I compartmentalize.

I stay there for as long as is socially acceptable and only then force myself to move in case I miss boarding. The harsh fluorescent lights overhead do nothing to help my confidence. I've been playing with my hair all night and it now hangs limply around my face, while my makeup has all but melted into my pores. I look like a mess. Which is understandable and not something I would usually care about with Andrew, but now I feel uncharacteristically self-conscious as I wet a paper towel and wash my face as best I can. It doesn't help that I changed clothes back in O'Hare, trading my skirt and blouse for sweatpants and an oversized hoodie. They're comfortable but aren't exactly helping the whole girl-in-the-before-photo vibe. Especially when there's not going to be an after photo anytime soon.

I give up on my halfhearted makeover, practice my I'm-totally-normal-and-just-a-little-tired smile, and open the restroom door, fully committed to acting like everything's fine and—

"Finally."

Andrew's waiting outside.

I freeze when I see him and he scowls when I do, straightening from his slump against the wall as I stand there like a cornered mouse.

"All right," he says, peering down at me. "What the hell is going on with you?"

CHAPTER EIGHT

"What do you mean?" My nerves skyrocket at the suspicion on his face. He's standing way too close to me, as close as we stood under the mistletoe, and nope, no thank you. Not needed right now.

"You're being weird," he says when I try to skirt around him. He immediately moves to the side, blocking my way.

"Because it's been a weird night. Day. However long it's been."

His hand shoots out when I try to get past again, pushing me gently against the wall. Only you'd swear he'd pulled me into his arms the way I react, sucking in a breath so loud that he rears back like I hit him.

He looks at me like I'm a stranger. Probably because I'm acting like one.

"You look like you're going to puke," he says, some of his wariness morphing into concern. "Do you want to sit down?"

"I'm fine." I push the hair back from my face, feeling a flush in my cheeks. Maybe I do need to sit down. Maybe I'm ill! That would explain everything.

"What is it?" he asks. "You can tell me. Is it your period?"

"No," I mutter, annoyed until I force myself to meet his gaze. The worry I see there only makes me feel worse. This is *Andrew*. I can talk to Andrew.

Just not about this. If Andrew is my one constant right now, then I refuse to let him go, since casually revealing to your friend that *Hey! I liked it when our bodies touched! Let's do that again!* might come across the wrong way.

"Can we go now?" I ask. "Trust us to miss this flight."

"We've got time." His expression softens at the panic he no doubt sees on my face. "Come on, Moll. What's up?"

"Beyond the giant mess of this trip?" I hesitate when he just looks at me like the stubborn asshole he is. "It's nothing," I say eventually. "I've just been super busy lately."

"You're always busy." He doesn't say it in a judging way, more like a statement of fact, but it still stings.

"I know," I say. "But work feels especially manic right now."

"Okay, well—"

"I also think I'm at the beginning of an early midlife crisis? And I was excited about seeing you and the flight and probably put way too much expectation on the whole thing and it's just—"

"Molly—"

"It's stupid," I finish.

"What's stupid?"

I ignore him, noticing his empty hands for the first time. "Who's watching our stuff?"

"A shifty-eyed man who tried to sell me a Rolex," he says without missing a beat. "What's stupid?"

"The..." What is happening to me? "The mistletoe thing... I shouldn't have..." I lift my hands helplessly, but he gives me nothing, staring at me with a blank look like he has no idea what I'm talking about. Because of course, he doesn't. He's probably already forgotten about it.

"You know what?" I say. "Maybe I am going to puke."

"Are you talking about when you kissed me?"

I am full-on sweating now.

"Molly?"

"Yeah. Yes." I shift my weight from one foot to the other. "I shouldn't have done it."

His brow furrows. "Why not?"

"Because it's *dumb!*" I exclaim. "The whole thing was dumb and I liked it and maybe I'm tired of spending every year with people thinking I hate Christmas and I just wanted to show that I could have a little good-natured, festive fun and—"

"You liked it?" he interrupts.

"What?"

"You liked the kiss?"

I stop talking, biting the inside of my cheek so hard I'm surprised it doesn't bleed. Maybe I should just get a flight to Greece and meet Zoe there. I bet Greece is lovely in December. "I guess."

"You guess," he repeats slowly. "And that... makes you want to puke?"

"I think it's because I've been going through a dry spell since Brandon," I tell him, and he blinks. "That and the champagne and all my aforementioned stress. It messed up my mind. Made me all floopy."

"That's not a word."

"You're right." I poke him in the chest, ignoring the immediate tingle in my finger. "It's not. Another indication of how floopy I am. That's all."

Andrew's gaze narrows as he examines me, but I actually feel a little relieved. Confessing to him has already started to heal me like the good little lapsed Catholic I am.

"Okay?" I ask, and he pulls back, putting some much-needed space between us.

"Okay," he says. "I get it."

"You do?"

"Yeah. When you kissed me under the mistletoe, it didn't go as you expected."

"Right."

"You were tired and stressed and haven't kissed anyone in a while so, when you kissed me, your wires got crossed."

"Exactly."

"It confused you."

"It *did*." I'm beaming at him now, relieved he understands.

Andrew nods. "So, we should do it again."

"Yes, we ... What?"

"We should kiss again to clear things up," he says, completely serious. "So you'll be less confused."

I pause. The words individually make sense, that much I understand. But together... "How would that make me any less confused?" I ask.

"Because if you feel nothing, you'll know it was just a random, stress-induced moment of madness. And if you feel the same way..."

"What?" I demand when he doesn't continue. "If I feel the same way, what?"

"It doesn't matter," he says simply. "You probably won't. Seeing as how you were just tired."

"I *am* tired."

"Right."

I stare at him as a speaker close to us blares to life with an announcement, but it's not for our flight. Andrew doesn't move an inch and I realize belatedly that he's waiting for me to make the next move.

And I know what that move should be. I know he expects me to laugh and drag him back to the gate. I know that's what I should do.

But looking up at that familiar face, I know it's not what I *want* to do. And isn't that just terrifying?

"You don't think it would be weird?" I ask.

"I don't think it will be any weirder than how you're being right now," he says flatly. "It's worth a shot, isn't it?"

I have no idea. But the man kind of has a point.

"Okay," I say, calling his bluff. If he's surprised, he doesn't show it. "Great idea." I straighten my shoulders, hands clenching into fists at my side as I fight the urge to pull my hair back. "You should probably do it. Kiss me, I mean. Seeing as I kissed you the first time. Although I guess, scientifically, we'd need to go back to O'Hare and find the mistletoe, but I don't think they'll still have it by the time we— Okay, okay! Jesus."

My back hits the wall as Andrew crowds me, stepping into my space until we're as close as we can be without touching. My hands shoot out, grabbing on to his shoulders to hold him there as my pulse starts to race.

"This is an experiment," I clarify, and I swear I see a faint glimmer of amusement in his eyes. For whatever reason, it makes me feel calmer. "It's for science."

"For science." He echoes it like a vow. "Do you want to hear a chemistry joke?"

"No."

He grins and I suddenly can't breathe. "You sure? It's a pretty good—"

I kiss him.

You know when people say that the anticipation of a kiss can be better than the actual event? Those people have never kissed Andrew Fitzpatrick.

It's a light one. A tame one. And yet again my reaction is not what it should be, my heart vaulting into my throat, my body surging up to meet his, following his warmth. And I should be disappointed, because with everything else going on in my life, this, this right here, is the last thing I need. The last thing I need and only thing I want.

That simple realization sends a spark of alarm through my mind, a blaring *Whoa there, time-out*, but then Andrew shifts, his mouth slanting over mine as his hands leave my hips to cup my face. He tilts my head to deepen the kiss and I make a noise, a little, dare I say it, whimper, that has me so embarrassed that, again, I'm the first to pull away. This time Andrew lets me go and I open my eyes, ready to apologize and make excuses or just downright *lie*, when I look up at him and see that I've wiped the smile right off his face.

A lock of hair falls across my forehead, tickling my cheek, and I watch as Andrew's eyes track the movement before he slowly, like I'm some sort of skittish animal (which, okay, yes), tucks it behind my ear. Goosebumps break out over my skin as he runs his fingers through the strands before dropping his hand to the side.

"No loose earrings this time?" I try to be sarcastic but only sound hoarse instead.

"Can only use that excuse once."

Neither of us moves. Neither of us speaks. The corridor we're in is bright and smells strongly of disinfectant. But it's also empty and we're both as alone as we're probably going to be for the next while.

"Feel better?" he finally asks, and it takes me a moment to figure out what he's talking about.

"Yep," I croak.

"All cleared up?"

"Uh-huh."

"Want to do it again?"

"Ye— *No*," I amend quickly, and just like that his smile is back, the intensity in his expression vanishing like he just flicked a switch.

"Still confused, huh?" He sighs. "I knew it wouldn't work."

"Then why did you suggest we do it?"

"I wanted to see what it would be like."

I stare at him. "And?"

"Yeah."

"What do you mean, *yeah*?"

"It was good," he says, turning to listen as another announcement blares across the terminal.

"It was more than good!" The gooey warmth I feel curdles into annoyance as his attention shifts away from me. "I am an excellent kisser. And that was an excellent kiss."

"Sure."

"No, not *sure*, you—" I break off when he turns, heading back down the corridor. "Andrew!"

"We're going to miss our flight," he calls over his shoulder.

I hurry after him, struggling to keep up with his long legs.

"I can't believe you scared me like that," he says when I do, typing something into his phone. Up ahead people are starting to get in line for boarding. "I thought there was something actually wrong with you, but you just have a little crush."

"I do not!"

"Think you do. I can tell."

"From one kiss?"

"Two kisses." He says it almost absently, reading a new message.

"The first one doesn't count," I tell him. "And the second one was *your* idea."

He doesn't answer as he retrieves our suit cases from a cheerful young woman with giant baubles attached to her T-shirt.

"Six out of ten," he says, turning back to me.

My mouth drops open. I know instantly what he means. "For our *kiss*?"

"Don't feel bad. You said so yourself, you're tired."

"I'm not—" I break off before I almost shout at him. "You're being annoying on purpose."

"Yeah," he says as if that's obvious. "Feel better?"

The line starts to shuffle forward as the doors open. I do feel better. As if he knew pissing me off would distract me above all else.

"Yes," I admit, trying not to fidget under his gaze. "I do."

"Good." He joins the end of the line and, after a second, I follow.

"You didn't have to kiss me just to distract me."

"Ah, sure we all have to make sacrifices." He glances over his shoulder and I swear there's a goddamn twinkle in his eye. "And you're an excellent kisser, Molly Kinsella."

"Stop teasing," I groan.

"I'm not teasing about that." He holds out his arm, wrapping it around my shoulder when I step into him like I always do. "Forget about it, okay? It's not weird and it's not a big deal. I'm just glad you're out of your funk."

"I know it's not a big deal. I never said it was a big deal."

"I'm telling this story at your wedding though. How you wanted to throw up at the thought of kissing me."

"Maybe I'll tell it at yours," I quip back. "How you came on to me in Buenos Aires during the worst Christmas ever."

"Fine. Whoever marries first gets the story."

"Deal."

"Deal."

I gaze up at him, eyes narrowing. "Six out of ten?"

He smiles. "Seven. Anything more and I need to see some tongue."

"That's gross. You're gross. Don't kiss me again."

"I will try and control myself," he says seriously, and I huff, but it's halfhearted. I'm mostly relieved. Relieved that

I'm no longer keeping things from him. That he truly doesn't seem to think it's a big deal that we've kissed each other twice in twenty-four hours after ten years of, you know, *not doing that at all.*

I stay silent as we shuffle toward the plane, trying not to overthink it. Andrew gets another text and is quickly distracted, though his hand remains tight around me.

I'm not teasing about that.

It's not a big deal. He just said it wasn't and now he's acting like it too. But my lips are still tingling. My lips are still tingling and even when I press them together, they don't stop.

CHAPTER NINE
FIVE YEARS AGO

Flight Five, Chicago

"Try it on."

"No."

"Just try it!"

"No, it would make you too happy."

"Try it on or I'm taking it back."

"That's not how gifts work, you weirdo." But Andrew shrugs off his sweater (*all the jingle ladies*) and unwraps the one I just gave to him.

"It's cashmere," I say as he holds it up. "And I know it's not exactly *fun*, but it's wintergreen, which is definitely a Christmas color, and it's light enough that you could wear it all year round if you wanted to."

He doesn't answer, too busy pulling it on over his head. I don't know why I'm so nervous. I've never been someone who worries about gifts, and yet I spent a whole weekend running around the city trying to find the perfect one for him. And I'm pretty sure I failed. I should have just gotten him a gift card. Everyone loves gift cards.

"I've kept the receipt," I say. "So, if you don't like it or it doesn't fit, we can—"

"It'll fit," he interrupts, his voice muffled by the fabric. His head pops through, his hair ruffled as he pulls it down over his chest.

I lean forward, brushing some lint from his sleeve before realizing I'm fussing. "Well? What do you think?"

"I *think*," he says, pulling the label free, "that this is now the nicest thing I own."

"Really?"

He smirks. "Is this moment about me getting a present or about you giving me a present?"

"Me," I say, and he laughs. "You're really hard to buy for."

"I'm easy to buy for. Get me anything."

"*Anything* is a code word for *hard to buy for*."

"Okay, we're definitely not doing this again," he says. "This is supposed to be fun, not stressful. Don't you exchange presents with your family?"

"Of course I do. But it's usually money, the greatest gift of all."

"You're a cold, sad woman."

"Give me my present."

Andrew smirks, reaching into the front pocket of his bag. He's the one who insisted on doing this, and I only agreed because I thought we would swap on the plane and open them in our respective houses. Alone. I didn't think he'd want to do the whole thing *now*. In front of everyone. We're due to board in a few minutes and the rows of seats by the gate are filling up, with a few people already waiting in line, their passports at the ready.

"Here you go."

He grabs my hand, pressing a small, tissue-wrapped rectangle into my palm that I quickly open.

Huh.

I truly didn't know what to expect. But I think if you'd given me a hundred guesses of what Andrew might get me as a Christmas gift, I would have needed a couple more attempts.

"It's a . . . fridge magnet?" I ask, and he nods.

"But it's also a fun one," he says. "It has a pun."

"I can see that."

"It says, 'Pasta la vista, baby,'" he continues, straight-faced as he points to the Comic Sans print. "And there's a picture of—"

"—some pasta, yes."

"I got it on eBay."

"Andrew."

"It cost me three dollars in postage."

A noise comes out of me before I can stop it, somewhere between a snort and a laugh, and I slap my hand over my mouth. "This is what you got me? I spent the last two weeks anxious out of my mind over this, and this is what you got me?"

"It's the thought that counts."

"You *thought* about this?" I narrow my eyes, not buying it for an instant. "Give me my real present."

"That is—"

"Andrew."

He grins, reaching back into his bag. "You're the spoiled child on Christmas morning, you know that? This was supposed to be a lesson in gracious disappointment."

"I'm returning your sweater."

"Again, not how this works, but here."

I drop the magnet onto my lap as he passes me a slim, red leather book.

The spine is cracked and the cover well-worn from being carried around. It has to be several years old at least. If not decades. *A Diner's Guide to Chicago* written in slanting letters on the front.

"It might not be the most up-to-date," he says, leaning into me as I open it. "But look." He flips forward a few pages, pointing to the margins.

"The owner wrote notes?"

"*Owners*," he says. "The handwriting changes. Looks like a few people got their hands on it."

He's right. There are some marked in pencil, some in red pen, and the writing switches from neat square letters to a tiny calligraphy I can barely read. "Where did you even get this?"

"I found it at a flea market months ago. Thought you might like it."

"I love it," I correct, tracing the scrawled words. *Ask for the handmade butter. Steal it if necessary.* "It's like reading a diary." *Tasting menu is worth the overtime. Flirt with Diane to get the good table.* "You got it months ago?"

"When you know, you know."

And he kept it all this time. Just to give to me.

"Uh-oh," Andrew says as I start to choke up. "Here they come."

"They're happy tears," I assure him. "Christmas tears. It's perfect, thank you." I clutch it to my chest, twisting so I can hug him.

"You're welcome," he murmurs, squeezing me back. "Happy Christmas, Moll."

A phantom voice echoes throughout the terminal, announcing a twenty-minute delay to our flight, but neither of us minds so much. In that moment I think I would have taken a twenty-hour delay so long as I got to spend it with him.

Now, Paris

"What do you mean, *my bag isn't here?*"

I stare at the woman behind the counter as she stares right back, her nude lipstick perfectly applied as she smiles apologetically at me.

"My stuff is in that bag," I say stupidly.

"I'm sorry."

"You lost it?" This is a joke. This is a terrible, very unfunny joke. I almost expect a camera crew to come leaping out, announcing I'm on some cheap reality show. I barely slept on the flight to Paris, after barely sleeping at the airport, after barely sleeping since I left Chicago. It's the 23rd of December. I have not had a shower in forty-eight hours, the timing of my contraceptive pill is *extremely* messed up, and they have *lost my bag?*

"They put our luggage in at the same time!" I exclaim. "How did they lose mine and not his?"

"Maybe yours was too small," Andrew mutters behind me, only to quickly look away at the death glare I send him.

"We didn't lose it," the woman reassures me. "We know where it is. It's in Argentina."

"But *I'm* in Paris."

"We'll have it on the next flight over."

I resist the urge to drop my head to the counter. "But we're not staying here. We're trying to get to Ireland."

"Again, I'm extremely sorry." Her polite tone doesn't change, but there's a hint of steel behind it that tells me I'm not the first wailing passenger she's had to and *will* have to deal with today. "We can compensate you per day your bag is not with you and fly it immediately to where you'd like it to go, but at the moment there is nothing more we can do for you."

"But—"

"I'm sorry, madam."

We hold each other's gaze for a long second, but for once I'm the first to blink as I force out that awful customer urge to yell at the person who has nothing to do with my problem.

"Okay," I say, sounding every inch the forlorn little girl that I feel like right now. "What do I need to do?"

One signed form and two minutes later, we trudge our way back through the entrance hall of Charles de Gaulle Airport. The place is predictably packed and I feel my mood slip further as I stare up at the departure board.

"We've missed the flight to Dublin, haven't we?" It was going to be a tight squeeze anyway but waiting for my bag that never came had made it impossible. I don't need to ask Andrew to know the rest of them are sold out.

"Don't worry about it," Andrew says gently. But I do. Because something as simple as getting home for Christmas should not be this complicated.

"There's a flight tonight that's booked out," he continues. "There's not much else we can do, but if we hang around, we can see if we can get on it, and there's always tomorrow."

Tomorrow. Tomorrow is Christmas Eve, which means we're cutting it close. Too close to waste another day hanging around at an airport. Not that that seems to have occurred to Andrew. He's not even looking at the board; he's gazing unblinkingly into space, his shoulders slumped in defeat. He's given up. Which is understandable. Giving up is by far the most appealing option right now. Definitely the easiest one.

It's just something I've never been a particular fan of.

"We're both exhausted," he continues. "Maybe the best thing to do is try and get a hotel room and then—"

"London."

"What?"

I turn to Andrew, doing the timings in my fuzzy, weary head. "We can try and get to London. We'll be able to get home from there."

He hesitates. "We're talking about a couple of hundred dollars, Molly."

"That's what credit cards are for. We've come this far. You really want to give up now?"

"I want you to sleep for a few hours before you collapse."

"I said I'd get you home," I dismiss. "So, I'm going to get you home."

I push past him to a bit of empty space along the wall, where I sit cross-legged and open my laptop. It takes a second, but he follows like I knew he would.

"Let's think about this," I say, frowning when he just looks at me. "Sit!"

He sighs heavily to show he's just humoring me but dumps his bag to the floor, sitting in front of me with a grumpy look. I know it's because a part of him has stopped believing he'll make it in time, so I don't hold it too much against him.

"London isn't a problem," I say, scanning the available flights. "There are seats this afternoon and this evening. And from there..." Shite. There are over a hundred flights from London to Dublin a day, but with the number of Irish people living in the UK, it's not exactly a surprise that they're all booked out.

I send Andrew a quick smile that he doesn't believe for a second.

"Molly—"

"You're not allowed to talk if you're sulking," I interrupt. His eyes bore a hole in my skull, but I keep looking, widening my search to surrounding cities. Anything to get him home. Anyway, anyhow, any . . .

My fingers freeze over the keyboard as a thought occurs to me, one so simple and so perfect that I can only sit there for a second, reflecting on my brilliance.

"We come from an island."

Andrew looks at me like I've lost my mind. "Yeah," he says slowly. "You want to swim home?"

"No." I straighten, going full smug-Molly mode as I open a new tab. "I want to get the ferry."

"The ferry? You don't think it will be booked out?"

"The car tickets might be," I say, adding in our dates. "But there's always room for foot passengers. We'll obviously miss the sailing today, but tomorrow . . ." I let out a shriek of victory that makes several people nearby jump.

"Paris to London," I say as I piece together the puzzle. "We grab a hotel room and in the morning get the train from Euston station to Wales. There's a lunchtime sailing from Holyhead. We'll be in Dublin on Christmas Eve. You can get the bus or I'll get my dad to drive you if we have to. That's it, Andrew. You'll be home for Christmas."

I glance up when he doesn't immediately praise my genius idea, only to find him watching me with a look in his eyes that throws me so much, I snap my attention back to my spreadsheet, suddenly self-conscious.

"You'll still be exhausted," I add. "But I think we can make it work. Unless you have any other—"

"I don't," he interrupts. "That sounds perfect. That's . . . Thank you."

I nod, still not looking at him. "I'll book the tickets then? We can be in London by late afternoon if we get the lunchtime flight. Maybe we could stay with your brother?"

"He's already gone home," Andrew says. "But I have a cousin there. Oliver. He's usually happy to have company."

"That's great. If he'll have us."

"I'll text him now." There's a pause before he speaks again. "I'm sorry, Molly."

I glance up at his words. "Me too. I'm sorry we missed the Dublin flight."

"Not your fault. And this is a good plan. I'm impressed."

"This is nothing," I dismiss. "Just wait until I've had a coffee."

He cracks a smile. It's a small one, but I'm counting it as a win. "Was that a subtle hint, Miss Kinsella?"

"Cream. No sugar."

He sighs exaggeratedly but gets to his feet. "Anything for my travel agent," he says, and I try not to look too pleased as I turn back to my laptop and start booking us in.

CHAPTER TEN

It takes another thirty minutes to sort the tickets and keep our various families updated on our new plan. Andrew's seems grateful. Mine just seems baffled that I'm going to so much effort. But at least his cousin is happy to put us up for the night, responding within a few minutes of Andrew's text that he was polishing the china as we spoke.

From the look on Andrew's face, I couldn't tell if he was joking or not.

It's only when everything's sorted that I begin to realize what being without my suitcase actually means. I'm not used to looking like I currently look. The corporate world demands a certain groomed appearance and, seeing as it's one of the few things in my job I am in complete control of, I take it seriously. So while I have no problem dressing comfortably for a long flight, there's only so many times a girl can turn her underwear inside out.

"I need to buy some clothes."

"In Paris?" Andrew makes a face. "They're not exactly known for their fashion sense."

"Cute," I deadpan, but I'm secretly glad he's perked up.

The coffee helped, and we both get another espresso before leaving his very-much-*not*-lost suitcase in luggage storage and risking a venture into the city. It does feel a little like tempting fate, but there's five hours to go before we need to be back for our flight and neither of us wants to spend another second more than we need to in an airport.

A brief consultation with my good friend Google and we get the RER train to Les Halles, an underground shopping mall near the Seine, where I head to the first decent store I see to grab a pair of jeans and a couple of plain T-shirts and sweaters.

Andrew is not impressed.

"It's literally two days before Christmas," he says, trailing me around the racks. "And that's what you want to wear."

"Yes, because I'm an adult."

"An adult who said she didn't want to be a grinch," he presses. "That means embracing the meaning of Christmas."

"The meaning of Christmas is not a T-shirt saying, 'Pull my cracker.'"

"No, it's family and friends. And as a friend, I would really appreciate it if you embraced a bit of glamour." He plucks a pair of snowmen earrings off a display, holding them up to me. "These, for example."

"No."

"I think they'd go really— Oh my God, they light up."

I roll my eyes as they start to flash in his hands and head to the counter, moving quickly at the thought of getting out of these clothes. The salesperson lets me do so in the changing room and I breathe a sigh of relief as I pull a fresh T-shirt over my head. I spend another minute arguing with myself before I take a quick detour back through the store and then leave to find Andrew waiting outside with a shopping bag in his hand.

"Tell me you didn't buy them," I say suspiciously.

"For my sister," he explains, glancing down at my outfit. "Feel better?"

"Hugely," I admit. "Though that could be the magic of the season coursing through my veins."

"Come again?"

I part my coat to reveal my last-minute purchase and Andrew's eyes widen at my new gold-and-black-striped sweater. *Joyeux Noel*, it says in slanted writing, decorated with an appropriate amount of glitter.

"Look at you, Cindy Lou Who." A slow smile spreads across his face. "I can't believe you went to such a minimal effort for me."

"Minimal? This is a big step! The glitter is itchy."

"Well, beauty is pain. You know, those earrings would go really well with—"

"No."

He smirks as I zip up my coat again but still seems amused, no hint of his previous bad mood left. And that was exactly what I wanted to happen when I bought it.

"I feel like we should do tourist stuff," Andrew says reluctantly, but one look at each other and we know neither of us has the energy.

"Something to eat?" I ask hopefully, and he grins. "But not around here," I add. "I'm not wasting our few hours in Paris on fast food."

"You love fast food."

"There is a time and a place," I say firmly, leading us away from the mall. We still have ages before we need to get back. "Trust me."

We head east, away from the Louvre and its tourists, just as it starts to rain. One of my favorite food bloggers raves about a small restaurant by Saint-Jacques Tower and it's there

I bring Andrew, finding it down a quiet side street. It's just open for lunch and we get a small table right by the window, the smell of rich food and the gentle chatter of voices immediately putting me in a better mood. I've always felt comfortable in restaurants, even when I'm by myself.

"Very French," Andrew declares as the waiter hands us our menus. "Do you want me to take your picture?"

"No."

"Why not? I've got my camera. You're in Paris. You're geeking out over yeast," he adds as I start admiring the breadbasket. I drop a roll on my side plate and make a face. "Let's create a memory."

"I don't particularly want to remember this trip," I tell him, and he gives me a look of mock hurt.

"*This* trip? This expensive, exhausting, terrible one?"

"The very same."

"I think we're having fun."

"That's because *you* still have your suitcase."

The waiter comes back for our drinks and I have to bite my tongue to stop myself ordering a glass of wine. Instead I ask for an ice water with some broken French and Andrew gets a ginger ale. Another one. It's what he got at the airport and on the flights. I wonder if it's his go-to whenever he wants something alcoholic. Is that something you do when you're trying to stay sober? I really have no idea. But I don't know how to ask him about it without sounding too prying.

"They do French fries in France, right?" Andrew asks, picking up the menu.

"*Frites*," I answer. "But I think you should go for—"

A sharp vibration comes from somewhere nearby and we both stare at each other before I realize it's my work phone. The automatic anxiety I get spikes through me and I dive into my laptop bag, taking it out to see a call from my boss go to voicemail.

"Are you working over Christmas again?" There's no judgment in the question, but for some reason that only makes me feel worse. I don't want to be the person who's always expected to be busy.

"Not officially," I say, checking my emails out of reflex before I realize what I'm doing.

Andrew watches me with a frown. "If you need to—"

"I don't."

"I don't mind. Do what you have to do."

"I don't have to do anything," I say, putting the phone down. "It can wait. What?" I add at the confused look on his face.

"Nothing," he says quickly. "It's just, I know how busy you are."

"I'm trying to get a better work/life balance," I say, even as my stomach drops. It's one thing to realize how much of your life has been consumed by your job; it's another to hear someone else say it.

But Andrew smiles. "Work/life balance, huh? What's brought on the change?"

"Nothing in particular. I just didn't want to..." I shrug, watching another email notification light up my screen. "I don't think that's who I am anymore," I say, trying to explain it. "I'm thinking about slowing down."

"Vastly underrated," he says, and I relax a little at how easily he accepts the thing that's been weighing me down for so long.

"Might be saying goodbye to any bonuses though."

"But you'll get the bonus of a hobby you'll give up after a few months."

I smile, playing with the edge of the tablecloth. "You won't mind if I can't get you first-class flights anymore?"

"I'm still not convinced you bought them in the first place. That was a *very* convenient storm."

I ignore him, glancing at the window as the rain falls harder. Passersby start to run, the unlucky few without umbrellas holding jackets and purses aloft, trying to protect themselves from the downpour.

Paris, I remind myself. We're in Paris. I just wish I weren't so jet-lagged and could care.

"We should go on a vacation," I say. "A real one."

"We can do that," he says, reading through the menu. "Where do you want to go?"

"Anywhere."

"Okay, that narrows it down."

I pick at my bread roll, restless as I watch him. He changed clothes back at the airport, switching his long-haul sweatpants and hoodie ensemble for jeans and a red sweater decorated in Christmas trees. It should be ridiculous, but he somehow pulls it off, the material fitted to his chest in a way that—

"You keep staring at me like that, I'm going to start charging," he murmurs, not looking up. I flush, caught red-handed as I take a sip of my water.

"I'm just not used to your stubble."

"Beard," he corrects. "It's an attractive and impressive beard."

"You can't see your dimple."

Andrew drops the menu onto the table, leaning back as his eyes flick to mine.

Uh-oh.

"You like my dimple?" he asks.

"I didn't say that. I just said you can't see it."

"And that upsets you, does it?"

"What are you getting to eat?" I ask, and he smirks at the warning in my voice.

"What are you getting?" he counters.

"The Andouillette grillée."

"And what's that when it's at home?"

"A sausage."

He makes a face. "Sausages freak me out."

"Which is why you should get the pesto tagliatelle," I say primly. "And then you're going to get the chocolate mousse."

"I've never been the biggest fan of mousse."

My mouth drops open. "That's a bald-faced lie. You love chocolate. Why wouldn't you like chocolate mousse?"

"I don't know, I went through a phase of buying those little pots from the grocery store and—"

"That's not the same," I interrupt, exasperated. "It will taste completely different here. Fresh, for a start. Handmade. I read they add a little touch of lavender to— Stop looking at me like that!"

"I can't help it." He laughs. "You get so excited about whipped eggs."

"*Beaten* eggs." Christ, it's like he enjoys annoying me. "You beat eggs for a mousse. And not even eggs, egg whites. You beat them and then you fold them into—" I break off as my work phone rings again and I feel a surge of anger as I reach for it, thumb hovering for a second before I turn the thing off.

Oh, they're not going to like that.

"Molly?"

My gaze darts to Andrew, who's watching me with concern.

"I seriously don't mind if you need to take a call or—"

"I'm on vacation," I say sharply. "They know I'm on vacation." I shove the thing back into my bag, glancing at the laptop and folders inside. I have a brief, overwhelming urge to throw everything into the largest puddle I can find.

"I'm thinking about quitting," I say abruptly, and Andrew sits up in surprise.

"Your job? You want to go to another firm?"

"No, I want to get out completely. I want to stop practicing law." It's the first time I've said the words out loud. I haven't even said them to myself. But as soon as I do, I know it's the right decision. There's no panic, no sick feeling twisting in my gut. Only a sense of relief.

Andrew doesn't say anything for a long moment, looking as though I've completely blindsided him. Which, I guess I have, in a way. My job is all I've been since we first started getting to know each other. I've never given any indication otherwise.

"To do what?" he asks eventually.

"I have no idea."

To my surprise, he almost looks disappointed. "Come on, Moll. You have no idea what you want to do? Seriously?"

"I don't," I protest. "At least not realistically. I've had a look at—"

He stops me with a quiet laugh. "You just said it. 'At least not realistically.' So, you do know what you want to do."

"Oh, *sorry* if I'm taking supermodel and Hollywood socialite off the table at this time."

"They were never on the table to begin with," he says flatly. "You hate any event that goes on past eleven p.m."

Okay, fair point.

"Tell me," he continues. "If money wasn't an issue. If you woke up tomorrow with a brand-new life and you could do anything. What would you do?"

"That's the problem. I don't know."

"You're lying. It's something bohemian, isn't it?"

"Andrew—"

"You're going to start making hats."

"I don't know what I want to do," I repeat, frustrated. "I just know that right now I'm unhappy."

Going by his sudden scowl, it's the wrong thing to say. "How unhappy?"

"I'm not... It's..." Backtrack, Molly. Backtrack. "It's just something I've been thinking about. It's not like I'm handing in my notice tomorrow."

"Why not?"

"Because I'm not an idiot? Leaving without a plan would be a really dumb move financially. And even with one, it could be a huge mistake. It's going to take a few years."

"A few..." He looks incredulous. "You've just admitted you're unhappy and now you're going to stay like that for, what? Five more years?"

"Not *five*," I mutter. Maybe three.

"Mistakes can be fixed," Andrew continues.

"They can also be prevented."

"I can't believe you're already talking yourself out of this."

"I'm not!"

"You are. You're—"

"Excusez-moi?"

It's at that moment our waiter chooses to appear, his pen poised over his notepad with that stressed air all service staff at Christmas have. Yet another reason to dislike the holidays.

The man hesitates, taking in our matching glares as we turn toward him. "Encore une petite minute?"

My eyes dart back to Andrew, who waits a beat before pushing his menu to the side. "You pick," he says to me. "I trust you."

"Even if I order you the sausage?"

He smiles a little at that. A temporary truce. "I trust you not to order me the sausage," he amends, and lets me take charge, watching me thoughtfully as the rain falls in sheets outside.

CHAPTER ELEVEN

I order him the pasta, followed by the mousse, and we spend the meal going over the plan to get to Dublin and not talking about mistakes or jobs or anything beyond what the next twenty-four hours will bring.

We head back to the airport with hours to spare and are the first people at our gate. Andrew doesn't even risk going to the restroom, waiting until we board despite the fact he grows visibly uncomfortable as the minutes tick by. We take off five minutes early and there's hardly any wait for his suitcase on the other side. Everything goes smoothly.

And doesn't that just make me suspicious as hell?

"It's like you *want* something to go wrong," Andrew says as I double-check the sailing for tomorrow one final time.

"We should make a backup plan."

"This is our backup plan. We're here. The tickets are booked. The weather looks good. We'll be fine."

"The train could break down."

"Then we'll get a bus," he says firmly, and I nod despite the niggling feeling in my gut.

"Where does your cousin live anyway?" I ask as we make our way through the crowds outside Heathrow Airport.

"He moves around a lot. But he's in Notting Hill right now."

I perk up at that. "Like the movie?"

"Exactly like the movie. You've been to London before, right?"

"Mam took my sister and me for a weekend when we were younger. We almost got separated on the Tube and I've never recovered from it."

"So *that's* why you scream every time you take the L."

I nod. "People think it's the screeching sound of the tracks, but no."

"Just your childhood trauma."

We wait in line for a taxi and end up with a blissfully silent driver who, other than saying hello, makes no attempt at conversation. And just like that, we're off on the next stage of our cursed adventure.

"We should try and see some stuff if we have time," Andrew says, peering out at the M4. West London passes by in a blur of cars and houses. "Especially since we didn't get to see Paris that much. I haven't been here in years."

"I don't think we'll have time."

"We will," he insists, glancing over at my reluctance. "We have all day."

"We'll see," I say in a perfect imitation of my mother. (It means "no.")

Our surroundings grow increasingly fancier as we leave the highway and near Notting Hill. The houses lining the roads look finer, the cars slicker; shiny Teslas and SUVs that I don't think anyone really needs to navigate the narrow residential streets. My nose is practically glued to the window as I take it in, especially when we pull up outside a white terraced townhouse that looks like something out of *Mary Poppins*.

I am instantly confused.

"Is your family secretly rich?" I ask Andrew as we get out. London real estate isn't exactly cheap, though I know looks can be deceiving. Maybe the building has been split into tiny apartments and his cousin is subletting from a sub-letter who's squatting. But I don't think so. The place looks too maintained, the painted shutters and window boxes too matching. A tasteful string of lights hangs from the roof and a fat white candle sits in the window, waiting to be lit. "You have to tell me right now," I say as the cabbie drives off. "I'll know if you're lying."

Andrew only laughs. "We're not rich."

"But *someone* is," I insist.

At this, he hesitates. "Well—"

"Cousin!"

The front door flies open as a man emerges from the shadowy interior. He steps into the daylight in a thick burgundy dressing gown and matching slippers, both of which look out of place for the middle of the afternoon. Even at Christmas.

Oliver.

He's younger than I thought he would be, late twenties maybe, and handsome, with an angular acne-scarred face and a thick head of blond hair in desperate need of a cut. He almost seems surprised to see us, despite the fact he knew we were coming.

"We didn't mean to wake you," Andrew calls, only sounding a little sarcastic.

"You're referring to my outfit?" Oliver looks down at himself. "This is loungewear. I've been up for hours."

"That's because you didn't go to sleep."

He smiles ruefully. "You always were the smart one." Oliver waits until we've walked up the stone steps before hugging Andrew hard enough that he almost falls backward.

To my surprise, he does the same to me, wrapping his arms tightly around my body. He smells oddly like cinnamon and I don't hate it, but when he pulls back, I see that his eyes are bloodshot and suddenly his attire makes a little more sense.

"Late one last night?" Andrew asks, coming to the same conclusion.

Oliver pats him on the cheek. "'Tis the season," he says faintly. "Come in! My favorite Irish cousin and his beautiful Irish friend. Has Christian met her yet? She seems his type."

His voice fades as he disappears inside, not bothering to check if we're following. I glance at Andrew, who's staring tiredly after him.

"Is he always—"

"Yes," Andrew sighs. His hand goes to the small of my back and he presses me forward into the house. "Yes, he is."

"I used to spend every summer in Cork," Oliver says when we enter. My eyes adjust to the dim light to find him standing on the bottom step of a stately, carpeted stairway. "Are you from Cork, Molly?"

"Dublin," I say, trying to glance around without being too obvious about it.

"I hated going to Cork. Weeks of constantly being made fun of for my English accent. Namely by this man."

"It was more of a family activity," Andrew tells me, and I try not to smile.

"He was my greatest bully," Oliver says, pointing to him. "Except for the day one of the village kids tried to do the same and he punched him in the nose."

"What?" I turn to Andrew, who doesn't even have the decency to look ashamed.

"He had an excellent right hook," Oliver continues. "Even when he was ten."

"He's still family," Andrew says with a shrug. "We were the only ones allowed to make fun of him."

"That's not what I—" I glare at him. "You broke a kid's nose?"

"Fractured," he says, as if that's any better.

"It was magnificent," Oliver adds fondly. "Well, then! Do you want a tour?"

Andrew stretches, eyeing his suitcase. "I think we'd rather—"

But Oliver is already off, shuffling into the next room, and despite my exhaustion, I hurry after him, too nosy not to.

I've been around rich people in my life, you meet them a lot in my line of work, new money and old, but this is next level. This is like... *movie* rich.

The house is small in the way I suspect most London homes are. The opulence is in the details, the ornate furniture and polished floorboards, the vases of flowers and matching gold and silver Christmas decorations. They're classy and restrained but also make me scared to touch anything in case they immediately crack into a million pieces.

Oliver leads us through the living room and then another living room and then a goddamn *library* before the kitchen, dining room, and pantry that's almost the size of my bedroom in Chicago. Eventually we end up back where we started in the hall, where a grandfather clock I hadn't noticed chimes grandly.

"And now for upstairs!" Oliver declares, but this is where Andrew puts his foot down.

"Can we do this later, Oli? I need to stand under running water and stare at the wall until I feel normal."

"But the... Oh, all right," he says, obviously disappointed. "At least let me show you to your rooms. I've given you my favorite ones." He looks at him pointedly. "Because I'm nice."

Andrew wrestles with his suitcase as Oliver leads me up the stairs, pointing out the paintings that line the wall along the way.

"How do you feel about floral patterns?" he asks when we reach the top.

"I feel completely neutral about them."

"Wonderful!" He throws open a door and gestures me grandly inside.

It is, by far, nicer than any hotel room I've ever stayed in. It's really the size of two rooms, with large windows overlooking the street below. A four-poster bed dominates the space and the wallpaper is indeed floral, as are the bedspread, the upholstery on the chair, and the love seat that's placed against the window. A solemn, possibly haunted closet takes up the other wall, and to my right, by the bed, is a door that I'm guessing leads to a bathroom or maybe the chambermaid's room because honestly who knows? It should be stuffy, maybe a little old-fashioned, but there's a charm to it I didn't expect. One that makes me feel instantly comfortable.

"Do you like it?" Oliver asks.

"I like all of it," I confess. "You have a beautiful home."

He beams, delighted with my response. "I'll leave you to get settled. Let me know if you need anything!" His voice echoes at the last bit, already vanished down the hall, and I take a moment to inhale, breathing in the scent of furniture polish. As I do, I slip my coat off and step farther into the room, running a hand down the thick quilt cover.

What a weird twenty-four hours.

"Looks comfy."

I spin around at Andrew's voice to find him standing in the doorway, gazing at the bed.

He gives me an innocent look and leaves my laptop bag just inside my door. I hesitate only briefly before following him out to his own room, which turns out to be directly next to mine.

"From the way he spoke about your childhood, I thought he would have put you in the attic," I say.

"The attic here is probably bigger than my entire apartment."

I glance around, taking it all in. It's just as nice as mine, but with a stereotypically more masculine feel, all dark wood and navy shades of wallpaper. It's also . . .

"Smaller," I say promptly, glancing around. "Your room is smaller. I win."

"Congratulations." He unzips his case, his attention annoyingly not on me.

"I can't believe you didn't tell me your cousin's rich."

"He's not."

"Please. This place is like something out of a storybook." I cross my arms when Andrew fails to suppress a smile, smirking to himself like there's some joke I'm not in on. "What?"

"It's not his."

"What do you mean?"

"This isn't his house, Moll."

Oh, God. "Please don't tell me we're squatting in—"

"No." He cuts me off as he straightens, a toiletry bag in his hands. "A police officer is not going to come knocking on the door. At least not for that. Oliver is a gallery assistant at some tiny, ridiculous place in Mayfair. This is the owner's house. Or one of them anyway."

"He lives with the owner?" My voice drops to a whisper. "Is it, like, a sex thing?"

"Would you— *No*." He laughs. "The *owner* is a seventy-five-year-old man with dubious royal connections who stays on some Greek island during the winter because he can't stand the cold. He doesn't like the place being empty when he's gone and is convinced someone's going to steal all his artwork so, for the past three years when he's not here, Oliver stays."

"That's *nuts*."

"It could only happen to Oli," Andrew agrees, laying out a fresh pair of jeans on the bed. "Just don't tell him I told you, okay? He thought it would be fun to pretend. He always wants a little drama."

"Well, who am I to spoil his Christmas?"

Andrew just nods, continuing to sort through his clothes until my presence becomes awkward lingering.

"I might take a nap," I announce, lacing my hands behind my back.

"Go for it."

"I'm pretty tired."

"I bet."

"Then maybe after I'll— What are you doing?" I blurt the words out as Andrew pulls his sweater *and* T-shirt up over his head. My eyes immediately drop to his bare chest before I snap them back to his face.

"Undressing."

"Why?"

He looks at me like I'm crazy. "Because I'm going to have a shower." He reaches for his belt buckle, one brow raised when I just stand there. "I can put on a show if you—"

"I'm going!" I say, ignoring his smirk, and I spin out of the room, slamming the door shut behind me.

CHAPTER TWELVE
FOUR YEARS AGO

Flight Six, Chicago

"Don't go."

"I have to go."

"Then let me come with you."

"No." I spin around, laughing when I'm met with a pouting face. "Since when did you get so clingy?" I tease.

Mark steps toward me, his hands going to my waist. "Since you're going to be away from me for two weeks."

"One week," I correct. "You're the one that's making it two."

"So come see me when you're done. My family won't mind."

"I need to work."

"And I need to see you." His voice drops to a murmur and I lean into his touch as he kisses me. It's not that I don't understand his insistence. This will be our first proper break apart since we made things official and I'm not exactly looking forward to it either.

Mark breaks the kiss, hands sliding around my hips to hold me against him.

"I love you."

"I love you too," I say, smiling against his lips.

His grip tightens. "Let me go with you."

"Maybe next year. Or we could—" I break off as someone clears their throat loudly behind me and I turn awkwardly in Mark's arms to find Andrew standing a few feet away.

He is, bizarrely, dressed in a suit, and I stare at him for a moment before I remember that he said he'd be coming straight from a wedding gig.

"Oh, don't let me interrupt," he says, his amusement clear. "Just feeling a little phlegmy today."

I give him a look as I pry myself away from my boyfriend, hoisting my backpack over my shoulder.

"You're early."

"Yes. You must be Mark." Andrew strides the two steps toward us, holding out his hand.

"And you're the friend," Mark says as he clasps it.

"To all that will have me. Andrew."

"Nice to meet you."

The shake goes on a little longer than necessary and I find my eyes drifting back to Andrew. He looks different, all clean cut and dressed up. His suit is deep blue, his shoes a polished brown, and there's a faint hint of stubble along his jaw that makes him more handsome than boyish. More grown-up than I've ever seen him.

"Where's Alison?" I ask, tearing my gaze away to look for his new girlfriend.

"Oh, we're not at the accompany-the-partner-to-the-airport stage of the relationship yet," Andrew says. "Though she says if I'm good I might be able to start holding her hand by the spring, so fingers crossed."

"He likes to make jokes," I explain to a frowning Mark.

"Sure," Mark says, sounding confused, and I turn back to him before this can get any more awkward.

"We should probably head through. It's getting busy."

"You've got some time."

"I need to do some shopping," I lie as Andrew wanders a few steps away, pretending to give us privacy.

"Call me when you land?"

"It will be the middle of the night!"

"I don't care. I'll stay up." He kisses me again as his hands drift lower, grabbing a quick squeeze that I swiftly pull away from, glancing at Andrew who's miraculously not looking our way. It's another minute of "I love you"s and "I'll miss you"s before I finally convince him to leave, and even then he stays exactly where he is, watching us walk toward security. Andrew stays quiet, which makes me *very* suspicious, and sure enough, as soon as we round the corner, he turns to me.

"Don't," I warn him.

"Don't what? Talk about how nice your new boyfriend is?"

"Shut up."

"He's very nice. And so tall."

"Andrew—"

"Clearly an ass man though."

My face heats as a woman in the line beside us glances our way. "Are you going to be like this the entire flight?" I ask tersely.

"If you keep reacting like that, I will," he says with a grin. "I think I made him jealous."

"I think you think very highly of yourself."

"Oh, come on. That man was clearly marking his territory back there."

"He was not!"

"He was five minutes away from pissing on your leg."

I try to hold back my laugh, but that turns it into a snort, which only makes him smile harder.

"I can't help that I inspire such possessiveness in people," I finally say.

"Must be the hair."

"Stop."

"I mean it. It's very chic. You cut it yourself?"

I hit him with one hand while the other tugs self-consciously on my newly shorn strands.

"It suits you," he says, spotting the movement.

"Yeah?"

"Yeah. Really shows off your ears."

I scowl at him before I turn to face the front. "I hate you."

"No, you don't," he says, bumping gently into me from behind. "And that man is completely in love with you."

I glance over my shoulder to find that this time he's not joking. My lips twitch as I try to hold my frown against the sudden burst of happiness at his words.

"Whatever," I say, catching the start of his grin before I turn back around.

Now, London

Gabriela calls me five minutes after I shut myself in my room. I spend those five minutes analyzing every word Andrew's ever said to me and trying to remember the exact tone of his voice when he told me my dress looked nice one year, so when the call comes through, I'm so relieved for the distraction, I could cry.

"They lost my bag!"

"Who did?" she demands like she's going to come straight over and beat them up for me.

"Argentina." I collapse back onto the bed, my body

immediately sinking into the soft mattress. "They lost it and we missed our flight to Dublin so now we're in London and we're staying with Andrew's fake-rich cousin for the night."

"*Fun.* How fake-rich?"

"He lives in his boss's mansion and his name is Oliver."

"Shut up." She sighs. "When are you flying to Ireland?"

"We're not," I say, staring up at the ceiling. "We're getting the ferry."

"*Cute.*"

"Long," I correct. "The ferry goes from Wales, which means we have to get a train there in the morning. And then Andrew has another bus from Dublin. We're both already exhausted. I'll be surprised if he doesn't sleep through Christmas at this stage."

"Is he okay?"

"He's . . . fine."

There's a long pause at the other end of the line as she probably reads a million things into my hesitation. And then: "What happened?"

"Nothing."

"Oh my God."

"*Nothing!*"

"That's your something voice," she says. "I knew something was up. I *knew* it."

"That's not why I was—" I sigh, rubbing my eyes. "That's a whole different thing."

"Oh, we are having the biggest lunch date when you get back. We're going to order some crab salad from Morillo's and lock ourselves in the east meeting room and you are not coming out until you tell me everything. In fact—"

"He kissed me."

Gabriela immediately stops talking, like all the air's been sucked from her lungs by my words. "Who did?"

"Andrew!" I roll over so I'm faceplanting into the mattress. "Twice."

"Twice?"

"I guess technically I was the one that kissed him. There was mistletoe the first time."

"Okay."

"And it kind of threw me. Because I was all, oh, friendly mistletoe kiss between friends because we're friends—"

"Sure."

"—But then it was *not* that. And then in Argentina, he followed me to the restroom—"

"He *what?*"

"It's less creepy than it sounds," I assure her, twirling a strand of hair so tight around my finger that it hurts. "Anyway, he followed me and we kissed again."

"In the restroom?"

"In the hallway *outside* the restroom. Because I told him that the first kiss messed me up and he said we should try it again, so we tried it again."

"Molly." She sounds extremely disappointed in me. "That's such a line."

"It only sounds like one."

"Because it is one!" She mutters something under her breath and I picture her pacing up and down the office. A quick check of the time tells me it's four p.m. London time, which means it's ten a.m. Chicago time, and I feel a familiar stab of guilt. I haven't responded to a single email since we left Buenos Aires.

"What are you going to do?"

"I was hoping you would tell me."

"Do you like him like that?"

"I don't know. Maybe. But what if that's exhaustion?

What if it's stress and exhaustion and instead of manifesting as a gray hair or a nose pimple, it's made me super horny?"

"Or what if you're just super dumb and you've never realized what's right in front of you?"

I flip onto my back, closing my eyes. Somewhere in the house, soft jazz music begins to play because of course it does.

Am I dumb? Sometimes, obviously, but this time I don't think so. There have been times when we've both been single, but even then . . .

I frown as I think back to his previous girlfriends. A bunch of perfectly nice women (give or take) whose Instagrams I definitely stalked for at least a few minutes when they were together. And when they were together, they were *together*. Photos of them on vacation and at parties with friends. At thrift stores and cafés and parks. They never seemed like the kind of people who would cancel plans because they had to go to work on a Sunday.

They would have put him first.

I don't think I've ever put a partner first. And I've tended to date people who understood that and did the same. I didn't want to move to Seattle with Brandon. But he didn't want to stay in Chicago with me. Is that why I've never thought about Andrew like that before? Why I've never even let myself *think* it? Because I knew I wouldn't be able to give him the attention he deserves and I didn't want to do that to him?

Because I knew I could never put him first. And it was only when I decided to make a different life for myself that I . . .

"Hey, Gab?" I sit up, drawing my knees to my chest. "If you didn't get into law school, what would you have done?"

"Change of subject much?"

"Indulge me."

She makes an unhappy sound, but she does. "I don't

know. Probably I'd have had a breakdown, dyed my hair, and tried again."

"No, I mean if you weren't a lawyer. If for whatever reason you couldn't have this career, what would you do?"

"Oh, that's easy," she dismisses. "Probably the violin thing."

"The vio... You play the violin?"

"Yep."

"Since *when*?"

"Since I was five?" She laughs. "I wanted to be in an orchestra. I still get lessons once a week. Helps me calm down."

"How do you have the time?"

"Asks the girl who once did a three-hour round trip on a Monday night because she read about a food truck she wanted to try. Same as you, Moll. I make the time. You always make the time when you want to. That's why you're traveling around the world right now, isn't it?" She pauses, her voice turning so casual that it's almost funny. "Why?" she asks. "What would you have done?"

"I don't know."

"But it's something you've been thinking about?" she presses lightly.

"Maybe."

There's a bang on her end, like she's hit her desk in triumph. "I totally called it! Something's wrong. Something's wrong and I knew it because I'm attuned to you."

"Gab—"

"Because of our close bond."

"Are you going to let me talk or what?"

"Talk. I'm listening. Tell me everything. What are you thinking?"

I bite back a smile even as the urge to lie threatens to take over. "I *think*," I begin, "that I decided to become a lawyer when I was sixteen years old because it sounded impressive and was an acceptable thing to want to be. And now I think I've spent a third of my life devoted to a career that I don't even like that much."

"At all?"

"I like *you*," I say, dropping back to the mattress. "I like the competitiveness. I like the adrenaline kick when we close a deal and I like having the cash to buy nice things and that my family is proud of me because I've got a good job and a good life. But the thought of looking ahead five, ten, fifteen years from now and seeing myself in the same office at two a.m. on a Tuesday makes me want to cry."

"Jesus, Molly. Is that what this is about? You want to quit?"

"I've been thinking about it. But I don't know if I'm ready yet."

Gabriela goes quiet and I gear myself up for her counter-argument, which is why I'm so surprised by her next words. "Then I'll help you."

"You will?"

"Yes," she says determinedly. "Women help women. I will help you quit. I'll take you to a life coach. We'll make some lists. I'll teach you the violin."

I laugh. "I thought you'd try and talk me out of it."

"Are you kidding me? I need new non-lawyer friends, Molly. This is a blessing." She pauses. "Is that why you didn't tell me?"

"That and I'm still figuring it out for myself."

"No, you've decided," she says. "I can hear it in your voice even if you can't. But this is good! This is a project. You know I love projects."

"I do," I say. "I'm not going to look at my email until I get back."

"Good. Screw them."

"But *you* can text me if you need me."

"Okay, thank God," she says in a rush. "Spencer's still out. Who gets mono anymore? Seriously."

I grin, feeling a bit of the weight I'd been carrying around lift. Two people down, only everyone else in my life to go. "It feels realer when I talk about it. Less scary."

"I also feel like I'm helping? Which makes me feel good, so it's a win for both of us."

I go to reply when my phone buzzes with a text by my ear.

"If it's anyone from the team, just send them to me," she says as she hears it too. "The revolution starts now."

"It's Andrew," I say, checking the message.

Oliver says you can help yourself to anything in the kitchen if you're hungry. I told him you're always hungry.

"I said I was taking a nap. He probably thinks I'm asleep."

"Ah yes, your other issue."

"He's not an issue."

"A conundrum, then."

"Gabriela—"

"I mean, we're on such a roll now, we might as well keep going. He's not seeing anyone, is he?"

"No," I say reluctantly. "He was, but they broke up during the summer."

"And you haven't been with anyone seriously since Brandon."

"No."

"So I say, why not explore?"

"Because what happens if he kisses me again and I hate it?" I ask. "And then it's ruined. A perfectly good friendship gone just like that."

"What if that doesn't happen and instead the kiss leads to mind-blowing sex and becomes the best decision you ever made? I think you need to talk to him seriously about this. Maybe he's freaking out too."

"He doesn't look like he's freaking out," I grumble, plucking at a loose thread on the bedspread. "He's acting like the whole thing is funny. Like it's a joke."

"Molly, I don't know him, but I guarantee you no one would think kissing you is a joke." Her voice hardens. "In *fact*, if he says even *one* thing to make you feel—"

"All right," I cut her off. "Thank you, babe."

"You're a catch, you hear me?"

"I do," I say dryly, but I smile. "But right now, I think I actually need to have that nap. Jet lag is not fun."

"Okay, but if you have any more problems about *anything* at all—"

"I will come to you. I will confide."

"That's my girl."

We say our goodbyes and I hang up. I do nap, but it only makes me feel worse and I wake forty minutes later with a dry mouth, a growling stomach, and the beginnings of a headache. With that added grossness on top of my plane grossness, I decide to check out the shower for the first time. There's a neatly folded towel on the vanity so I grab that and the toiletries left by the sink and hope to God there's hot water. There is.

And it is *blissful*.

The water pressure is what I imagine those shampoo commercial waterfalls must feel like and I stay there for way too long. I even do a deep conditioner but have no choice other than to let my hair dry naturally, seeing as I can't find a hairdryer in the room. I *do* find a handheld clothes steamer though, which I immediately put to use unwrinkling everything I bought in Paris and having way too much fun doing it.

I'm working on the pillowcase just for kicks when there's a knock on the door and I open it to find Andrew on the other side, dressed like he's about to head out.

"What are you doing?" I ask, nodding at his coat.

"What are *you* doing?" he counters. He stares at my steamer like it's a space gun from a cheap sci-fi movie.

"I found it under the bed. Just because we're traveling doesn't mean we have to show up all wrinkly. If you ask nicely, I'll steam your stuff too."

He slumps against the doorframe. "I'm trying desperately to think of a way to twist that into an innuendo."

"And you've got nothing?"

"I've had a long day. And to answer your question, I'm going out and so are you. Oliver suggested we go soak up the atmosphere."

"Now?"

He pauses at the disbelief in my voice. "You don't want to see London at Christmas?"

"You mean go see an already overcrowded city at one of the busiest times of the year? No. It will be full of tourists."

"We *are* tourists." He grins as I unplug the steamer. "It's just for an hour."

"We have to be up early."

"And we will be. Tell me the last time you slept in past eight a.m."

I open my mouth, but the man has a point.

"Look," he continues, seeing my hesitation. "You can stay here by yourself and . . . steam, but I'm going to get a hot chocolate." He pinches his fingers together. "With a little bit of cinnamon. And three marshmallows. We deserve to have some fun."

I sigh, glancing at the bed. I wish I was sleepy, but I'm not. I'm wide awake and growing restless. And he knows it.

"An hour?" I ask.

"Tops."

"Fine." I start to shrug my robe from my shoulders and his smile disappears. It's at that moment I remember I have nothing but a bra on underneath. Everything else was getting steamed.

"Okay," I snap, pulling it back on. "Sorry to tantalize you with my bold display of skin."

Andrew recovers just as quickly, his grin back in place. "So, you're tantalizing now, are you?"

"And with that comment, I'm not steaming your clothes. I hope you're happy with yourself." I point to the door and he straightens, hands in the air.

"I'll see you downstairs," he calls, swinging the door shut behind him. "Preferably clothed."

CHAPTER THIRTEEN

I stay in my new pair of jeans but put on a fresh T-shirt under my Christmas sweater. I don't bother doing anything with my hair, leaving it damp around my shoulders and risking the chill. I still have Andrew's scarf from when he gave it to me in Chicago and, after a moment's hesitation, I wrap it around my neck and tuck it into my coat.

Oliver and Andrew are waiting for me by the front door when I come down. Oliver's dressed like he's going to some fancy restaurant and Andrew is dressed like Andrew. He's swapped his heavy Chicago coat for one of Oliver's and his camera bag is slung over one shoulder. I try not to stare at him as I come down, but I don't miss the way his eyes flick to his scarf when I appear. I expect him to ask for it back, but a hint of satisfaction flickers across his face, as though he's pleased to see me wearing it.

"Beautiful!" Oliver declares when I hit the bottom step. "You descend the stairs like you were born to."

"Huh?"

Andrew just shakes his head as Oliver picks up a black backpack I hadn't noticed before.

"Where exactly are we going?" I ask as he tugs it on.

"I thought we could see the lights," he says vaguely. "And then I have one quick pit stop to make so I can drop something off and then... pub?"

The thought of a cozy English pub where I can plonk myself next to a fire isn't the worst idea in the world, but I glance at Andrew, ready to say no. He's expecting it and just winks at me before giving a look that says, *I told you it was fine.* And he did, but still, there's no need to make it any harder on the man. With everything that's happened in the last few days, he's probably hoping I've forgotten all about his casual "I'm sober now" bomb, but it's something we're going to have to talk about at some point.

Now, however, is not that time and so I try and push it from my mind as Oliver shepherds us out the door. As soon as we hit Portobello Road, I see instantly what he means by "lights." I hadn't noticed the decorations in the taxi, mostly because it was daytime, and they were all off. But now the narrow, winding streets are lit up. Strings of fairy lights crisscross overhead and the houses get solidly merrier as we move away from the extremely posh to the moderately posh. Warm golden glows give way to multicolored bonanzas that I can't help but smile at as we make our way slowly through the crowds.

Oliver doesn't seem in a rush and is practically indulgent as he lets Andrew take pictures of the houses and storefronts, the packed restaurants and pubs. He even makes him take pictures of him, posing regally around the town until Andrew threatens to only send him the bad ones.

Oliver's kind of hilarious. Just on the edge of annoying. But he seems genuinely happy to have Andrew here and me by extension, asking about my life in Chicago and my childhood in Dublin, as well as buying me a fragrant mulled wine from one of the stalls dotted around. It's the first bit of Christmas fun that I could see myself getting used to, and the way Andrew keeps smiling at me every time Oliver makes me laugh makes it all the better.

Eventually, we leave the brightly lit streets behind, moving into a quieter, more residential area. It's not as fancy as where Oliver is staying—I can tell most of these houses are split into separate apartments—but it's nice and peaceful and, through the open curtains of many rooms, I spy young families and groups of friends sitting around dining tables. I assume he's taking us to some small neighborhood pub and so am surprised when he comes to a stop in front of a tiny redbrick house halfway down the street.

It's at the end of a small row of houses, with a narrow alleyway in between it and its neighbor. Unlike all the others we've passed, it's completely dark, with no car parked outside.

"We're here," he announces, turning to us with a smile.

"We're where?" Andrew asks, and I'm glad I'm not the only one confused. "Are you house-sitting this one too?"

"Oh no," Oliver says cheerfully. "This one I'm breaking into."

"You're— What?" Andrew hisses the last word as his cousin takes off down the alleyway, vanishing into the shadows. "Oliver!"

"He's obviously joking," I say, but Andrew doesn't seem to think so.

"Stay here," he mutters as he heads after him, but to hell with that. I ignore his annoyed look as I follow them both into the darkness, my eyes adjusting in time to see Oliver toss his backpack over a tall brick wall that blocks off what must be the backyard.

"Explain," Andrew says, catching him by the elbow before he can go any farther. "Now."

Oliver gives a world-weary sigh and shrugs him off. "You used to be fun, you know that?"

"I'm telling Aunt Rachel," Andrew warns, but Oliver just rolls his eyes and then, before I can so much as blink, takes a step back and leaps, grabbing hold of the top of the wall and pulling himself nimbly up before disappearing down the other side.

"Are you coming?" he calls way too loudly. Andrew looks horrified, but I feel a thrill shoot through me. Even though I just met the man, he's Andrew's cousin and I highly doubt that whatever we're doing is that illegal or dangerous.

I mean, maybe it's *slightly* illegal.

And maybe it's the mulled wine or maybe it's because I'm having a surprisingly nice time, but whatever it is, I'm feeling a little reckless tonight.

"I dare you," I say, and Andrew scoffs. But he knows he doesn't really have a choice and so, with a final pointed glare at me, copies his cousin's movement and jumps. He manages impressively well, while my effort is less graceful. I've never done anything like it before and there's a moment when I'm straddling the top of the wall where I'm pretty sure I'm going to simply fall down the other side, but Andrew lingers below and helps me climb down while my arms shake like Jell-O.

"Nice one," Oliver cheers as I dust off my sore, slightly grazed hands and look around. We're in a small, pleasantly overgrown backyard, the patch of grass illuminated dimly by the lights coming from the surrounding homes. But through the windows of the veranda doors, the house looks as it did from the front, empty and dark.

"Are we really breaking in?" I ask.

Andrew huffs. "We're not breaking in."

"We're kind of breaking in," Oliver says, making his way to the stone patio bracketing the back of the house. "But we're leaving things, not taking things. And we'll be fine. This is a nice neighborhood. They probably think we're cleaners."

I follow him to the sunroom, picking my way through the withered winter flower beds while Andrew remains tense by the wall.

"Are you going to smash the window in?" I ask, worried.

"Of course not," Oliver says, gazing at the various garden pots dotted around us. "We're going to find the key." He kneels abruptly beside a small terra-cotta one, picking it up. "It must be under— No." He reaches for the blue one next to it. "This one looks— No."

Andrew's mood grows increasingly worse as Oliver uses the flashlight on his phone to look through the shrubs.

It seems a little too obvious to me, but I leave him to it as I take a closer look at my surroundings. The place is cared for, despite the wild look about it. Beside a weathered bench, there's a covered barbecue and a small table and chairs. Butterflies made of colored glass dangle on the walls and the grass looks like it's been mowed recently. In fact, the whole garden is mostly swept clear of debris and leaves... except for a few pointedly arranged ones around the gutter.

"Molly," Andrew says in a warning tone as I wander off, but I'm like a hound catching a scent. I did a lot of teambuilding days during my various internships. Escape rooms are nothing new to me.

"Don't encourage him," he continues.

"Why are you in such a bad mood?" I ask, crouching beside the drain.

"I'm not."

I don't even bother to reply as I copy Oliver with my light, plucking out the leaves. They're muddied and gross, but it doesn't take long to find a discarded metal tin of mints hidden at the bottom. Bingo.

Oliver is by my shoulder in an instant. "Excellent work. You get a prize."

"I do?"

"Don't encourage *her* either," Andrew says as he joins us. Oliver wipes the key clean on Andrew's sleeve before Andrew can stop him and hurries back to unlock the door. A flick of his wrist and it swings open, and for two seconds the three of us simply stare inside before a loud beeping starts.

Oliver strides inside and I follow, too caught up in it all to stop.

Maybe I should become a criminal? Some kind of mysterious jewel thief.

I enter a tiny kitchen that leads into an open-plan living room. Oliver strides through it as though he's been here a million times before and I go after him, with Andrew so close he bumps into me at every step, as though getting ready to grab me and flee.

"We have twenty seconds to figure this out," Oliver says, coming to a stop in the small entranceway beside the door. He flicks open the lid to the beeping alarm and cracks his knuckles. "Pick a number between one and nine."

Andrew makes a choking sound behind me. "Are you serious?"

"Of course not." His fingers fly across the pad, promptly shutting the beeping off. "You're too easy to annoy this evening, you know that?"

"Not as easy as you'll be to *murder*," Andrew snaps, and I wrap a hand around his wrist, squeezing briefly. I have no idea what's gotten into him.

"Is this your real house?" I ask suspiciously. Oliver laughs, slipping past us back into the living room. Like the yard, it's a little messy, just as all homes should be, but yet it feels empty. Even more so with the small, bare tree in the corner as though the owner had put it up and didn't have time to do anything more.

"Who lives here?" I ask, gazing at a photo near me. A tall woman with curly black hair beams out at me, standing in front of the Eiffel Tower.

"Lara," Oliver says casually.

"And who is Lara?" Andrew asks when he doesn't explain further.

Oliver glances between us before he settles back on Andrew with a pleasant smile. "My Molly." He drops his backpack to the ground as Andrew's face creases in confusion. Like a clown pulling out a string of handkerchiefs from his pocket, he proceeds to unravel handfuls of homemade Christmas bunting. "You're tall," he adds. "You're in charge of hanging."

"Oliver—"

"We went to uni together," he interrupts. "During Freshers' week, I got drunk and tried to jump off the science building into the lake. She called me an idiot and kneed me in my unmentionables to stop me. We've been best friends ever since." He looks up, his expression unnervingly serious. "Lara loves Christmas and usually has the best-decorated house on the street, but this year her mother is sick and so she is in Berlin by her bedside, where she has been for the past three weeks. They're both coming back tomorrow and I can't have her return to an empty, cold house. I simply refuse. And so here we are, decorating it like we're trying to win a daytime reality TV show." He hesitates. "If you'll help me, that is."

Oh my God. I glance at Andrew with a pleading look that has him rolling his eyes.

"You don't even like decorations."

"Now I do."

He turns to Oliver, ignoring me. "You could have just told us this."

It's Oliver's turn to look confused. "But that wouldn't have been as fun."

"Oliver, I swear to—"

"A compromise," he interrupts, glancing at his watch. "Seeing as how we're short on time, thirty minutes tops. Let's see how much we can get done."

I pull out a bag of snowflake confetti. "Like a game?"

Andrew drops his head back with a groan, but Oliver just nods, pleased at my interest. "Exactly. I'll even set a timer."

"Christ." Andrew sighs, taking one look at my face and knowing I'm a goner. I don't really know what the big deal is. This kind of thing seems right up his street, but his scowl only deepens as he straps his camera bag tighter to his chest and looks at his cousin. "Where do we start?"

After a brief discussion, we agree to play to our strengths and I'm put in charge of the kitchen. Oliver passes me small boxes of party food from the local supermarket, along with novelty cakes and cookies. I put everything away in their respective places but can't help but arrange a few plates ready to be eaten for tomorrow. Sparkling apple cider and wine complete the edible portion of the décor and, by the time I turn back to the front room, the place has been transformed.

The bunting hangs cheerfully over the open fireplace along with dozens of fairy lights emitting a soft, warm glow. A different, colored set is strung around the tree, which Andrew is in the middle of decorating, a look of fierce concentration on his face as he tries to space out the baubles. Oliver is on stocking duty, stuffing the two he's taped to the mantelpiece with more treats.

I'm not exactly experienced in this kind of thing but figure it can't be too hard and do my best with the last of the decorations, little Santa Claus figurines and glittering snowflakes. By the time we're done, the place couldn't look more different than where Oliver's staying. The ornaments are mismatched both in tone and style, giving the room a chaotic feel, but one that can't help but make you smile. It looks like a festive fever dream. It should be my nightmare, but it's kind of . . . fun. Not that I'm going to tell Andrew that.

"I'm taking all the credit, by the way," Oliver says as he stuffs the leftover packaging back into his bag. "Neither of you were here. All me."

"What a surprise." Andrew straightens from where he sits by the window. "Happy?" he asks.

"Deliriously so. Just one final thing." Gently, almost reverently, he places one small, wrapped present under the tree, arranging the tag just so. *To Lara*, it says, and knowing what he got her immediately becomes the most important thing in my entire life. Against all odds, I manage to keep my mouth shut.

"Thank you very much for all your help," he says after a moment. "Even if I did initially trick you into it."

I nudge Andrew with my elbow and he sighs.

"We're happy to help," he says, only a little reluctantly. "Though next time, I'd prefer if you—"

He breaks off as flashing blue lights sweep suddenly across the front room. "Oliver—"

"All right!" Oliver claps his hands together, ushering us toward the back door. "All done."

"You said—"

"Time to go!" he says cheerfully, turning back to set the alarm.

Andrew and I make a beeline for the yard where he gives me a leg up the wall. Twenty seconds later Oliver joins us and walks briskly down the lane, leaving us to follow. I glance a few times behind us, apparently just to make sure I look extra suspicious, but no one comes chasing after us and no sirens start blaring. We're safe, even if Andrew is back to looking agitated again.

No one speaks until we reach the next street, at which point Oliver comes to a sudden stop, rubbing his hands together.

"Right then!" he says. "Thanks for that. Pub?"

Andrew shakes his head. "We're going home."

"What?" Oliver sounds aghast. "Why?"

"Because I don't trust you tonight."

"What are you talking about? It went fine."

"We're going back to the house," Andrew says firmly. "We're up early."

Oliver turns to me for backup but all I can offer is a sympathetic smile.

"Fine," he sighs. "I guess I'll go find some like-minded people."

"You do that," Andrew says, steering me firmly into the direction we came.

Oliver catcalls us for another few moments before he gives up and, when I glance over my shoulder, I see him walking the other way.

"That was kind of fun," I say. Andrew only grunts. "Are all your family like that?"

"Just him."

"All my family are boring. The only black sheep we have

is my aunt who has an Etsy store for her bracelets." He doesn't answer and, not for the first time that evening, I find myself ticked off at his sudden change in attitude.

"Would you stop?" I ask. "I've never seen you this grumpy before."

"I'm fine."

"You sound like me," I tell him. "What is it?"

He shakes his head, jaw still clenched tight as he glances back the way we came. "He could have gotten us into trouble. He should have told us what was going on."

"He was just messing with you."

"If the police had knocked on the door—"

"They would have contacted Lara," I say. "It would have been fine."

But it might not have been. It's only then I realize what he means. By the time they contacted Lara, chances are we would be stuck in a police station somewhere, very much missing our window to get home. And while that hadn't even occurred to me, of course, it would have been at the forefront of Andrew's mind. Of course, he would have been worried about getting over another hurdle to see his family.

Guilt trickles through me as he opens the map on his phone, searching for the quickest way to Oliver's place. My mind wavers for only an instant before I make it up.

"Why don't we stay out?"

He doesn't even spare me a glance. "You're the one who wanted to stay in."

"Yeah, but I'm awake now. And the night is young. Let's go explore the city."

"The night is young?" He looks up and I can tell he's suspicious at my change of heart. "I thought you didn't like London at Christmas."

"All the more reason to prove me wrong."

"Molly—"

"Come on. Just for an hour. Before I get tired and cranky. Like you."

"Funny," he says, but he moves when I tug on his arm and lead him toward the station.

CHAPTER FOURTEEN

Andrew relaxes the farther we travel into Central London and by the time we get off at a crowded Westminster station, he's back to his usual self, grinning at the crowds of holiday tourists around us. I hadn't planned any further than "go to the city, find something dipped in sugar" and after one disorienting moment, we decide to follow everyone else crossing the bridge beside Big Ben, where we soon spy a Christmas market on the south bank of the river.

It's kitschy, even for Andrew, with quaint mom-and-pop stalls filled with sweet treats and plastic trinkets that don't fool me as authentic for a second. But I guess it's not the worst place to be on a clear December evening. It's busy, but not so busy that we can't move around, and once we get past the stalls, there are benches to sit at and games to play. A classic carousel spins shrieking children and their indulgent parents around and around, and Christmas pop music plays over the speakers, one hit song after the next.

I buy us both a bag of churros and Andrew his promised hot chocolate as we walk along the Thames and I'm feeling weirdly content and perfectly comfortable, so I don't even think when the next words pop out of my mouth.

"This would be a great date night." I go still as soon as I say it, only to double down when Andrew turns to me with a smirk. "It would!"

"Is that what we're doing?"

"*No*," I say childishly, but then, with my conversation with Gabriela echoing through my mind: "Maybe."

Andrew's expression doesn't change, but it takes a moment for him to look away. "This isn't a date," he says. "I wouldn't take you somewhere Christmassy on a date."

"Where would you take me?"

"I haven't thought about it."

"You've thought about it enough that you know you wouldn't take me here," I point out, and I know I've caught him when he goes quiet. "Tell me," I say, and I shake the churros before him like a bribe. He snatches one in his hand, examining it for a second before he eats half of it in one bite. Men.

"Okay," he says as we keep walking. "I guess it's more of what you don't like rather than what you do like."

"And what don't I like?"

"Picnics."

"I like picnics," I protest. "I just don't like insects. Which picnics usually involve."

"You also don't like sitting in the sun."

"I burn."

"Or paper plates."

"They're flimsy."

"You don't like picnics," he concludes. "You *do* like the cinema, so I could take you to some old fancy movie and pay crazy ticket prices, but I've never liked things like that for a first date. Why waste an evening sitting in silence when I could be talking to you instead?"

"So, that rules out the theater."

"Which is handy seeing as you also hate the theater."

"Now, see, I don't hate the theater. What I hate are places that don't let you pee when you need to pee. And sometimes you've just got to sneeze. I mean, I'm sorry it's your big dumb monologue, but you can't hold something like that in. It damages your brain."

"No, it doesn't."

"Yes, it does. I read it online."

"No theater," he says. "Museums and galleries are tough. Everyone has their own pace and they can be tiring too. A bookshop can be romantic, but you don't read—"

"I read!" Sometimes.

"Hikes and walks, you're back to the pace thing. Plus, the sun, the insects."

"Plenty of places to pee though."

"True. If the weather's nice we could go to the water, but again the—"

"I get it," I interrupt flatly. "I'm undatable."

"I didn't say that." He eats the other half of his churro and I'm so distracted by a fleck of sugar at the corner of his mouth that I almost miss his next words. "Ax throwing."

"Ax . . . what?"

"I would take you ax throwing," he says.

I stare at him. "What the hell is ax throwing?"

"Exactly what—"

"It sounds like," I finish. "All right, Mr. Smart-Ass. That doesn't seem very romantic."

"Have you ever been?"

"Obviously not."

"You get these little axes and these round blocks of wood,

like archery or a dartboard. It has a bull's-eye and everything. And then you go to your lane, and you just throw." He mimes the movement. "You ever feel like screaming sometimes?" he asks. "Ever have a bad day where everything is going wrong, and you just want to stand up and yell?"

"Only three to four times a week."

"Hot yoga doesn't cure everything," he says evenly. "So, I would take you ax throwing. After which, we'll both have built up an appetite, so I'd take you to dinner. Somewhere quiet so we could talk. Of your choosing, of course. And that would be our date." He downs the last of his hot chocolate and tosses the empty cup into a nearby trash can as though he didn't just describe what might be the weirdest and possibly greatest day ever.

"What would you do for me?" he asks.

"On a date?" I frown. "I have no clue."

"Well, that doesn't seem fair."

"I'm terrible at date ideas."

"Then make an effort."

I groan inwardly. I wasn't lying. With my line of work, dating follows a predictive pattern. An alcoholic beverage after work, usually late, and then maybe a formal dinner. I haven't done anything anyone would consider "fun" since college.

"Well, since you *love* picnics," I begin, and he laughs. "Dinner," I say, more seriously. "But not out. I would invite you over to my apartment and I'd cook."

"I didn't know you could cook."

"I can make pasta, garlic bread, and cheesy garlic bread."

"Ah, the three food groups."

"I wouldn't attempt dessert though. I'd buy that, but I'd plate it nicely and most likely lie and say I made it from scratch so you'd be impressed with me."

"And I would pretend to believe you because I'm nice."

He would. I know he would. And I would get two desserts in case he didn't like one. But I know what Andrew likes. Anything with melting chocolate in the middle. I would wear something casual that I was comfortable in because, between cooking and plating, I wouldn't have time to dress up. Afterward, we'd go over to the couch and we'd watch one of his dumb comedies or maybe he'd let me pick the movie and he'd suffer through it silently. And then the credits would roll and it would be dark outside and I'd kiss him because it would be a date and it's perfectly normal to kiss someone on a date and even more normal to feel your heart race when you do.

"So, you're going to woo me with food, is that it?"

I blink away the image of us, clearing my throat for good measure. "Are you complaining?"

"Absolutely not. That sounds right up my street."

"I can do it after the ax throwing," I say airily, and he smiles.

"Sold."

Our eyes meet and there it is again, the spark of something that seems to happen more and more.

And Andrew knows it. He stops along the walkway, pausing to lean against the railing. In the distance, Big Ben looms across the river, while directly behind him the market continues in all its festive spirit. But it's quieter here, mainly couples and solo visitors wandering like us, taking pictures of the lights as they eat roasted chestnuts and lick melting marshmallows from their fingers.

But I'm not looking at them. I'm looking at Andrew, Andrew who's gazing at me with such a serious expression that I suddenly feel like I'm being pulled in front of the school principal. And I know he's going to ask me about it. About the kiss. About us. He's going to ask the question and I don't know the answer and I get so panicked, so worried, that I distract him with the first thing I can think of.

"Take my picture."

"What?"

"Take my picture," I repeat, more confident this time.

His brows rise. "You hate having your picture taken."

I do. It wasn't just because I looked like a wreck in Paris. I've always been uncomfortable in front of the camera. I can barely stand the professional headshots they make us do at work and my Instagram feed doesn't have a single selfie of me. Not even when I was rocking that bob cut everyone complimented me on but that was way too much maintenance to keep up. I don't do pictures. But my distraction is working.

"I feel pretty," I say. "And I want to document this ridiculous day."

He doesn't respond at first, as though waiting for the punchline. I just stand there.

"Okay," he says, reaching for his camera.

"You also could have told me I always look pretty," I tell him.

"I could have," he agrees, and gestures for me to pose.

Predictably, I feel instantly self-conscious.

What do I do with my hands? How do I pose? Do I tilt my head? Do I smile? Do I jump into the river and swim far, far away?

Andrew glances through the lens and makes an adjustment, eyes flicking up when he sees me flailing.

"You're terrible at this."

"Andrew!"

He laughs and some of my awkwardness changes to annoyance.

"Never mind," I say. "Put it away."

"Oh, absolutely not. I'm having too much fun now."

I almost pout, squirming under his attention as he gets ready.

"Put your left hand on the railing," he says. "Not like you're holding on to the *Titanic* ... Perfect. Look at me."

"I am looking at you."

"Look at me like you did before."

"Which was how?" I ask, confused, but he only shakes his head, his attention on the camera.

"Whatever you do," he says as he goes almost unnaturally still. "Don't smile."

"Shut up."

The lens shutters.

"What did I just say?" he says in mock outrage as my lips twitch. He clicks again. "You know what they say about cameras stealing your soul, don't you?"

"Is that what you're doing?"

"I just want you to know what you're getting into," he says, and finally lowers the camera, looking pleased as he checks the screen.

"Done?" I ask. I weirdly feel a little out of breath, but I suppose that's the effect when Andrew Fitzpatrick turns his full attention on you.

He nods and I hold out my hand. "Let me see it."

"Nope."

"Let me see it!" I grab it off him, but only because he lets me, pulling the strap over his head as he clicks something and a screen appears, showing me the last photo he took.

For a moment I don't recognize myself.

My hair has dried naturally in gentle, frizzy waves and the cold has left my nose and cheeks pink while the rest of me is bathed in the soft glow of the fair. I'm not looking at the camera. I'm looking at Andrew. Looking at him with a smile I've never seen before. Whenever I pose for a photo, I usually smile with my lips closed thanks to my two crooked front teeth. Someone made a passing comment about them when I was fourteen and I've never forgotten it. Honestly, I've never had a photo taken of myself where I haven't anticipated how I was going to look. And how I thought others would look at me.

My lips are open in this photo, my eyes creased, caught mid-laugh as I turn slightly away from him. I look like I'm having the time of my life. I look like I'm in a winter wonderland. I look...

"I look *amazing*."

"I'm just a really good photographer."

I'm far too pleased to even think of a retort. "Can you send me this one?"

"Of course."

I start to hand the camera back, but change my mind at the last second, cradling it to my chest. "Can I take one of you?"

He pauses. "I won't lie, I know you're a capable, professional adult, but that camera cost three grand so if you—"

"Thanks," I say, ignoring his sigh as I peer through the lens. That much I know how to do. "What do I press?"

"The big red button."

I make a face at him but to be fair, I guess that's the answer.

"Say cheese," I mutter, trying to frame him as he did me. For someone who's used to being on the other side of the camera, he doesn't look awkward, just leans against the railing, his body facing the water, while his face tilts my way.

I hesitate. "It won't be as good as yours."

"I hope not, seeing as I'm a professional," he deadpans. But his expression softens. "Just feel it," he says simply. "It's not all about science and angles and light. Sometimes you just... feel."

Feel. I guess I can do that.

"Think about something that makes you happy," I say, clicking the button again.

He smirks. "Like you?"

"Maybe not me," I say without missing a beat. "Let's try and keep this shoot PG-13."

And there it is. His grin is instant, lighting up his whole face, and the carousel in the background is a blur of so much color and movement that it's like the noise of it is captured alongside everything else. And with a small click of my finger, I've saved it forever.

I don't even need to look at it to know I did a good job and I pass the camera back to him, feeling so happy that it almost hurts. "There," I say. "Now we're even."

"Even?" he asks, still smiling.

I nod, turning back to the water as he examines the photo. "Now I've got your soul too."

CHAPTER FIFTEEN

The house is dark when we get back, but even though we need to be up in a few hours, I'm not ready for the night to end just yet. I think about proposing a movie, maybe raiding the fridge for some snacks and re-creating the Christmas we would have had if we'd stayed in Chicago. But my grand plan goes out the window as soon as we step through the door and see a line of discarded clothes scattered down the hallway leading to the kitchen.

"Huh," I say as Andrew sighs. He runs his hand along the wall, searching for a light switch, and when he finds it, I see the clothes are accompanied by receipts and what looks like bank cards, as though someone (Oliver) had gone through his pockets as he undressed, leaving a trail of bizarre bread-crumbs behind him.

Andrew turns the light off again. "I say we just go to bed."

"What if he's hurt himself?" I ask, already heading to the kitchen.

"What if he has company and you're interrupting him?"

"It's just *his* clothes," I point out, though I get ready to close my eyes quickly in the event of a naked Oliver plus company roaming around the house. Thankfully, it doesn't happen, and I find our gracious host slumped on the kitchen floor beside the fridge dressed in a full Santa suit, white beard and all.

"Cousin!" he proclaims when he sees me.

"I'm the friend," I tell him.

"And yet you already feel like family, such is our connection."

He's wasted. Pissed. *Inebriated*. Whatever you want to call it, the man is going to feel it in the morning.

"You should have worn that back at Lara's house," I joke as Andrew comes into the room behind me.

"You'll have to forgive me, I'm usually much more civilized than this but I met up with my friend Zac in Chelsea and he insisted."

"Did he?" Andrew asks flatly.

"Well, I didn't want to be rude," Oliver says, looking wounded that Andrew would even think of such a thing.

"Do I need to take you to the hospital?"

"I'd much rather you order me a tikka masala."

"How about a glass of water and some toast?"

Oliver sighs loudly but doesn't protest and, as Andrew finds his way around the kitchen, I reach into my pocket and hand him the box of gingersnap cookies I picked up as we were leaving the market.

He smiles at me, turning it over in his hands. "You got me a present?"

"As a thank you for letting us stay."

"That is almost questionably thoughtful of you, Molly, but I shall accept it in the spirit in which I'm sure it's intended."

"... Great."

His eyes latch on to my face, surprisingly focused. "Did you have a nice time?" he asks, suddenly urgent.

"We had a lovely time."

"You'll come back to visit then. With or without Andrew, I have no strong feelings toward the man."

I laugh and he starts prying open the box. "You know, I'm pretty sure there's a ready-made pizza in the freezer," he calls to Andrew. "I wouldn't dare make it myself, however. Not in this state." He lowers his voice to a faux whisper. "Much too dangerous."

I smirk, glancing over my shoulder, but Andrew's not listening to us as he pulls white bread out of a plastic packet, a look of fierce concentration on his face. It's only then that I take in the messy surroundings of the kitchen, the numerous wine and spirit bottles lining the counter. Oliver must have attempted to raid the cabinets before he got too tired.

"Hey," I call softly, twisting fully to face Andrew.

It takes a moment for his attention to come back to me. "Yeah?"

"Could you get his stuff ready for bed? I'll take care of the toast."

"Pizza," Oliver protests, but I shake my head.

"Toast will do the same job *and* you won't wake up in the morning with half of it stuck to your face."

"Wanna bet?"

I ignore him, watching Andrew as he lays a slice of bread carefully on the counter, his eyes flicking between it and the alcohol at his fingertips.

"Sure," he says after a second, and disappears without another word.

"I love a woman in charge," Oliver says as I make the food before forcing him to drink a pint of water. By the time he's done, Andrew has returned and together we haul Oliver to his feet.

His bedroom is, of course, all the way in the attic, and I'm disappointed to find his room incredibly ordinary compared to the rest of the house, with whitewashed walls and a plain navy bedspread. It's also a mess. His belongings are thrown everywhere, but I smile as I see the leftovers of Lara's Christmas decorations littering the floor, discarded colored paper and cotton wool, as though he'd spent the day doing arts and crafts just for her.

"Only two more sleeps until Christmas," Oliver says grandly as Andrew helps him onto the mattress. "I'll get up in the morning to see you off."

"I'm willing to bet everything in my suitcase that you won't," Andrew says. "And I have a giant Toblerone in there."

Oliver looks aghast as his cousin crouches before him. "You're only telling me this now?"

"Thanks for letting us stay. Get a real job."

"Anytime. And absolutely not. And, Molly!" He cranes his neck to where I stand in the doorway. "A delight to meet you. Thank you for my present."

"Thank you for having us."

"Always, always."

We leave him to sleep it off and head back down the stairs, pausing outside our respective doors on the floor below.

"Sorry about all that," Andrew says. "There's one in every family."

"I like him," I say. "I'm glad I got to meet him."

"Yeah, well..." He smiles a goodnight smile, turning toward his room.

"Andrew?" I step closer to him, trying to guess where his mind's at but unable to tell anything from his expression. "Are you okay?"

"With Oliver?" He shrugs. "He's melodramatic, but he means well."

"I meant with... He's pretty drunk," I finish, and Andrew tenses in understanding.

"I'm fine," he says. "No wagon-falling here. My cousin isn't exactly a glittering advertisement for the wonders of drinking."

"Still," I try again. "We can talk if you want to."

"I'm okay, Moll. Stop worrying."

"I will if you stop lying." We're both surprised by the exasperation in my voice, but I go with it, not caring anymore. "I'm going to worry," I tell him. "Of course I'm going to worry. You can't just tell me you're going through this incredibly hard thing and not expect me to want to help."

"Molly—"

"You don't have to do this by yourself." As soon as I say the words, I get a flashback to Gabriela following me around the office, begging me to talk to her. She knew something was up with me just like I know something's up with him. And I guess now I finally understand her frustration. "You can talk to me."

"I know I can." His gaze gentles at the obvious hurt in my voice. "I know, I'm just... This is all pretty new to me too. Besides my roommates, you're the first person I've told."

Now, that shocks me. "Really? Not even your family?"

He shakes his head. "Not yet. I'm still figuring out how to explain it to them without freaking them out."

"But what about Christmas?"

He knows what I mean. No one likes the stereotype, but the culture of casual drinking is very much alive in Ireland. Even more so at this time of the year when my social media feeds fill up with breakfast mimosas and lunchtime pints with captions of *'Tis the season* and *Might as well*. It's expected. Almost encouraged. And if you don't join in, it means something is wrong.

"I'll tell them I'm on antibiotics or something," Andrew says. "Christian's usually too hungover to touch anything anyway. I won't be alone. I guess I just don't want anyone to treat me any differently."

"But they will," I say. "They have to." I take another step toward him, relieved he's finally talking to me, furious I didn't ask sooner. I didn't realize how guilty I'd felt since he told me. I mean, talk about being a bad friend. So caught up in my own problems, year in and year out, that I didn't even see it.

Andrew smiles, reading my thoughts like I spoke them out loud. "You can't take the blame for this one, Moll. This is all on me. I got very, very good at hiding it. Even from myself."

"When did you know?"

"That I had a problem?" He shrugs, trying to play it casual even as a stiffness creeps into his body. "There weren't any warning signs," he says. "At least not the ones you think you know to look out for. I didn't wake up hungover all the time. I wasn't angry or moody. Or at least I told myself I wasn't. But it was becoming an everyday thing. Every meal, every event. Every time I went anywhere, anytime I did anything, it was all I could focus on. But I kept telling myself that as long as I didn't get too drunk, it wouldn't be an issue." He pauses, scratching the side of his neck. It's a nervous gesture. One that I'm not used to seeing from him. "I was in denial," he says eventually. "And I guess I lied just now. I couldn't hide it from everyone. It's why Marissa and I..."

I straighten, realizing what he's saying. "Oh my God, Andrew."

"She asked me to stop and I didn't. I was convinced she was blowing it out of proportion. But she could see it. Her dad had problems when she was growing up and she didn't want that in her life."

I have no idea what to say, so I don't say anything, listening like I need to start doing.

"It got worse after she left," he says after a beat. "Just to be predictable. But I realize now I couldn't stop for her. I had to stop for me. And I did."

"That's good," I say. "That's *great*."

He smiles at my earnestness. "I still get the odd moment," he admits. "The guy running the program says it's helpful to avoid places with excessive drinking, but it's the little moments that get to me. The quiet times when you think... maybe it wouldn't be so bad. Maybe I could just have one and then I could stop. Even though I know deep down I won't. And tonight? Spending it with you, knowing I'm seeing my family tomorrow? What better way to finish a perfect day?"

"So tell me when that happens," I say. "Let me be there for you. Even if it's just as a distraction."

"A distraction, huh?" His voice goes soft as he gazes down at me. "You want to be my distraction, Moll?"

I don't answer, feeling like I'm pinned in place as I swallow, my mouth suddenly dry. His eyes drop to my throat at the movement before trailing down to the necklace he gave me. I don't think I'm even breathing as he reaches up, tugging the chain from under my sweater so that it sits on top.

"Thank you for telling me," I whisper as he plays with it. "You can tell me anything. You know that, right?"

"I do." He lets go of the pendant, but his hand stays where it is, tucking a strand of hair behind my ear in what's fast becoming his signature move. "But just for the record," he says, "you can't tell me stuff."

He smiles as he dodges my hit, taking a step back from me and putting some much-needed distance between us in the process.

"I promise to tell you when it gets too much," he says. "And you can distract me however you want."

I grimace, thinking he's back to joking, but he shakes his head.

"I promise," he repeats, and he looks so sincere that this time I believe him.

"We should get some sleep," I say eventually, thinking about our final day of travel tomorrow. "If we wake up and the ferry is canceled, I say we buy as much food as we can carry and make s'mores in that giant fireplace downstairs."

"And you say you don't do Christmas."

"Goodnight, Andrew." I open the door to my room, dragging my gaze from his as I step inside.

"Sweet dreams," he calls after me, and I listen for his own door to shut before I do the same to mine.

Inside, I flick on the bedside light and change out of my clothes, leaving on my underwear and T-shirt to use as pajamas before washing my face in the bathroom. With barely anything with me, it doesn't take long to pack for the morning. My laptop bag remains untouched where Andrew left it that afternoon and I have one spare T-shirt to wear for the journey. The rest I fold into the small bag I got them in, and I put them beside my shoes, lined up neatly at the end of the bed.

When I'm done, I pull on the thick gray robe hanging on the back of the bathroom door and stand staring at the bed.

I know I need to at least try and get some sleep. That I'll hate myself tomorrow if I don't. But I don't think I've ever been more awake, my mind jumping from one thing to the other.

My skin feels tight. My body restless.

A perfect day.

That's what he said today was. Perfect.

There's a shuffling noise at the wall separating us, most

likely him just plugging something in, but at the sound of it I tense, suddenly achingly aware of how close he is.

Before I know what I'm doing I'm out my door, marching the two steps it takes to get to his where I knock, almost bruising my knuckles against the wood until I hear him cursing on the other side.

"Oliver," he growls as he opens it. "I swear to God if you—"

Andrew stops talking as soon as he sees me. "Are you okay?" he asks, instantly concerned.

Am I? I think seriously about my answer as I take in his messy hair and his kind eyes and his stupid shirt saying, *Yule got this*.

"No," I say and press a hand against the center of his chest, pushing him back into the room.

CHAPTER SIXTEEN

It's dark on the other side of the door. He hasn't put a lamp on yet, and the streetlights outside cast everything in an odd purple-and-orange glow. Behind him, the room is tidy. He's barely unpacked other than his toiletry bag and a spare T-shirt thrown on the bed, ready to wake up and go tomorrow. Ready to leave all this behind.

I shut the door at the thought, though I keep one hand on the handle just in case I chicken out.

"Molly?"

"Just don't talk for a second." To my surprise he does as I request, letting me stand there, taking him in silently. And I do take him in, my eyes traveling from his face, down down down to his chest, his jeans, and back up again.

Or what if you're just super dumb and you've never realized what's right in front of you?

Gabriela's words echo through my mind as I stare at him. I stare at him for so long my hand starts to cramp against the handle and I have to let go.

"You kissed me back," I say, and he goes so still I swear he isn't breathing. "Not to clear my mind. Not because you thought I was being funny. You kissed me back because you wanted to."

"I did," he says, and my heart stutters at those two simple words. But it's still not enough. I don't understand and I'm not leaving here until I do.

"Have you ever wanted to kiss me before?"

"Molly—"

"Have you?"

A muscle jumps in his jaw, fascinating me before he answers. "Once," he admits, forcing the word out. "Years ago."

"When?"

"We have to be up in five hours. Do you really want to do this now?"

"You want to wait another ten years?"

He scoffs but doesn't argue further, looking almost embarrassed the more I watch him. "Our third flight," he says eventually, and then, so quietly that I'm not even sure I heard him right: "You were wearing a red scrunchie."

I frown at him, confused. "That's our first real flight."

"I guess."

"That was seven years ago."

"I—"

"You've wanted to kiss me for seven—"

"I wanted to kiss you *then*," he stresses. "But you wouldn't shut up about your boyfriend, would you? So I left it alone."

He left it alone.

"What about you?" he asks while I freak out. "Have you ever wanted to kiss me before?"

"No."

He waits a beat for me to continue, huffing when I don't. "All right, thanks, Molly."

"I didn't!" It's the truth. "Not until the other day." When it became the only thing I ever wanted. Like someone had turned a spotlight on and aimed it straight at him. "I liked it when we kissed," I say, because it feels like something that needs to be made clear to him. "But then you started joking around—"

"You said you didn't want to do it again."

"I was obviously *lying*!" I exclaim. "And you said it wasn't a big deal."

"Because you were acting weird!"

"Because it *is* weird! *This* is weird. I've never felt like this before with you."

"Like what?"

"Well, right now, like I want to push you over," I snap. "And otherwise..." Otherwise, like my entire life was leading up to that very moment. "I liked it when we kissed," I repeat, folding my arms under my chest.

"So why did you freak out?"

"Because I didn't want to ruin our friendship. I like our friendship. It's important to me and I didn't want to lose it."

"You're not going to."

"You don't know that. You don't. And for all I knew, you felt nothing more than friendship for me, which means I would be making things majorly awkward for both of us and if you *did* feel more..." I fumble with the words, flustered now that we're getting to the heart of things. "If you did and we tried something, there's no saying if it would last or not, and then that's it. Ten years gone. You can't go back on something like that. Some things can't be unsaid."

"So, you're scared of liking me because you're scared of losing me?"

The urge to hide is strong. "Well, when you say it like that it makes me sound pathetic, so no."

"Moll..." His voice is filled with tenderness as he takes a step toward me. "Look at me. I'm not going anywhere."

"I know."

"You don't. And that's the problem. Everything you just said? I worry about it too. And I'm not going to let go of something like that, someone like *you*, that easy." He pauses, frowning slightly. "I shouldn't have tricked you into kissing me back in Argentina. It was selfish. And you're right. I wanted to kiss you. When I realized that you wanted me as well . . ." He shakes his head, his gaze intense as he stares down at me. "I snapped."

Snapped.

No one's ever snapped for me before.

I don't know why that turns me on so much.

"I guess everyone gets a little crazy during the holidays," I whisper, and I honest to God blush at the look in his eyes.

It becomes very clear to me then that I have two options. I can go back to my room and go to sleep and we'll keep tiptoeing until one of us cracks.

Or I can stay where I am. I can stay where I am and I can . . .

"Seven out of ten?" I ask.

His confusion lasts only a second before he realizes what I'm saying. "I guess practice makes perfect," he says evenly.

And then everything happens at once.

I close the space between us and step into him, fully into him. Chest to chest, hip to hip *into* him until it's only our faces that aren't pressed together. Andrew tenses against me, but I don't let myself read too much into it and when he doesn't move away, I tilt my head up and press my lips to his.

It's not the smoothest move I've ever done. More *I dare you to stop this* as opposed to *let's explore this newfound delicate thing between us*, and yet, it does the trick. Warmth flows through me again, a heavy feeling of rightness that fills and soothes every inch of me. Places I didn't even know needed soothing, like the nervous coil in my belly and the tightness in my shoulders. It all melts away with ridiculous ease as if to say, *Look, you idiot, this was all you had to do. It was right in front of you all along.*

There's still some sugar by his mouth, leftover from his churros, and when I flick my tongue out to lick it off, he makes a noise I've never heard from him before. My hands go to his hair, moving from a caress to a clutch as I hold him to me, our kisses growing deeper, needier until the gaps between them grow shorter, until we barely stop touching. And I never want to stop touching. Kissing Andrew Fitzpatrick was the best decision I ever made and I'm brazenly about to tell him this when he pulls back, pushing me an inch away so there's space between us.

My breathing is ragged, his just as bad, and I think maybe that's it and we'll go back to talking or he'll bid me goodnight and I'll have whatever the female equivalent of blue balls is, but instead his eyes drop from my face to where my robe is tied loosely around my waist. There he reaches out, running his finger along the halfhearted knot before a gentle tug pulls it free.

I'm not exactly wearing the sexiest of lingerie underneath. The T-shirt is plain white cotton, the underwear black and practical, but Andrew doesn't seem to care, his gaze intense as his hands slide under the hem of the shirt and around my waist, growing surer with every inch until he's holding me steady.

"This okay?" he asks.

I can only nod, barely able to form a thought as he draws a path up the sensitive skin of my rib cage. My top drags up as he goes, revealing my stomach as he stops just short of my breasts. His fingers feel hot enough to burn.

"Words, Molly."

"I'm good," I bite out, but he pauses at whatever he hears in my voice and brings his touch back to my hips. Before I can tell him to keep going, he drops his lips to mine, and okay, this is good too.

I respond with an enthusiasm I might have been embarrassed to show with another partner, but with Andrew I don't hesitate, wrapping one arm around his shoulders as I press myself into him, giving him no doubt this time as to what I want. He gets the hint.

He kisses me. Harder than before. Hard enough that I'm gasping into him, doing my best to keep up, and my back hits the door before he spins us both away from it. He does it so fast that I almost trip and I try to concentrate on the kiss while concentrating on keeping upright while concentrating on Andrew. Andrew who's steering me toward the bed and following me down onto it. Who's overwhelming me until he's all I know, until I stop thinking about anything other than the heat from him and the heat because of him.

My legs fall apart and he falls into the cradle of my thighs, our bodies pushing against each other until a pulse goes through me, deep and needy.

I want his shirt off. I want his shirt off and my shirt off. I want my skin against his and my body against his and I want it now and for the rest of the night and forever and ever and ever.

And still, he kisses me as his fingers move up again under my top, finally going right where I want them to, where I *need* them to, and screw our friendship. I have one life to live here and I want this to be it. And with my lips never leaving his, I reach for the bottom of his T-shirt, intending to pull it off and give in to everything I want, when we're interrupted by a firm, mocking knock on the door.

I didn't know knocks could sound mocking, but somehow this one pulls it off.

"Oh, lover boy?"

Andrew freezes above me, his expression almost comical.

"You've got to be kidding," he says, so close to me that his breath skims across my lips.

"Romeo?" Oliver calls again.

"I'm sleeping," Andrew yells.

"I'm not falling for that one again," Oliver says, his words slurring. "You know I'm not one to stop a man from relaxing, but I'm afraid I need a little help. I won't lie to you, after all that water I'm in desperate need of a piss but can't seem to find my way out of this bloody suit."

Andrew stares at me and, before I can stop myself, I run my finger down his nose. An almost pained expression crosses his face. "I'm tired, Oliver."

"Molly's welcome too," his cousin says conversationally, and I clamp a hand over my mouth as embarrassment shoots through me.

"She's also sleeping," Andrew shouts.

"I don't think that was snoring I heard."

Christ on a bike.

"Or maybe it was just a very good dream?"

Andrew rolls his eyes and starts to lean down but I stop him with a hand to his chest.

"What are you doing?" I whisper.

"What does it look like?" he asks, and I can't help but smile at his irritated tone. I push him again and he follows the movement, collapsing beside me.

"Not when he's still outside," I tell him.

"He's not."

"Oh, no, I'm still here," Oliver calls. "Listening too. Surprisingly thin walls, you see." He knocks again and Andrew shoots a glare at the door before turning back to me. One look at my face and he recognizes defeat.

"Give me a minute," he says, and I pat his arm.

"Excellent!" Oliver sounds delighted, and a moment later I hear the gentle shuffle of his slippers against the floorboards.

Neither of us moves, Andrew still looking at me as though he's hoping I'll change my mind.

"You should go," I say as I glance down his body, to the evidence of what I felt against me a few moments ago.

"He'll have to wait a minute," Andrew grumbles, and I bite my lip, trying not to look smug. I certainly feel smug. And Andrew knows it too, huffing as he climbs off the bed and snatches my robe from the floor. He sits back on the mattress as I pull it on.

"Are you okay?" he asks carefully.

I nod, pausing to look at him. "You?"

"Yeah."

"Okay then," I whisper, and we smile at each other as though sharing a joke, or maybe just sharing how ridiculous this is. In the best possible way.

"Goodnight, Andrew," I say, pulling my gaze away from the sight of him, deliciously rumpled at the end of the bed. I feel his eyes on me as I head to the door and it's not until I'm on the other side, closing it, that I hear his low response.

"Night, Moll."

CHAPTER SEVENTEEN
THREE YEARS AGO

Flight Seven, Chicago

"I hate men. I hate them. I mean, look at this crap. *Look.*"

Andrew rears back as I shove the phone into his face, showing him a picture of Mark and his new girlfriend. *Naomi.* The woman with the poreless skin.

"See?" I demand when he doesn't say anything.

"See what? Your screen's locked."

I drop my arm with a scowl, tapping in my password so hard I hurt my thumb.

"Molly—"

"Hang on," I mutter as I put in the right digits. "There." I turn my phone back his way with one hand and reach into my giant bag of duty-free toffees with the other. "It's been three weeks since we broke up. Three weeks and they're already on vacation. Do you know what that means?"

"I can't think of a single answer that would make you not yell at me."

"That it's been going on much longer," I say, ignoring him. "Mark cheated on me."

"You don't know that."

"They're at the *beach*," I say, going to the next photo. "Drinking out of *coconuts*."

He starts to nod before shaking his head when I just glare at him. "Moll, I won't lie to you; I am extremely bad at girl talk so this entire conversation is just making me nervous that I'll say the wrong thing."

"Well, tough," I snap. "Because you're sitting next to me for seven hours, which means you have to contribute to my breakdown. That's the friendship rule."

"But is it a *plane* rule?" he begins as I start scrolling through Mark's last few posts. Bitterness stabs me with each one, like my heart is breaking all over again.

I've been dumped three times in my life and each time it's *sucked*. It's sucked *balls*. And—

"I think that's enough of those," Andrew says, taking the packet of toffee from me. "I'm pretty sure everyone here would prefer if those vomit bags remained decorative for the rest of the flight."

I swallow the lump of sugar in my mouth, aware that I'm acting like a child throwing a tantrum and yet unable to stop. Between Mark and more responsibility at work, some days it feels like I'm hanging on by a thread.

"That's what 'meeting someone else' means," I say, continuing the conversation I'd been having in my head. "It means 'I've been cheating on you.'" I'd just been too stupid to realize it. No one breaks up with someone because they see another person across the street and go, "Yes! Her!" He would have started something with her weeks ago. Maybe not going all the way, but emotionally moving on before blindsiding me on a rainy Tuesday night with a well-rehearsed speech and a packet of tissues because he knew I was going to cry and I did. "Can I have my toffee back?"

"No."

I scowl as Andrew shoves the packet down the side of his seat. He's wearing a sweater with a dog on it that says, *Dachshund through the snow*, which honestly just feels a little lazy, but he told me his girlfriend had bought it for him so it's not like I can tell him that.

"I think you should get dumped too so we can be miserable together," I say at the thought of her.

"That *was* part of our contract."

Contract. Ugh. I'm still waiting to hear back from one of my clients about—

"Stop thinking about him," Andrew says.

"I'm not. I'm thinking about work."

"Just as bad. Why don't you think about *Home Alone* 2 colon *Lost in New York*?"

"Nobody says the title like that."

"Because they don't have the proper respect for *Home Alone* 2 colon—"

I cut him off with a groan as he starts flicking through the options on my screen. He's already loaded up the movie on his.

"You're going to marry Alison," I say as he plugs the headphones in. "You're going to marry Alison and *I* am going to have to hook up with someone at your wedding. Is your brother still single?"

"You're not hooking up with my brother."

I huff at the clear dismissal in his voice. "Why not? I'm a delight. You don't want me in your family?"

"Not like that, no."

"I'd settle for a third cousin," I say, but that only seems to make him madder.

"No settling at all."

"Well, I'm going to have to do *some* settling, seeing as I

can't seem to hold down a relationship for more than a year. I mean, there's got to be something wrong with me at this stage." I regret the words as soon as I say them, wincing as Andrew glances at me. Why not just lay out all my insecurities for everyone in my life to know? Why not everyone on the plane! Seems like a great plan. Super healthy. "Sorry," I say. "I may or may not be having a bad day; I don't know if you can tell."

Andrew doesn't respond, just holds up an earbud until I accept it, slotting it in place and placing a finger over the play button so we can sync. But Andrew doesn't move, still watching me with that serious expression that makes me desperate to fill the silence.

"Okay, so I may have overreacted about the coconuts as well. But—"

"Mark doesn't deserve you," he interrupts. "And I don't care if he's found his soulmate or if he spends his weekend rescuing stray dogs. He hurt you, so I hate him. And I would very much like to punch him for breaking your heart. In fact, if anyone ever makes you think you are less than what you are, or that you don't deserve everything that you reach for, I will make their lives as miserable as you want me to. Prank phone calls. Stones in their shoes. Whatever you ask me to do, I will do it. You are hardworking and passionate and kind and one day ... one day you are going to find someone who lights you up even more than you already do. And they'll be lucky to have you."

I can only stare at him as he sits back, so lost for words that I don't notice him retrieving my bag of toffee until he drops it in my lap.

"Okay?" he asks as I jump.

"Okay."

"No settling?"

"No settling." The word comes out as a whisper, but something in my face must satisfy him because he nods, turning his attention back to the screen.

"Good," he says, hitting play. "Now watch the damn movie."

Now, London

The next morning, I stand in the concourse of Euston Station, waiting for Andrew to return with our promised coffees as what honestly feels like eleven million people converge around me. It is six forty a.m. on Christmas Eve and no one looks particularly happy to be here. Parents clutch the hands of bleary-eyed children and single travelers and couples stand grimly just like I do, laden down with bags and sweating in their coats. Everyone either stares at their phones or at the large board overhead, which flickers every thirty seconds with rolling destinations and departure times.

It's chaos. And once again, I think about how this was not supposed to end up this way. Andrew and I were supposed to enjoy an hour in the first-class lounge before floating to our seats. We were supposed to enjoy our flight in comfort and luxury before parting as usual at the airport, me into a taxi and him to a bus to bring him home. We were supposed to be at our respective houses by now, which means I wouldn't be standing here, cold and grumpy and exhausted.

I also wouldn't have kissed him.

I wouldn't have nearly done much more than just kiss him.

Or maybe I still would have.

I peer up at the board, waiting for our platform to appear

as I fiddle with the scarf around my neck. Andrew's scarf. Underneath it lies the necklace he gave me, the one I have yet to take off. I run my finger over the pendant, shivering when I remember the feel of him last night. I don't even want to think about what would have happened if Oliver hadn't interrupted us.

I mean, I want to think about it a *lot*, but—

"Three-fifty for a croissant," Andrew announces as he appears through the crowd with our breakfast. "There's London prices and then there's just daylight robbery."

"So you didn't get any?"

"No, I got two. I've seen you when you're hungry; no one wants that."

I smirk as he passes me a coffee, taking a sip as he bites into one of the pastries.

"Why the face?" he asks. I'm surprised at the hint of worry I hear. As though he's afraid he's the reason for my mood.

"I'm thinking of those first-class tickets," I say. "And how very much that experience would not have been this experience."

"Ah, it's good to be among the people," he says. "Keeps you grounded."

"I feel like I'm one wrong look away from screaming the whole place down."

He shrugs, his gaze flicking absently over the crowd. "We can handle that. What's your line?"

"My line?"

"Your I've-had-enough-and-I-don't-care-how-bad-a-mood-I'm-in line." Andrew takes another sip of his coffee. "Mine is if we break down. I don't mind a wait to change drivers but if we break down, I am officially losing my shit."

"I don't know what mine is yet."

"You can take a crying baby? Crying baby is a good one. There's also strong-smelling food, considering how early it is in the morning. That would be a hard number one line for me if I wasn't so sure something extremely bad was going to happen."

"Don't say that."

"I don't mean a crash," he says casually. "But at the very least, a three-hour delay resulting in a missed ferry."

"You're being pessimistic. *I'm* the pessimistic one. I'm the most pessimistic."

"Are you seriously trying to beat me at pessimism?"

"Trying?" I ask, and he grins, letting the conversation drop.

We haven't talked about last night yet. It's not like we've ignored it. We only left the house an hour ago and before that we were getting ready. We'll have to acknowledge it at some point. And say what, I have no idea. No idea because I don't know how I feel about it yet.

I don't regret it. But I'm not sure what it means either. I've never been one of those people who overanalyzed their relationships. But that's because they've followed a traditional, set pattern. Meet a guy, talk to a guy, date a guy. That's it. Not whatever this is. Not whatever we—

"You know you make these faces when you're thinking really hard about something?"

I start, spilling my coffee over the lid as I squeeze the cup too tightly. "Huh?"

"Like you're having an internal conversation," Andrew continues, watching me curiously. "You start making these expressions. Did you know that?"

I did not.

"What are you talking to yourself about?"

"You."

His eyebrows rise, a smile beginning before I shut it down.

"You've got crumbs all down the front of your coat."

His smile drops as he brushes them off and I turn, a little primly it must be said, back to the concourse.

Maybe he's waiting for me to bring up last night. And that's fine. That's totally fine. I have, after all, initiated the majority of non-platonic friendship events between us. I know he doesn't regret it because he's acting completely normal just like he promised he would, so maybe he's just waiting. For me. For a *Hey, remember when we almost had sex a few hours ago? Remember when we made out for a good several minutes and felt each other up and—*

"I will give you one hundred dollars if you tell me what you're thinking about right now."

"Just don't look at me!" I exclaim, and I step in front of him so he can only see the back of my head. Almost as soon as I do, the board changes and Andrew points to where our platform number has just appeared.

"A seacht," he says, speaking in Irish as he pulls the handle of his suitcase up. "Numero siete. Lucky number seven."

"Okay."

"This way, Molly. Let me show you the way to go home. To the green hills of Ireland. The old Emerald—"

"I get it," I snap, and he laughs.

One good thing about his ridiculous suitcase: it carves a neat little path for me through the crowd. Around us, dozens of people break away, doing the same. This train, like all the others, is standing room only. There are lines at the barrier and again on the platform, with some people going so far as to hoist their luggage over their heads in order to squeeze their way to the doors.

It gets a bit tense, and it isn't long until something bumps into my shoulder, followed by a muffled apology as a man with an acoustic guitar shoves past.

I gaze after him suspiciously. "If he starts playing that thing, we're moving to a different carriage," I tell Andrew.

"That's your line?"

"That's my line."

By some miracle, we manage to find a spot for our bags and no one is sitting in our booked seats, so we don't have to make anyone move either.

Still, I hold my breath, waiting for something to happen. For a tree on the tracks or a failed engine. But everyone gets onboard and eventually, warily, we pull out of the station and chug our way through the buildings of North London.

I start to feel a little better.

I think Andrew does too. He doesn't do anything for the first few minutes of the journey, sitting rigidly beside me before his shoulders lower with a quiet sigh. Another minute and he unfurls the same *National Geographic* he had back in Chicago, along with a paperback thriller he must have picked up with our coffees.

I fight back a yawn and turn to the window, watching as the sky begins to lighten and the city gives way to the green fields of the countryside that make up my view for the next few hours. I must doze off, because the next thing I know, Andrew is shaking me awake as the conductor announces our impending arrival into Holyhead. We still have another twenty minutes or so, but everyone predictably gets up to stretch their legs and the carriage is soon filled with people passing down bags and gathering their belongings.

There's a marked difference in mood from when we got on the train to getting off it. There's no jostling this time around. Everyone is smiling, suddenly chatty now we're halfway home. I do start to get a little antsy as we wait for our turn to exit, but it vanishes as soon as I step onto the platform and stretch my legs. I can't see the sea, but I can smell it, fresh and salty and alive. I can hear it too, the shriek of the gulls, the blasting horn of a departing ship. It's a sunny day in Wales, the clouds white wisps above us, and the air is the clearest I've experienced in months.

I take a deep breath of it, turning to Andrew as he passes me my bag. "I just remembered something."

"Yeah?" He's distracted, making sure we have everything as he pulls his coat back on.

"Yeah. I freaking love the ferry."

He laughs so loud a nearby child glances at him in alarm. "I've never been on one."

"Seriously?"

He hesitates. "I've just gone way down in your estimation, haven't I?"

"You've never been on the ferry? It's the best!"

"I believe you."

"I'm going to take you up on deck when we get to Dublin."

"You can do whatever you like to me," he says, only to grin at the look I give him.

We check in his suitcase and then it's a short wait at passport control before we file down a long hallway, straight onto the ship.

It's smaller than I remember, probably because the last time I was on one I was a child, but there's still lots of room to move around, and we spend a few minutes exploring before grabbing turkey and ham sandwiches from the cafeteria. Santa himself makes an appearance, which sends every child onboard into a frenzy. Everyone's inner child too, considering Andrew makes us stand in line for twenty minutes to say hello and get a company branded keyring for our efforts. The rest of the journey is spent watching *Elf* on one of the giant television screens before I drag him out to join the other brave souls on the open deck. A sharp wind hits us as soon as we do, but we find a bit of shelter as we near the port, Andrew a warming presence as he crowds my back, sheltering me from the worst of the wind.

It's late afternoon by this stage and day is turning to night, but a thousand lights welcome us where Dublin city hugs the bay.

"Ten bucks says we sink," Andrew says, his mouth right by my ear so he can be heard over the noise of the engine.

"*You'll* sink," I say. "I'm an excellent swimmer."

He laughs as he moves closer, his arms bracketing me in as he holds on to the railing on either side of me. I stay very still, practically holding my breath as he leans in.

"Thank you," he says.

"For what?"

"For getting me home for Christmas."

"You're not home yet," I warn, but he ignores me. His lips skim my cheek, his gloved hands coming to rest on mine, which exactly two seconds ago, I would have been more than okay with, so I can understand his surprise when I immediately knock him off, moving up the ship.

"Okay, so that's what we call a mixed signal," he calls after me, but I barely hear him, my attention on the rapidly approaching coastline. "And can we not do that?" He pulls me sharply back as I lean over the railing.

"It's fine."

"So is standing behind the safety line."

The ship's horn blares as we near the port and I motion for Andrew to stand beside me before we miss it. "We have to wave!"

"To who?" he asks, still sounding a little disgruntled that I ruined the moment.

"To them."

I point over the railing to the flat stone wall leading to Dublin's Poolbeg Lighthouse. People dot the pathway, getting in their Christmas Eve walks, and they raise their arms overhead as we sail past.

We're too far away to see them clearly, too far away to really see them at all in the dim light, but I can just make out their faint shouts, can see their exaggerated movements as they say hello.

"It's like they're welcoming you home," I say, glancing at Andrew when he doesn't respond. He's not even looking at them, his gaze trained on me with the biggest smile on his face.

"Don't laugh," I warn, suddenly self-conscious.

"I'm not."

"You're about to."

"Because you're adorable."

"Wave at the good people of Dublin," I order, and he nods, schooling his features into a serious expression as he joins me at the railing.

"Can I yell?" he asks.

"Within reason."

He seems to consider this for a moment before holding his hands aloft. "*Hello!*" he screams over the noise. "*Merry Christmas!*"

"Andrew—"

"*And Happy New Year!*"

"You can stop now."

"It's cathartic," he says. "Try it."

"No."

"I dare you."

I huff, but as the horn blares again, it's not like anyone can hear us.

"Go on," Andrew urges, and I press my lips together before copying him.

"*Merry Christmas!*" I screech, and he grins.

"Again," he says, so I do. And together we scream and we wave until our voices grow hoarse and our arms grow tired and an announcement calls over the intercom, urging us back inside to disembark.

Only then does Andrew tug me free of the rail and we laugh, breathless as we follow the others down the stairs and get ready to go home.

CHAPTER EIGHTEEN

A cheery coach driver in a Santa hat is there to greet us as we trickle out of the port, his accent so strong that it takes me a moment to adjust.

"Well?" he jokes as we put our luggage in the hold. "What did yis bring me?"

Andrew can't wipe the smile from his face as we find our seats. We pick two near the back, with him at the window, and I text Zoe that not only are we still alive, but she now has to do as promised and pick me up.

"What time is your bus?" I ask, my voice a little hoarse from all our yelling.

Andrew shrugs, watching the world outside as we leave the port and head into the city. "On the hour every hour. They run up to eleven."

"Really?"

He glances over his shoulder at how pleased I sound. "According to the website."

"Well, why don't you swing by mine first? You can finally meet everyone. Have a shower, some dinner. We're not that far." My enthusiasm wanes when he just looks at me. "Unless you want to head straight—"

"That sounds great," he interrupts. "The shower part in particular. Plus I'd love to meet your folks. And Zoe."

"You're not allowed to like her more than me," I say, only half-joking.

"Well, then you'll have to up your game in the next twenty minutes now, won't you?"

And it's twenty minutes exactly until my sister messages back, confirming the new plan. By then the bus has dropped us at the top of O'Connell Street, a broad sweeping avenue in the center of the city that might as well have been in the North Pole by the look of it.

The air is full of noise, of voices and laughter and Christmas music coming from every direction. Women call out as they sell pots of poinsettias and bouquets of red berries, clutching cups of coffee to keep warm. Enthusiastic teenagers collecting for charity shake rattling buckets of coins at passersby. Every single store I can see has its doors thrown open, crammed with last-minute shoppers and people who apparently just live for chaos.

Even the cars have made an effort, dressed up in Rudolph noses and reindeer antlers as they crawl so slowly through the traffic that most people simply weave between them to cross the roads.

I gaze around at it all with a strange feeling in my gut, surprised at how happy the scene makes me. It's like my head knows they're just the same old decorations they put up every year, but something about them now makes my heart beat a little faster, makes me smile at the passing strangers, and even the exuberant choir belting out some Mariah Carey across the street is a little less irritating than it would usually be.

It's Dublin at Christmas and there's excitement in the air.

And yes, you would have to be a grinch not to be taken in by it all.

We need to go to Merrion Square to meet my sister, so we collect our luggage and start walking past the glittering hotels and impressively large Christmas trees down toward the Liffey, the river that splits the city into the north and south side. Even that hasn't escaped the festive cheer, with the numerous bridges that cross it lit up in bright neon lights that shimmer gleefully in the reflection of the water, ready to be posted to a thousand Instagram accounts. Including mine, I guess, seeing as Andrew stops us halfway across to take a selfie.

We round the curve of Trinity College next, where giant snowflakes are projected onto the front entrance. Our progress slows considerably here, the narrow sidewalks congested with people, but Andrew doesn't seem to mind, navigating his suitcase with good humor even as mine starts to sour. Eventually, I slide in front of him, intent on politely pushing people out of the way, but Andrew tugs me back and I follow his gaze toward Grafton Street, the busy shopping thoroughfare with its famed Christmas lights strung elegantly overhead.

"No," I say as he raises a brow.

"Come on."

"It's jammed."

"It's Christmas."

It's Christmas.

And the smile on his face is so boyish, so hopeful, that I don't resist too hard when he tugs me again, and we wind our way through the traffic and onto the busy street. The stores are still open here too, and people move in and out of them with cones of gelato and cups of hot chocolate, numerous shopping bags dangling from their arms.

We edge around a tight circle singing along to a busker, a rosy-cheeked teenager who looks like he's having the night of his life, before Andrew brings us to a halt at the mouth of an alleyway to get our bearings.

"I feel like I should pop in somewhere and get your parents something," he says, peering into the nearest store. "I'd offer the giant Toblerone, but I'm not that grateful."

"What about one of your photos?" I suggest. "They'd love one. Truly."

"You think?" He sounds distracted and I look over to see his face tilted to the sky, or more specifically, to the mistletoe hanging from the stone archway above.

"That could be anything," I say. "It could be drugs. A lot of drugs in this city. It's a big problem."

"Worried you're going to freak out again, huh?"

"*No*, I—"

"Because I'm too hot to handle? It's the bobble hat, isn't it? Nothing screams sex appeal like a knitted bobble—"

I kiss him, and both of us smile when I do.

Maybe we don't need to talk about us. Maybe we'll talk about it when we have time, without Christmas and family looming over us. We'll talk when we're back in Chicago. And in the meantime, we'll share a kiss goodbye.

Except I don't want this to be goodbye.

The thought comes to me as soon as his lips touch mine, sending a sharp spark of panic through me, and though he obviously means this to just be a quick one, I keep myself pressed firmly against him, clutching the ends of his coat as his hands settle on my arms.

"Do you know what?" he murmurs when he breaks away. "I think we're both really good at that. Eight out of ten."

"Shut up," I groan, but I'm more embarrassed than annoyed. More pleased than embarrassed. And he knows it.

The way he looks at me now makes me wonder if he's thinking the same thing I am, which is, why the hell have we never tried this whole kissing thing before? Though maybe if we had it wouldn't have been the same. These feelings felt sudden to me back in Chicago, confusing and strange. But now I can't help but think that maybe they're not so sudden after all. Maybe they were more gradual than that. A slowly cresting wave just waiting to break on the shore. Maybe it was always coming. Maybe that's why it feels so right and the thought of leaving him now, even just for the next few days, has me feeling hollower than I have any right to be.

"Come on," he says, slipping his gloved hand back into mine. "I want to meander."

"We've been meandering for *three days*."

He doesn't care.

Andrew makes us walk all the way to the top of the street, which takes twice as long as it should seeing as how he stops at every window display.

Finally, we turn left at the Christmas tree, walking parallel to St. Stephen's Green park. It's shut for the night, but the line of horse-drawn carriages is still operating outside it and they take turns clopping off with delighted tourists taking videos as they go. We keep moving, past more hotels and pubs and restaurants where people spill out onto the streets and straight into taxis, before completing the block down the quieter and darker Merrion Square. And there, halfway down by the towering government buildings, a woman in a bright pink coat leans against a car, her head bent as she scrolls through her phone.

My sister.

"That's her," I say unnecessarily, seeing as she's the only person around. My steps quicken as excitement bubbles inside and as we draw closer she glances up, waving when she sees us.

Andrew makes a surprised noise behind me. "So, she's like, *identical* identical."

I laugh. "I've definitely shown you a picture before."

"Yeah, but in person it's..."

A lot. I know that. Zoe and I look the same down to the last freckle at times, though she's always kept her hair longer than mine. And of course, now there's one pretty big difference.

"You're alive!" she proclaims, throwing her arms wide. I have to step to the side to hug her, her pregnant belly making it impossible to meet her face-to-face. When I pull back, she grabs my hands, placing them where my soon-to-be nephew rests.

"Meet Logan," she says.

"I thought it was Patrick."

"Patrick was last week. Now it's Logan."

I smirk. "And next week it will be?"

"I met a really nice Ryan the other day," she says as her eyes flick behind me.

"Meet Andrew," I say, welcoming him into the family reunion.

Zoe holds out a hand as though she expects him to kiss it. "Charmed."

"Would you stop?"

"What? My child needs a father." She says this while shaking Andrew's hand, Andrew who isn't quick enough to mask his confusion.

Her expression turns serious. "He left me when he found out."

And here we go. "Zoe—"

"I thought I meant something to him, you know? But he left me. Penniless and alone and—"

"She went through a donor," I say loudly. "And she earns more than I do."

Zoe huffs. "Spoilsport. I paid a stupid amount of money for a small bit of semen," she tells him, pinching her fingers together. "A complete rip-off. I was perfectly fine chancing it with a couple of one-night stands but Molly was like '*Noooo*, that's unethical.'"

"Being the sarcastic twin is all she has," I say, and Zoe tilts her head, looking at him thoughtfully as she rubs her belly.

"I never had an Andrew on my name list."

"Okay," I say, stepping in front of him. As I do, I draw her attention back to me and a smile lights up her face.

"I can't believe you're here," she says, and draws me into another hug. This one is a proper one and I feel the same twinge of sadness I always do when I see her for the first time after a few months. I don't think it will ever be easy being so far away from her, even if it is what I want.

"You need to sit down," I say. "How are you even standing right now?"

"With great difficulty." She unlocks the car as Andrew brings his stuff around to the trunk. "Have you seen these ankles? Of course, whenever I complain to Mam, I get a twenty-minute lecture about how she had to carry *two* babies. She's *thrilled* about finally getting to meet this guy, by the way. The famous Andrew in the flesh."

He smiles. "Famous, huh? No pressure, then."

"We also expect our guests to repay our hospitality with solid gold. Molly, I don't know if you told him the rules?"

"There's a giant tube of M&M's in here if you play your cards right," he says, hefting his case inside. Zoe plants a hand over her heart.

"And there we go. Andrew is at the top of the list.

Goodbye, Logan! We barely knew you." She glances at me. "He gets shotgun."

"But I'm your sister!"

"And he's the *guest*. Get in before I make you walk; my baby's cold."

And with that, we get into the car.

CHAPTER NINETEEN

The unease starts to kick in the closer we get to the house. Zoe peppers Andrew with questions the entire way, which gives me the chance to sit back and not think for a few minutes. Or at least, try not to think. I guess I should feel a sense of relief. All that money, all that stress, all those chocolates given to grumpy cabdrivers, and here we are. We made it.

But all I feel is apprehension. I can't help but wonder if as soon as we step foot back in Chicago, this will be over. That we'll go back to just being Andrew and Molly. I mean, sure, we had a cute time in London. A little back-and-forth, oh, I'll take you ax throwing. But that was said with twinkling fairy lights and an eccentric cousin and that new warm contentment that didn't have anything to do with our real lives. With our friends and jobs and responsibilities. Throw those into the mix and anything could happen.

"Did you see the O'Reillys got an extension?" Zoe asks as we turn onto our road. We pass a familiar redbrick house on the corner with a very notable box taped onto the side. "Mam's fuming. Says it's ruining the whole street."

"She's just jealous."

"Of course she's jealous." She pulls in sharply, parallel parking with enviable ease. "Home sweet home," she says, sending me a smirk.

I ignore her, gazing up at the small, terraced house of my childhood. "They've seriously made you move in with them?"

Zoe lives in a decent apartment down by the docks. One of those fancy buildings with its own Pilates studio and at least five independent, *very* serious coffee shops within walking distance.

"Only for a few weeks," she says as we get out of the car. "Not going to lie, I kind of like being looked after. Just don't tell them."

We follow her up the small lane, Andrew grinning at the lit-up reindeer in the garden next door.

"*Mam?*" Zoe calls as we step inside. "I found your second-favorite daughter!"

"Zoe."

"And she brought a boy home!"

"Zoe!"

She ignores me, waddling a few steps into the house. "They must be at Mary's," she says, already turning back when there's no answer. "Give me five minutes."

"Mary's?" Andrew asks when she disappears outside again.

"Our neighbor. She's been by herself since her husband died. They spend a lot of time there."

"That's kind of them," Andrew says, following me into the room. "You must miss it, knowing everyone on the street."

"Are you kidding me? Do you know how nosy people can get? The woman four doors down baked me a cake the day I first started my period. I don't even know how she knew."

He laughs. "I still think that sounds nice."

"It was red velvet."

I shrug off my coat and scarf, already sweltering at the balmy conditions they like to keep the house in. A few of Zoe's things are scattered about as well as a couple of noticeable presents for the baby, but otherwise the place looks exactly the same as it always does. A small front room and an extended kitchen at the back, with three bedrooms and a bathroom upstairs. It's small and basic but loved and cared for, and I have nothing but good memories of it growing up.

"Where's the tree?" Andrew asks, flicking the tassel at the end of one of Mam's cushions. She's had them since before I was born, along with the brown couch and the heavy wooden bureau that belonged to my grandmother. That sits where it always has, in the corner of the room, groaning under the weight of a million family photographs.

"We never get a tree."

From the look on his face, I might as well have told him Santa isn't real.

"Where would we put it?" I continue, gesturing around the small room.

"You really did nothing?"

"I guess we used to decorate the pine tree outside when we were younger. Dad pretended there were fairies inside."

"Okay, well, that's completely charming."

"I was a charming child." I point to a beaming photo of four-year-old me as proof. "Up until about twelve."

"All went downhill, huh?"

"Puberty was not my friend."

He scans the row of photographs, lingering over a few.

"This is the part where you tell me I grew into myself," I remind him.

"Did you though?"

"*Okay*, Mr. Sarcasm. You're a guest in this house, lest you forget."

Andrew just points at another photo of one of us atop a donkey. "What's going on here?"

"Zoe's birthday."

"Which is also your birthday," he says, only to frown when I shake my head. "Were you one of those one minute before midnight, one minute after situations?"

"Nope. We just celebrated on different days. We got to pick them."

He stares at me. "You got to pick your own birthday?"

"Uh-huh." I grin as I realize I'm blowing his mind. "My parents were very keen that we each got to feel unique. So, we celebrated our real birthday *and* we got another day."

"That's just greedy."

I laugh. "It felt very normal to us."

"Which one do we celebrate?"

"My real one," I assure him.

"And your other one?"

"March tenth. There's no significance," I add. "None. I picked it at random. I haven't done anything on it since I moved away, but my parents still send me a card."

"I can't believe you get two birthdays."

"I'm special."

He falls silent, examining each picture with intense focus, as though trying to glean as much as he can from them before he finally pulls away, asking about the shower. Despite not technically living here anymore, I fall quickly into the role of host, heading upstairs to make sure the place is clean while he runs outside to get what he needs from his suitcase.

"I'll just be in here," I say, pointing to my old room when

he returns. "Mam will probably make stew because it's the only thing she can cook."

"Stew sounds great," he says, hanging up the spare towel I pass him.

"Give me a shout if you need anything."

He flashes me a brief smile and disappears behind the closed door.

This is where a normal person would leave him to it. But I don't move. It's like my feet are stuck to the carpet, my body weighted to the spot as I listen to the scrape of the lock against the wood, the gentle rustling of clothing before the shower turns on. The hallway fills with the noise of our boiler heating the water, of the water itself splashing against the tiles.

It's only when the front door opens below that I force myself back into my bedroom. Zoe left out some of her (non-maternity) clothes for me and I throw on a pair of her jeans and a hoodie before scraping my hair back into a bun. The water shuts off barely a few seconds later and I quickly tidy my things as I hear Andrew fumble with the lock.

We meet in the hallway, him with only that ragged towel wrapped around his waist. His clothes are in his arms, hiding half his chest, but I still get an eyeful of smooth wet skin and a shadowy trail of dark hair that disappears beneath the—

"No six-pack, sorry."

My eyes snap up to the small, knowing smile on his face.

"You don't need one," I say, and his smile widens. "That was quick," I add.

"I figured you might want one."

"Oh. Nah." I wave a hand, my eyes trained somewhere above his left shoulder. I don't want to waste a second more away from him than I have to. "I'll, uh . . . You can change in my room."

I don't give him a chance to respond, slipping past him into the now empty bathroom as we switch places. It's steamed up from his shower, the air warm and scented with soap. *His* soap. That stupid sandalwood/pine/going-to-take-you-into-the-woods-on-a-summer's-day-and-kiss-you-on-the-soft-forest-floor soap.

What *is* that?

I move automatically, trying to keep busy. I wipe the mirror clean and shake out the shower curtain. I hang up the mat and wash my hands. I stand in the middle of the room and try not to cry.

They're tired tears, I know they are. Emotional, physical, someone-look-after-me tears that burn behind my eyes. That I refuse to let fall.

Maybe I should have just brought him straight to the bus stop. It would have been easier that way. A clean break. No seeing him in my house, joking with my sister, probably about to charm my mother. I should have said goodbye in town, but I don't want to say goodbye at all.

I don't want him to go.

I don't want him to go. I don't want him to go. I don't want him to go.

I stare at the shower, taking a few steadying breaths until I'm sure I have myself under control. When I do, I return to my bedroom, where I knock softly, entering when Andrew tells me to. He's still only half-dressed, his chest and feet bare as he looks between the shirt options he's laid out on my bed.

"How formal is dinner here?" he asks.

"Tuxedos or get out."

"I figured."

I step farther into the room as he grabs a T-shirt with one hand and rubs the damp towel over his hair with the other. The muscles of his stomach pull taut as he does. The same muscles I touched last night. And just as the kiss in Buenos Aires seemed a whole other world away, the dark bedroom in London feels like a lifetime ago, one we still haven't talked about.

"You're making a face."

"I know."

Andrew frowns, draping the towel against the back of a chair. "What's up?"

"I want to decide what this is before Christmas," I say. "I don't want to wait until we get back to Chicago. That's too long. You said you're not going anywhere, but I need to know where we stand or I'll just go crazy." I pause, sliding my hands down my thighs. "Does that make sense?"

"Of course it does."

I nod, waiting.

"Well," he says when I just stare at him. "What do you want this to be?"

Damn. I should have asked that first. "I don't know," I say honestly. "I know I don't want to stop."

"Neither do I."

"But don't you feel like we're moving too fast?" I ask. "I mean, we've gone from nothing to something pretty quickly, haven't we?"

"Maybe." He shrugs. "Maybe not. It doesn't feel wrong to me." He hesitates, looking at me curiously. "Does it feel wrong to you?"

I shake my head. Because that's the problem, it doesn't feel wrong at all. It feels right.

"Because if Oliver hadn't interrupted us..." Andrew continues.

"I know."

"I was ready to use some of my best moves, that's all I'm saying."

"Shut up," I groan, sitting on the edge of the bed. I catch a brief glimpse of his smirk before I drop my head into my hands.

"We have time," he says when I meet his gaze. "We have lots of time. So, if you want to go back to the beginning, we can do that."

"The beginning?"

"Yeah." He grins as he crouches before me. "Like first-date beginning. I mean, sure, we'll have a leg up on other couples, but it's not like they could compete with us anyway."

Other couples. A fizzing kind of pleasure shoots through me at the words.

"You say you don't think it's wrong. But if you're worried it could be, we'll just ... chill. Take things as they come. Okay?"

"Okay," I mumble, fidgeting with the hem of my sleeve.

"When do you get back to Chicago?"

"The twenty-eighth."

"I'm back on the seventh," he says formally. "Would you like to get a coffee with me, Molly?"

"I guess."

"Would you like to show a little more enthusiasm?"

"Would you like to put your shirt on?" I respond, and he laughs, doing as requested.

"I'll see you on the seventh."

"You'll just be back!"

"And I'll come straight to you. We can get dinner."

Dinner. I can do dinner. I've had dinner with lots of people. "I get to pick where we eat."

"I wouldn't dream of it any other way."

I nod, distracted as his hands find mine. It's getting harder to think when he's near me like this. But dinner is good. "There's this Nepalese place in Wicker Park that I think you'll really—"

The way his gaze drops to my mouth is the only warning I get before he kisses me. It only lasts a few seconds, nowhere near long enough, and I try to curb my annoyance when he pulls back.

"When you say taking it slow," I mutter, and he smiles before kissing me again.

"You want to make out on your bed?"

"And make all my teenage dreams come true?" Yes, yes, I do. But before I can push him down on the sagging mattress and act out seventeen-year-old me's fantasies, we're interrupted by Zoe calling my name from below.

"If this interrupting family thing becomes a habit for us," I begin, and he laughs, sitting back on his heels. "Ready to meet my parents?" I ask, accepting his hand as he helps me to my feet. "Mam is—"

I break off with an annoyed huff as Zoe calls me again. And even though it's been years, I'm so used to the sound of my sister shrieking at me that my first instinct is to ignore it. But a second later she yells it a third time, only this one is followed by a short, piercing scream.

CHAPTER TWENTY

I go down the stairs so fast I almost trip. Andrew actually does, stumbling over the bottom step as we find Zoe standing in the middle of the kitchen. She's bent double, one hand grasping the back of a chair, her face screwed up in pain.

"I'm fine," she says when she sees us. "Sorry, I'm fine."

"You screamed!"

"I'm dramatic. I just—" Her lips press together as she barely holds back a groan. Andrew curses softly beside me.

"Are you having contractions?"

She shakes her head. "Fake ones."

"They don't look fake," I say.

"They're Braxton-Hicks. It's a thing. It's a known thing." She has to force the last word out as another one hits, her knuckles turning white as she collapses into the chair. "Jesus Christ."

"We should go to the hospital," I say as Andrew crouches beside her. She immediately grabs hold of his hand, and he doesn't even wince as she proceeds to squeeze the bones off him. "Zoe? Hospital?"

Zoe just rolls her eyes, or as much as she can roll her eyes while her uterus is gripping itself like a stress ball. "I'll just have a bath."

"How will that help!"

"I don't know! Stop yelling at me!"

Andrew acts as a steadying weight as she attempts to stand and she grunts a thank you as she gets to her feet.

As she does, I see a wet patch spreading rapidly down her pants. It's only through sheer force of will that I swallow my gasp.

Andrew follows my gaze and, to be fair to the man, he doesn't so much as flinch as he looks quickly back to me, eyebrows raised.

"Zoe? Honey?" I keep my voice as gentle as possible. "I think your water just broke."

"I probably just peed myself. You do that a lot when you have a human pressing on your bladder."

"I don't think you peed yourself and I don't think these are fake contractions. I think you're having your baby."

Zoe stares at me, looking genuinely confused and extremely irritated.

My sister is not an idiot. We battled it out at school together to get top of our classes. She beat me by three points in our final exams. She does the *New York Times* crossword every day and once learned Portuguese in six months because I bet her she couldn't.

She's not an idiot. But she is, and always has been, a stubborn brat, and right now seems so completely set in her ways that the alternative is unthinkable to her.

I try again. "You're going into—"

"I'm not going into labor," she says, irritation winning out over confusion. "Don't be stupid. You're stupid."

"Zoe—"

"I'm not due for three weeks."

"It's not like the baby is checking its calendar!"

"The hospital?" Andrew asks.

I start to nod before remembering how little I have with me. "I don't have my license."

"I can drive her."

"Hello?" Zoe calls, waving a hand. "Stop talking about me like I'm not here."

"Stop being a dumbass," I counter. "Where's Mam and Dad?"

"They're dropping Mary at the church."

"Which church?"

"I don't know!"

"Well, how long will it take them to—"

"Maybe they should meet us there?" Andrew asks.

"This isn't happening," Zoe groans as Andrew and I share a look over her bent head.

"Look, if they're fake, then they're fake," I say. "No problem. But it won't hurt to hear it from someone who didn't learn their medical knowledge from *Grey's Anatomy*. Please just let us take you."

Zoe gives me a look like *I'm* the unreasonable one in this situation, but something in my face must convince her that she's not getting out of this.

"Maybe they'll give me painkillers," she says, and I nod encouragingly.

The contractions seem to ease once we get her into the car and she calms down when we're on the road, texting our parents as well as a few of her friends to let them know what an idiot I'm being. Despite her refusal to believe this is happening, she thankfully has the directions saved on her GPS and Andrew makes quick work of the traffic as he drives us back into the city. The maternity hospital is right in the center of town and we end up paying an extortionate amount for parking three streets away but, right now, I couldn't give a crap.

In reception, a nurse with Christmas puddings as earrings takes one look at us and immediately jumps into action.

"I'm *fine*," Zoe says for the millionth time as the woman—Cara, according to her lanyard—tries to lead her toward a wheelchair. "I'm not even having them anymore."

I clamp a hand around her forearm when she tries to shrug me off. "Can we maybe listen to the nice medical professionals?"

"I *will* when it's *time* to." But she gets into the chair, her eyes wide and her face pale, and I see her attitude for what it really is, sheer undiluted terror.

Despite her jokes about baby daddies, she's never wanted to be in a relationship. I've never seen her go out with someone for more than a few weeks, and even then, I think it's because she was curious about what all the fuss was about. But she wanted to be a mother, so she became one. It would never have occurred to her that she couldn't at least try. And like everything else she did, she tried her best.

As a single parent, that meant plans. Five-year plans and ten-year plans, complicated financial charts, and a tight network of friends and family to help her out. I know she planned for so long and tried for so long that a part of her had forgotten about the actual event, especially when that event was two and a half weeks early.

"Are we going to another waiting room?" she asks, sounding very young as she blindly signs a form.

"We're going to the labor ward," Cara says.

"The . . . Why?"

She doesn't even blink. "Because you're going into labor."

"This can't be happening," Zoe repeats for the twelfth time. She passes the clipboard back and turns her wild gaze to me. "I can't have a December Capricorn."

"It turned out okay for Jesus."

"The man was *crucified*, Molly!"

Cara takes up her position at the back of the chair, looking at us expectantly. "Do you want to follow me?"

It takes us all a moment to realize she's talking to Andrew.

"I'm not the father," he says, startled.

"Oh, I'm sorry. I thought—"

"I'm a single mother," Zoe interrupts, texting furiously into her phone. "Modern and strong and brave. Can we wait for my mam?"

The nurse is already wheeling her through the doors. "If she makes herself known when she arrives, we'll be sure to—"

"No, we need to wait for them," Zoe says, starting to panic again. "We need to— Mam!"

At that moment, our mother chooses to stride through the reception doors, coatless and hatless despite the weather outside.

"I'm here, love. I'm here." Her previously blond hair is now a white-silver and there're more lines around her face than I remember; there always are whenever I see her, but she looks as strong as ever as she hurries over to us, her gaze taking me in briefly before they snap to my sister.

Zoe grasps her wrist, holding her to her. "I think I'm having my baby," she says, like she's confessing something.

"We'll see what the doctors say."

"Where's Dad? Is Dad coming? Where—"

"He's gone back to the house to get your things, but we thought it best that I come straight in."

"Yes," Zoe says. "Yes, stay with me."

"I'll be there the whole time," she says, squeezing her.

"Are we ready to go now?" Cara asks with the patience of a saint. My mother nods and, with a frantic smile my way, she wheels my sister through the swinging doors of the labor ward, leaving us to stare after them.

"Is this the part where she finds out she's suddenly having triplets?" I say to Andrew, who looks a little out of breath.

"I was having visions of her going into full labor in the car," he says, running a hand down his face. "I always thought I was pretty good in an emergency, but..."

I laugh a little manic laugh and look around the waiting room. No one seems particularly bothered by our few minutes of drama, all too concerned with whoever they're waiting for themselves. "Well, I guess we should... Shit! Your bus! If you need to—"

"I've got plenty of time," he interrupts. "I can stay here if you like."

"Really?"

"On the hour, every hour," he reminds me, and I nod, relieved.

"At least until my dad gets here?"

"Of course." He drapes an arm over my shoulder, drawing me into him as he leads me to a row of empty chairs along the back wall where it looks like I'll be spending the rest of my Christmas Eve.

At some point, we sit there long enough that I fall asleep. I don't remember feeling tired, but the events of the last few days must be catching up with me because one moment I'm gazing blankly at a poster for quitting smoking and the next I'm horizontal, staring at the legs of one of the expectant fathers across the room.

I'm twisted along three seats in a very awkward position, one I know I'll be feeling in my back for days seeing as I'm no longer twenty and reaching down to pick up a sock too quickly has the potential to put me out of commission. But I don't move right away and not just because my left leg is dead and about to break into a thousand pins and needles. No, I stay where I am because there's a pleasant scrape against my scalp, a frankly semi-orgasmic experience that I never want to end.

Andrew's playing with my hair.

I open my eyes to see his own closed, his head tipped back against the wall as he runs his fingers absently across the crown of my head. One particular tug sends a shiver down my spine and he opens his eyes as I shift, looking down at me as though surprised to find me there. He immediately stops touching me, returning his hand to rest on his thigh.

"Sorry," he murmurs, and I shake my head.

"Keep going. That's better than any of the massages I pay a gazillion dollars for."

"I aim to please." He says it sarcastically but the look on his face is unsure, so I purposefully close my eyes and turn away from him, waiting.

After a moment, he starts back up again and, I swear to God, I almost purr.

"What time is it?" I ask instead.

"A little after eleven."

"What?" My eyes fly open. "Your—"

"I'll be grand," he says, his other hand pressing firmly on my shoulder as I try to sit up. My head spins as I shrug him off, moving too quickly.

"You missed the last bus."

"I'll get a taxi."

"But you'll—"

"I'm fine, Moll."

My panic eases at his calmness.

"Okay," I say, still hesitant as I slump back into the chair. "Is my dad here?"

"He left about twenty minutes ago. Sorry. Think he and your mam are going to take shifts sleeping so someone's always with Zoe. He didn't want to wake you. Said you looked as tired as a corpse." Andrew hesitates. "But in an affectionate way."

I snort. "Sounds like him." I take out my phone to shoot him a text and as I do, my attention catches on the duty-free bag next to us.

"He also dropped that in," he says when I pick it up. "Said he assumed it's for your sister."

"It is," I say, taking out the tissue-wrapped package. It feels like years since I bought it. "It's her terrible Christmas present."

"I'm sure you can get her something else," he says kindly. "The shops are still open."

I can only smile. "It's an on-purpose terrible Christmas present," I explain. "It's tradition to get each other bad gifts."

"It's tradition to get each other presents neither of you wants?" He sounds understandably confused.

"It's the thought that counts."

"Have you thought about getting each other something you'd actually like? Maybe you could start a new tradition. A, dare I say, much better one?"

"I know how it sounds," I laugh. "But it's something we've done since we were kids. We don't know why we do it except that we've always done it. And I don't know . . ." I shrug. "It's fun. I always get her perfume. The worst perfume I can find."

"What does she get you?"

"Food," I say. "Usually some disgusting novelty snack that I can only take one bite of. It then spends a month in the back of the cupboard before Dad finds it and eats it."

"Perfume," Andrew says slowly, realization dawning. "That's why you always smell awful on our flights. It's true!"

he adds when I whack his leg. "I thought you were just an eccentric. I've got to say I'm a little relieved. Though I still don't get it."

"Do you know how hard it is to get something someone will hate?" I ask. "Do you know how much thought I put into that gift? I think harder about her present than I do anyone else's."

"I know you're trying to make it seem like this is a logical thing, but it's really not."

I smirk, smoothing the bag against my lap. "It's tradition," I repeat. "It doesn't have to be logical."

"And you said you guys didn't know how to do Christmas."

Mam enters the waiting room before I can respond, carrying a tray of plastic cups filled with water. "The doctors are with your sister," she says, passing them to us. "Who sent me away because apparently I was looking at her too much." She sits beside me, taking in my Christmas sweater with a single eyebrow rise.

"It's from Paris," I say, a little defensively, and she shakes her head.

"You poor thing. You must be dead on your feet after all of that."

"It wasn't so bad," I say, glancing back at Andrew. It's only then that I realize we haven't exactly done introductions. "Mam, this is—"

"We've met," she interrupts, giving him a warm smile. "When you were asleep. He's told me all about your adventures."

Oh, he did, did he? Andrew looks innocently at me as she takes out her phone, reading a text before carefully typing out a one-fingered response. She's still texting when he stands suddenly, giving an exaggerated yawn.

"Just going to go stretch my legs," he says, wandering off before I can stop him.

"He's very handsome," Mam murmurs, still focusing on her phone. "You never told me he was handsome."

I make a noncommittal noise, waiting for her to send her message. "Your hair's nice."

"The new girl at the salon says I can pull off gray."

"You can."

"Hmm." The phone goes to her lap as she turns to me, rubbing her thumb across my cheek. Whatever she sees in my face must satisfy her because she lets me go, moving her attention back to the labor doors. "I'm glad you're still in one piece. You had us all in a panic thinking you wouldn't make it back."

"I didn't think it would be that big a deal."

"To not have you home?" She seems surprised by my surprise. "Why would you think that?"

"Just..." I trail off, a little embarrassed. "I don't know. We're not exactly big Christmas people."

"I still want you here," she says. "We both do. You should have seen your father. He usually tracks your plane by the minute. And this year, with the storm, we were terrified that you wouldn't be able to make it back at all. He stayed up all night waiting to see if they would put on extra flights."

"You didn't say anything," I protest, thinking of all the calls Andrew had to fend from his family.

"And stress you out even more?" Mam shakes her head. "That's the last thing you needed, to be worrying about us. Molly, you're an adult. One who's off living her own life. I never want to make you think that you have to drop everything to come back here. Only if you want to."

"I do want to," I say quickly. "I always want to."

She hesitates, her eyes dropping to my sweater. "If you want to start putting up decorations," she begins, and I almost smile at the reluctance in her voice.

"I don't. I really, really don't. I just want to be with you guys."

She seems a little mollified by that, leaning into me as though sharing a secret. "Did you see that light-up snowman the Brennans put up on the roof? Where they're finding the money for all the electricity, I don't know. But God forbid I say anything to them about it."

"I'll have to take a picture for Andrew," I say. "He loves all that stuff."

"Does he now? And that's what's rubbing off on you, is it?"

"Maybe a little bit."

"You'll be wearing reindeer antlers on your head next," she mutters.

"Or putting up stockings in the dead of night. Can you imagine if Dad walked down the stairs one year and the whole house was like Santa's grotto?"

"He probably wouldn't notice," she says dryly, and I laugh. Her expression softens at the sound.

"I'm glad you made it home," she says. "Never think that I don't want that." She draws me into a hug, kissing me firmly on the cheek.

"We're being watched," she adds when we pull away, and I glance over my shoulder to where Andrew lingers by the magazine rack, giving us our moment. "Should that boy not be on a bus somewhere?"

"I think he wants to be here in case something happens."

"I see. Well, you can tell me all about *that* when we're home."

"You'll like him," I say truthfully, and a warm smile breaks over her face as her phone chimes.

"Your sister wants me back," she says, getting up with a groan. "I'll try not to look her in the eye this time."

Andrew returns when she goes, a teasing look in his eyes. "Hah hah," he sings. "Your family loves you."

"Everyone loves me," I grumble, trying not to show how embarrassed I am. He can see right through me, of course, but thankfully knows not to push and merely settles back in his chair, both of us facing the swinging hospital doors as we wait for the latest miracle to occur.

CHAPTER TWENTY-ONE

My nephew is born ninety minutes later, three weeks premature, in the early hours of Christmas morning.

"He slid right out," Mam announces when she tells us the news. Andrew, to his credit, gives only the slightest wince. Because of course, Andrew is still here. Andrew who stayed with me, who just scoffed when I told him twice to get a taxi. Who held my hand without even asking, knowing I needed it. And I was glad of it. Selfishly so. I didn't want him to go. I want him here. I want him with me.

Because the baby was a little early, the nurses whisked him off for some checks, so it's a while before I'm able to see him. A while that soon has me pacing up and down the waiting room in frustration.

"If he's fine, then why do they need to do so many tests?" I say out loud for the millionth time. Andrew doesn't bother to respond, only pats my knee when I collapse back into the chair beside him.

"Distract me," I order.

"Sexy distraction or card trick distraction? Not that they're mutually exclusive, of course."

"Can you get me sugar?"

"Even better. I can get you the most processed, shouldn't-even-be-allowed-in-a-hospital sugar known to man." He squeezes my leg and makes the long, arduous trek across the waiting room while I try and catch the eye of the nurse manning the station, the nurse who has learned in the last twenty minutes to not even look in my direction.

As I do, another one appears through the main doors, a stack of paperwork in her hands. She's pretty, with long dark hair scraped back into a thick braid. She does a double-take as she passes Andrew, which doesn't exactly surprise me, but then she comes to a complete stop, her eyes going wide as she halts mid-step.

"Andrew?"

Andrew glances up, about to tap his card against the machine, when his face breaks into a smile.

"Ava?"

Ava? Who the hell is Ava?

I watch, bewildered, as the stranger leans in for a hug, thrown by the sharp spike of jealousy that runs through me.

Their voices lower as he draws her to the side and chats rapidly for a few minutes. Eventually, she hugs him again, smiling cheerfully as she disappears back around the corner. Andrew glances my way and my eyes immediately drop to my phone in the most obvious move ever.

"Making friends?" I ask when he returns, tossing a chocolate bar into my lap.

"I used to babysit her," he says, and I glance up in surprise. "Am I old now?"

"They're just getting younger," I say, relieved. "So she's working through Christmas?"

"Actually . . . no. Depending on her paperwork, she's out of here in an hour. She's driving back to her folks tonight."

I start to nod before I realize what he's telling me. "Oh."

"Yeah. She's going to give me a ride. I'll be home for breakfast."

"That's... perfect." I start to unwrap my snack even as my appetite shrinks. "Brilliant news."

"It will save me the taxi fare at least. But if you need me to—"

"Shut your face," I interrupt. "Shut it right up. Go home. This was the whole point of everything. You've already stayed way longer than you should have."

"It's a bit of a special situation."

"And I'm *sure* Zoe will understand that you, a stranger, are not here to mind her."

"And who's going to mind you?"

I still at his words, melting a little inside, and take a large bite of chocolate to hide it. I realize then how easy it would be to get him to stay with me. That all I need to do is ask and he would. I know it without a doubt and, weirdly, that helps me not to.

My mother appears through the doors a moment later, catching my eye. Time to see my sister.

"Go," I say gently. "Please. I am so sick of you."

He laughs, lounging back in the chair. "She's not going for a while yet," he says. "I'll see you back here?"

I nod, my knees creaking as I stand. I'm going to need to do some serious hot yoga after Christmas. "Text me if something changes."

"I will."

"Better go meet the newest Kinsella," I say, and think about leaning down to kiss him, the way couples do, but chicken out and do an incredibly corny finger-gun motion instead that makes him smile and me want to die.

Before I can do anything else to embarrass myself, I turn and follow the signs to the maternity ward.

Zoe's fancy job has paid for a fancy private room. It's small and bare, bar the giant hospital machines blinking at us, but Dad brought some of Zoe's things from home, including a card from the neighbors and a stuffed animal from our childhood. I remember Gabriela's Cubs bear waiting in the suitcase, which is still probably stuck in Argentina, and make a mental note to give it to her as soon as I can so the baby can imprint early.

And it's the baby I go to see first. My as-yet-nameless nephew lies pink and new in a plastic crib on the other side of the room and, as soon as I lay eyes on him, the predictable happens.

"You're not crying already," Zoe grumbles from the bed.

"It's okay to cry now, Zoe. All the cool kids are doing it." I lean over the crib, pressing my finger to the tip of his nose. "You are very small," I tell him.

"He didn't feel small when I was pushing him out."

"I'm trying to have a private moment with my nephew."

"Well, do it while passing me my juice. *Ow.*"

I turn around to see her fall back against the bed, a pillow propping up her torso. "You look like shit," I tell her, leaving the child to sleep while I focus on her.

"I just had a baby," she grumbles. "What's your excuse?"

"Days of traveling to be with you."

"Oh, that was for *me*, was it?"

"I knew the baby was coming. Sixth sense."

"Thanks for the heads-up."

I take a seat next to the bed, handing her the plastic cup on the nightstand. She really does look worn out, which is understandable, all things considered. And whereas my usual reaction to anything she does is to make fun of her, I feel like she should get a pass for today so, instead, I take her hand and pat it gingerly until she snorts and pulls it away.

"That's enough affection from you, thanks very much."

"Well done, Zoe."

She huffs a breath, but she smiles. "Thank you."

"The nurse said everything's fine?"

"Yeah. Just a few checks because he's an early bastard."

"An attention seeker like his mother. It's nothing we can't handle."

She watches me as I brush the hair back from her forehead, her face softening with each movement. "Sorry I freaked out before," she murmurs.

"I think you're allowed to. Plus, you're right. Christmas birthdays are the worst."

"I know." She groans. "It's going to be so freaking expensive. And when he grows up, he's just going to complain that he doesn't get any attention." She sighs. "He's going to have to get a fake birthday too, isn't he?"

"Maybe Mam and Dad were onto something."

"Hmm." She tilts her head away and pats the bed beside her. "Get up."

"What?"

"Get up!" she commands, tugging at the blanket. "I need a hug. All those hormones."

I roll my eyes but there's more than enough room in the bed for the two of us, so I do as requested, climbing carefully onto the mattress and twisting into her body, flinging an arm around her. We used to sleep like this when we were children and Mam first put us into our own rooms. It was a necessity, she claimed. She said we were too clingy and that we needed to learn to be independent. She wasn't wrong. Zoe and I were inseparable back then and those first few days I didn't know what to do without her. But Zoe especially found it hard. She started getting nightmares and eventually Mam let her come to me when she woke up (I think she only did it so that Zoe wouldn't go to *her*) and, more often than not, I'd wake in the morning to an elbow in my stomach.

Still, after all this time it feels natural to snuggle in next to her and lay my head on her shoulder. I think it always will be.

"Hey," I whisper, setting her present on her lap. "Happy Christmas."

"Oh no." She grimaces, poking it with one finger. "Perfume?"

I nod.

"Yours is at the house. Ugh." She lets the tissue paper fall to the bed as she turns the glittering pink bottle in her hands. It looks even worse than it did at the airport. "I can smell it already."

"No sniffing," I say as she brings it to her nose. "That's cheating."

"All right, all right."

I watch with a smile as Zoe scrunches her eyes shut and sprays it a few inches from her chest. She immediately starts coughing.

"Oh my *God*."

"It's good, right?"

"This can't be healthy for the baby. I smell like a twelve-year-old girls' magazine. From 2004."

"A vintage bouquet."

She winces again. "Don't try and make me laugh. It hurts my vagina."

"How does it—"

"I don't *know*," she moans. "It just does. Don't question me, I'm a new mother." She burrows deeper into me and I wrinkle my nose at the perfumed smell of her. "Andrew seems nice," she says after a minute.

"Smooth transition."

"You want to tell me what's going on there?"

"How did you—"

"Please," she scoffs. "It's obvious. *You're* obvious."

"We kissed."

"You did?" She makes a humming noise that I don't know what to make of. "What kind of kiss?"

I give her a brief rundown of the last few days, including the brief but memorable make-out session in London. "We've decided to try dating when we get back," I finish.

"*Dating?*" She looks appalled. "You don't need to date. You basically know everything about each other."

"Not like that."

"Yes, like that," she says. "You're just adding in boning."

"Zoe!"

"I'm *joking*," she says when I make to get off the bed. She pulls me quickly back down, her arm like an iron fist across my stomach. "Has he gone home, then?"

"He's going soon. He bumped into someone from his hometown because this is Ireland so of course he did. She's giving him a ride."

"He could always stay here for the night. Go back in the morning."

"He can't; he has to go home. That's the whole point of all the stress." I pick at the bedspread and then, when that doesn't satisfy me, my hair, suddenly restless.

"You don't want him to go," Zoe surmises.

I shrug, fooling no one. "I'll see him in a few days."

She just watches me, her face pale and tired but her eyes as shrewd as ever as she takes me in. "You could always go with him."

"Excuse me?"

"You could go home with him," she says. "For Christmas."

"That's ridiculous."

"No, it's not. Christmas is about spending time with people you love."

"I don't *love*—"

"As a friend, then," she interrupts. "And it's not like we'll be doing anything here. They're keeping me in overnight."

"I'm too tired for any more traveling," I say. "And I'm certainly not going to crash their Christmas."

"I'm sure they'd love to have you. I'm sure *he'd* love to have you. Why else do you think he's stuck around here as long as he has? If he didn't care so much about you, he would have left hours ago. He likes you."

"And I like him! No one is denying that, but I'm not leaving you. Not when you have stitches where no one should have stitches."

"But I'm not doing anything!" she says with a laugh. "I'm done. That's my baby and this is my Christmas. This bed. These walls. We're talking about a couple of hours down the road."

"You're reading too much into it."

"Will you ask him at least?"

"No!"

"Molly!"

We both freeze as a sound comes from the crib, a tiny hiccup that has us both turning to the baby. My nephew makes another noise and wriggles, as if testing out this strange new world, before falling still again. Neither Zoe nor I move, waiting to see if he does something else.

He does not.

"So, fun new thing about me," Zoe says as we stare at him. "I don't think I've ever loved or will ever love anyone as much as I love him. Even if he turns out to be a dick. Which with me as his mother is a real possibility."

"I kind of want to eat him. That's a thing, right? Like, I see his little fists and I just want to... eat him."

"How about you hold him instead?"

I make a face. "No."

"Why not?"

"You know me and babies," I say, even as I find it difficult to tear my eyes away from him.

"Yes, but this one is *my* baby. I expect you to show him more love and attention than this."

"Well, I expected to be a godmother."

"Would you get over that?" she snaps just as the door swings open and a nurse who does not look old enough to be in charge of, you know, keeping humans *alive* bustles into the room.

"Twins!" she proclaims, glancing between us. "Which one of you is Zoe? Just kidding. The one in the hospital gown, right?"

"Nothing gets past this one." Zoe sighs, pushing herself up. "Can I go home now?"

"No," the nurse says cheerfully. "You do that and you'll be back here in an hour. It's feeding time."

"I'm not hungry."

I roll my eyes as I climb off the bed. "For the baby, you idiot."

"Oh." Zoe looks down at her breasts with a doubtful look. "Will you send Mam in?"

I nod, rounding the bed to kiss my nephew's tiny little forehead. "I love you," I whisper because I do, and then hug my sister goodbye.

My mother is talking on the phone outside, but she hangs up when I exit.

"Zoe wants you to go in," I say, and she nods but doesn't move.

"Are you all right?"

"I'm fine. I was . . . Zoe actually . . ."

She just waits.

"I was thinking about maybe spending today with Andrew. With his family. For Christmas. Christmas Day. And then I could—"

"I think that sounds like a wonderful idea," she interrupts.

"You do?"

"Yes, it's not like we'll be doing anything here," she says, echoing Zoe. "We'll be able to celebrate properly tomorrow."

I raise my brows at that but don't say anything.

God, I mention briefly I thought she didn't want me home and now I'm going to come back next year to find out we've won most festive house in Dublin.

"I'll have to ask him first," I mutter, pulling my sleeves down over my hands. "He might say no."

Mam just gives me a look as the smiling nurse pops her head around the door.

"Can we have the mother of the mother?" she asks as Zoe's frustrated grunt comes from inside the room.

"I can't do it!" she calls. "My nipples are broken!"

"Just keep me updated," Mam says, cupping my cheek briefly as she follows the nurse back inside. "And best behavior."

"Why wouldn't I—"

"Pleases and thank yous."

"I'm not *nine*."

Though a few hours home and I feel like I am. I fight back a smile as the door swings shut, leaving me alone in the hallway. I stand there for a moment, stalling, before heading slowly back to the waiting area, past rooms of sleeping mothers and exhausted partners, past nurses and midwives and doctors as they get ready to spend Christmas Day in the hospital.

Andrew is in the same position I found him in at O'Hare, hunched in his seat, a magazine in his hands. Only this time it looks to be one for lactating mothers as opposed to a *National Geographic*. I linger just around the corner to watch him and know in my heart that whatever I'm feeling isn't going to go away anytime soon. This isn't me bouncing back after Brandon or losing my mind over a travel plan shot to hell. It's deeper than that. It's deeper and it's real and it's worth sticking my neck out for.

"Is Zoe okay?" he asks when I approach.

"She's fine," I say. "They're both fine. Fine and dandy." Oh my God, shut up. "Ava still around?"

"She should be done any second now. Though I realize I'm jinxing myself by saying that." He stands, stretching his arms over his head. "You good?"

"Yeah. Tired."

"I bet. Maybe you can—"

"I was actually thinking I could join you guys," I interrupt, the words spilling out of me in a rush.

Andrew looks confused, arms still raised as he bends his back. "For what?"

"For Christmas. Zoe suggested it and I thought it would be a nice opportunity to meet your family." I lose confidence by the second when he just stares at me. "I mean, only if that's okay with you. And no worries if it's not because I know you're excited to see everyone and we've come all this way to . . ." Nothing. He's giving me nothing. "You know what? I'm sorry. This is such short notice. Forget I ever said anything. Zoe's just—"

"I'd love for you to come." His arms drop to his side before he rubs his face, like he's trying to wake himself up. "That sounds great. If you're sure you're okay leaving Zoe?"

"She's not getting out until tomorrow," I say, a little awkward. "Shouldn't you check with your folks first?"

"I'll let them know." He shrugs.

"That a stranger is coming to visit on their biggest day of the year?"

He gives me an odd look. "You're not a stranger. They know who you are."

"They do?"

"Of course they do," he says, as if it's the most obvious thing in the world. "They've known about you for years. And the biggest day of the year is Hannah's birthday. She makes sure of it."

"If you're positive—"

"I am," he says firmly, looking much more awake now. "They'd love to meet you. Mam especially. Honestly, this will make her day."

"Well... okay. I guess I'll go tell everyone." I start to walk backward, not taking my eyes off him. "Meet you back here?"

He nods, watching me go, and it's only when I reach the double doors that I force myself to turn around, smiling so wide that my cheeks start to hurt.

CHAPTER TWENTY-TWO
TWO YEARS AGO

Flight Eight, Chicago

"I think I'm dying."

Andrew watches me sympathetically as I slump back into the chair, pressing the mini soda can to my temple. "You should have said something."

"I know," I moan, shifting around again. It's impossible to get comfortable in this stupid seat. Next year, we're flying business class. I'll pay for us both, I don't care. Though I don't think even that could save me right now.

My period's being a little bitch. The doctor said it might be stress. She did that thing where she asked me if I had a high-pressure job and I just started laughing. But yeah, stress. Who knew. I mean, the old crimson tides have always sucked but they've at least been *manageable*. Nothing a few painkillers and a night of feeling sorry for myself couldn't handle. This month it's like my body's just decided to give up. I'm as weak as a newborn kitten and the trip to the airport has completely drained me.

"Don't look at me," I complain. "I look gross."

"You've looked worse," he says, smiling when I glare at him. I'd tried my best when I arrived, using all the energy I had as we ate, listening and nodding in all the right places as he caught me up on dating post-Alison (shite) and his apartment (also shite). But the headache started when they called our gate and, by the time we made it onto the plane, I could barely keep my eyes open.

I shift again, drawing my legs up as I try desperately to get comfortable in the small space, as though if I contort my body in the right way, the ache will suddenly stop.

"Here."

"What— Hey!" I glare harder when Andrew steals the tiny airplane pillow from my lap, fluffing it out as best he can before placing it on his shoulder. When I just stare at him, he pats it invitingly, one brow raised.

"No," I say flatly.

"You're not going to get comfortable sitting like that." When I don't move, he takes the blanket and then his own pillow, building a kind of wall between us. "I once dated a girl who said the only way she could be comfortable on her period was if she lay flat on the floor with her legs up against the wall. I used to come back to the apartment and find her in different rooms, working away on her laptop like that. I didn't question her and I'm not going to question you." He pats the pillow. "Slump."

God, this is embarrassing. But I guess the good news for me is that I'm in too much pain to care. I push up the armrest, shuffling closer to him. The position immediately allows me to bring my legs up more comfortably as I rest my head gingerly against the pillow. God damn him, but it works.

"Okay, you're not allowed to move," I mutter, and can feel his laugh through the makeshift barrier as I tug my legs tighter to my body. "Don't let me fall asleep."

"I won't."

"I mean it, Andrew." My eyes are so damn heavy.

I test out more of my weight on him, leaning a little heavier when he doesn't comment, and finally start to relax.

"Sorry I'm ruining Christmas," I mutter, and he laughs.

"You're not ruining Christmas."

"I'm ruining the flight."

"The whole point of this flight is to spend time with you. I'm spending time with you, so do you see me complaining?"

He doesn't have any time to when I'm doing enough for the both of us.

"You're sick," he says firmly. "Let me look after you. I'll always look after you."

He says the last bit almost as if he's mad that I'd think otherwise and I nestle into the pillow, feeling a little better.

"Okay," I say. "I might have one very short nap."

"Good."

"But you have to wake me up for snacks."

"You got it."

There's movement above me as his head tilts, almost like he's placing a kiss to the top of my head. But it's too light for that, barely more than a whisper, and I think nothing more of it as unconsciousness pulls me under.

Now

It's another hour before Ava returns, looking heroically alert after a double shift, and at the sight of her, I'm reminded once again that whatever the world pays its nurses, it will never be enough. She's changed into sweatpants and a black fleece and accepts my added company with a more-the-merrier smile.

The city is a lot quieter when we emerge from the hospital, the sky dark and clear of any clouds. Ava leads us down the street to a small blue car that we somehow, with Tetris-like skill, manage to fit Andrew's suitcase inside. Of course, it means taking out Ava's bags and putting them in the back seat, but with only me to join them we have room.

As well as playing the radio at full volume, Andrew makes an effort to chat to her as we drive, helping to keep her awake, and she seems grateful as she catches him up on the latest news from the village and shares stories from home. Names and memories wash over me, meaning nothing, and despite the noise, the gentle rhythm of the car smoothly zipping along the empty streets soon has me closing my eyes.

At some point, I fall asleep. How, I don't know. It's uncomfortable in the back, and the roads grow increasingly bumpy once we're off the highway. But I'm beyond exhausted and so sleep I do, waking up only when a phantom finger drifts a path down my cheek.

Of course, it's not a phantom at all, but Andrew, and when I stir, he draws back, smiling softly in the dim glow of the dashboard as he twists in his seat to watch me.

"You all right?" he asks.

I nod, only to immediately regret doing so when my neck screams in protest. "How long was I out?"

"About an hour," Ava says. "We're almost there."

We are? I sit up, a smile pulling at my lips as I take in the passing fields before nestling back into my corner.

"Hey," Andrew says. "Don't fall asleep again."

"You're not the boss of me."

"I mean it, Molly. Don't make me wake you up."

I ignore him, trying to get comfortable. I don't actually intend to go back to sleep, but my lids are feeling heavier and heavier and—

"Ow!" My eyes fly open as Andrew pokes me sharply in the leg.

"I warned you," he says and turns back around. "We can walk from here," he continues, pointing to the side of the road.

Ava shoots him a confused glance. "Seriously?"

"Seriously. We're right over the hill. It's five minutes tops."

"What about your case?"

"We'll manage." His voice rises as he calls back to me. "We can walk, can't we, Moll?"

I make a face, seeing as how I'd much rather stay here in the warm car until it drops me off at the presumably warm house, but Andrew has other ideas.

"She can walk," he says.

After a minute, Ava pulls into the side of a field and unlocks the doors. She's too sleepy to protest further but still looks unsure as she hugs Andrew and then me goodbye, driving off with a "Merry Christmas" and a soft beep of the horn.

I wait until she disappears around the corner before I turn to Andrew with a frown. "Am I being punished?"

"What do you mean?"

"I'm freezing my ass off."

"Want me to warm it?"

I don't even dignify that with a response, walking ahead of him in what thankfully must be the right direction because he jogs a few steps to catch up with me.

The cold air wakes me up at least, though there's still that dull ache behind my eyes that will take more than a cup of coffee to counter. The thought of having to put on a bright smile for Andrew's family on top of awkwardly explaining my presence there makes me groan and I clench and unclench my gloved hands, doubt filling me as I lengthen my stride up the hill just as the dawn begins to break.

This was a stupid idea. I'm crashing their *Christmas*. I don't care how nice they are. I don't care how much Andrew likes me right now. No one really likes the strange lady who rocks up on Christmas morning. Way to make a first impression, Molly. Way to—

"So right now, what you're doing is city walking," Andrew calls to me. "When what you need to be doing is countryside walking. Especially on an incline."

I stop just as we reach the crest. "Sorry."

"No, please," he says, slightly out of breath. "I'm impressed."

"Do you want help with your suitcase?"

"Do you actually want to help?"

"No," I say, eyeing the thing. "But I don't have any sympathy for you. It was your idea to walk."

"It was. I was hoping to be romantic."

I blink at him. "Okay, we're going to need to have a serious conversation about what is and is not romantic, because if you think—"

"Just look over the hill, you idiot." And then muttering to himself, "Before I push you down it."

I make a "very funny" face and lunge my way up the final steps, pausing at the top as I wait for him. "Lovely," I proclaim, staring down at the small valley. "I'm so glad you made us . . ."

Oh.

Andrew reaches my side as I fall silent, and together we watch as slowly, gently, the world around us lightens, as though coming to life before our very eyes.

"That's why we're walking," he says. To his credit, he only sounds a little smug.

The first weak rays of the sun highlight the frost on the gently sloping hills. There'll be snow on the mountains this morning, but down here the grass is still green enough that you'd be forgiven for thinking it's summer. There is no one else in sight. No other car upon the road, no lone figure walking their dog. Just Andrew. Just me. Just this moment, peaceful and perfect and bright.

"We had snow one year," Andrew says, pointing across the fields. "We went sledding down that hill all day."

"I'm jealous. Snow in Dublin just melts. And in Chicago, it's..."

"Normal."

"Yeah." In Ireland, it was rare and usually a cause for celebration if not huge traffic problems. "I feel like you planned this," I add.

"Nah. Just got lucky with the weather. Wouldn't have the same effect if it was raining."

I hum in agreement. "Is this the part where you tell me you live in a hobbit hole?"

"I live there."

"Where?"

He reaches out and gently grasps my chin, turning my face to a sprawling white farmhouse to our right.

"You live on a farm," I say, unable to hide my surprise.

"I do."

"With animals?"

He looks like he's trying very hard not to laugh. "We have cows."

"How many cows?"

"Fifty."

My eyes go wide. "That's so many!"

This time he does laugh at me, but I'm too charmed to care.

"And to think you were going to spend today in Chicago," I say. "With no cows at all."

"I was going to spend it with *you*," he corrects quietly. "And I still am."

I press my lips together, trying not to show how warm

and fuzzy that makes me feel, but of course, he picks up on it, smiling at me knowingly.

"All right," he says. "Let's get inside. Before you run away from the embarrassment."

"I'm not going to run away. I'm too cold to run."

He nods down the hill. "We should stick to the grass," he says. "The roads will be icy."

We make our way carefully down, Andrew's pace quickening with each step we take.

"Will anyone be up this early?" I ask, almost whispering as he wheels the case up the drive. There are three cars along with a tractor parked outside, but the house itself looks like it's still asleep.

"Dad will be up with the animals already," he says. "He'll be out all day and Mam's probably still in bed, though Christmas is kind of her forte so she might..." Andrew trails off as he comes to a sudden halt. "Oh. Christ."

"What?" I ask in alarm. "What is it?"

"Are you allergic to—"

But whatever he was going to ask is drowned out as the front door opens and the air fills with excited barking. Two dogs bound toward us and I barely have time to brace myself as they aim for Andrew, almost knocking him down before they come to me.

"Whoa whoa whoa!"

Andrew lunges, grabbing the brown one by the collar, but the bigger one jumps up, his paws hitting my shoulders as he tries to lick my face.

"Uisce! Polly!"

A hissed whisper comes from the direction of the house and I peer around the slobbering tongue to see a shadow emerge from the porch. That shadow becomes a woman who hurries toward us, arms outstretched to grab the dogs.

"Inside, inside," she chastises, tugging the dog off me. "Now!" Andrew lets his one go at the command and to my surprise, they immediately do as told, hurtling back to the house.

"My mother," Andrew introduces, checking to see if I'm all right before he turns to her. "I was just saying, I didn't know if you—"

He's cut off as she draws him into a firm hug, her arms wrapped around his shoulders, head burying into his chest. Andrew immediately reciprocates, holding her tight, and I feel immediately like an intruder witnessing their reunion. I take a step away, trying to give them their moment, but the movement draws his mother's attention and she pulls back, wiping a hand across her cheek.

"Ridiculous," she says. "Scaring us like that for nothing." With an appraising eye that reminds me of my own parents, she gives him a once-over as though checking to make sure he's still in one piece before turning to me. "Won't be home for Christmas, he says."

"I almost wasn't," Andrew reminds her before reaching out to grab my hand, tugging me into his side. "This is Molly. Molly, this is my mother."

"Call me Colleen," she corrects, and then I get my own hug. "Thank you for bringing him to us," she whispers in my ear, and all I can do is pat her shoulder in response because, honestly, what am I supposed to say to that that won't make me immediately tear up?

With a final squeeze, she steps back, and I get a good look at her for the first time. She's a little taller than me, with thick salt-and-pepper hair pulled back into a bun and a weather-worn face that speaks to days spent outside. She's still only half-dressed, a short duffel coat over her pajamas, the legs of which she's stuffed into a pair of muddy, no-nonsense rubber boots.

"We were planning on sneaking in," Andrew says apologetically. "I thought you'd still be in bed."

"On Christmas morning?" She huffs. "I suppose you'll be wanting your breakfast. I'm doing a fry later but there's no reason I can't whip you up something now."

Andrew and I share a glance and I'm relieved to see an echo of my own exhaustion in his eyes.

"We need to get some proper sleep," he says. "Or we won't make it to lunch."

"Of course! The others won't be up for a few hours anyway. I've got Liam's old room made up for you. The radiator has a mind of its own and we're a little tight for space, but it's the best I can do. Now, if you don't like it, we're going to have to—"

"I'm sure it's fine, Mam," Andrew interrupts, nudging me after her as we head toward the house.

I don't even have the energy to look around once we get inside, saying goodbye to Colleen before following him up the stairs.

Liam's old room is halfway down a long hallway and is small and simple with faded blue wallpaper and worn beige carpet. A queen-size bed takes up most of the space, along with an old wooden dresser and a box of books marked for charity.

"Where's your room?" I ask.

"I shared one with Christian," Andrew says as he positions his suitcase against the wall.

"And Liam doesn't stay here as well?"

"He lives in the town over. He'll bring the kids for dinner but won't stay the night." He frowns as he presses a hand to the radiator. "I'm going to get a hot water bottle. Mam wasn't lying; these things take ages to heat up."

I nod, my mind starting to shut down as he leaves me alone. Chilly air hits me as I take off my coat so I don't remove anything else but my shoes while I wait for him. I even keep the scarf on as I perch at the end of the bed, stroking a hand down the quilt. I hadn't thought about what Colleen meant when she said we'd be tight for space. Of course, they can't just magically drum up an extra bed at such short notice, but it never occurred to me that we'd be sharing one.

The door opens before I can worry too much about it and Andrew slips back inside, clutching a hot water bottle to his chest. He hesitates by the wall, no doubt seeing the warring thoughts on my face. Lord knows I'm too tired to hide them.

"Here," he says, handing it to me. "I'll go kick Christian out of bed."

"Don't be silly. We'll fit."

His eyes flick between me and the mattress. "Are you sure?"

"Am I sure I don't want to be the person who ruins your brother's Christmas morning? Yes."

"There's a couch downstairs I can—"

"Andrew," I interrupt. "Please take this literally—I want you to sleep with me."

He laughs, looking relieved. "Okay," he says, and goes to take off his sweater before thinking the better of it. I understand. It's not that he doesn't think I can handle him in a T-shirt, but it is *cold* in here.

"I'm keeping your scarf on," I say, and turn to the bed to strip back the blankets. I hear him kick off his shoes and then he closes the curtains before climbing in beside me.

It is, predictably, immediately awkward. The three layers of clothing we're both wearing don't help. Nor does the fact that we're both frozen, with only the hot water bottle to keep us warm. I'm about to ask him if he'd prefer to keep said water bottle where it is or put it down by our feet when he huffs out an annoyed breath and promptly turns on his side, drawing me into him.

"Is this okay?" he asks, arranging us so he's spooning me. I can only nod as I try to ignore how incredibly comfortable it is and how much I like the warmth of him and the smell of him and the everything of him.

"Should we set an alarm?" I whisper.

"My family is the alarm."

"But what if—"

"I'll wake you, Moll. I promise. Try and get some rest."

I don't need to be told twice, and as his head sinks into the pillow next to me and his body heat slowly transfers to me, I slip quickly, blissfully, into a deep and dreamless sleep.

CHAPTER TWENTY-THREE

I may have fallen asleep with Andrew wrapped around me, but I wake wrapped around him. My arm is tossed over his broad chest, my thigh hooked over his hip and nestled between his legs, pressing against him like I'm unconsciously trying to climb over the man. Or on top of him.

I don't move away. A little because I just don't want to. Mostly because I still feel tired. It takes me a few minutes to gain enough awareness to move my limbs and, even when I do, they feel so heavy that I don't try much more than a half-hearted twitch.

Eventually, I register noises other than the sound of Andrew's breathing. Murmured voices, a cabinet door slamming. They're faint, probably from downstairs, but the thought of someone walking in and seeing me like this, a stranger draped over their son or brother, is enough to make me get up.

I do it as gently as I can, trying not to wake him, but Andrew moves as soon as I raise my head, rolling us over so he's on top of me, pressing me gently into the mattress. At first, I think he's still asleep and that I'm trapped, but then his breath tickles my ear and I feel the ghost of his smile against my skin.

"Where are you going?" His voice is a quiet rasp that sends goosebumps down my arms and I realize I could get happily used to Andrew in the morning. But there'll be plenty of time for that.

"To pee," I grumble, and he laughs, peeling himself off me before turning over onto his side, tugging the blanket up to his chin.

"Two doors down. Put a sock on the doorknob or someone will walk in."

"What?" I ask, mildly alarmed.

"Christmas with the Fitzpatricks," he says as if that explains everything. Which it kind of does and also doesn't. I wait for him to say more, but he already looks as if he's gone back to sleep and, with my bladder now doing that I'll-let-out-a-little-tinkle-if-you-don't-move-soon warning, I slip out of bed, wincing as my bare feet meet the chilly air. I must have kicked off my socks sometime during the night. Or the morning. Or whatever part of the day we've just spent unconscious.

I move over to the curtain to check, drawing it back to find it fully light outside. Andrew groans when the sunshine hits the bed, but we need to get up, so I leave them open and dart out of the room before he can complain.

It's warmer in the hallway, as well as more... delicious? The smell of garlic and onions wafts from downstairs and my stomach rumbles loudly, despite the fact my internal body clock is now well and truly busted. God knows how I'm going to get back into a routine.

I count the doors as I head toward the bathroom. There's a sock on the handle, just as Andrew said, but I can't hear anyone on the other side. And though I don't want to meet any more of his family members standing outside the toilet, I also really, *really* need to pee. I'm weighing up the pros and cons of trying to find another one, thighs pressed together, when the door flies open, revealing a young woman in mismatched pajamas.

She yelps when she sees me, dropping the toothbrush that was dangling from her mouth.

"Hannah!" Colleen rounds the top of the stairs, carrying an armful of folded towels. "What did I say about waking them? And why aren't you getting dressed?"

"I'm brushing my teeth!" the girl says, affronted. She's tall, with green eyes set far apart and a button nose with a small piercing at the side. Her long brown hair is tinged bright red at the ends, half of it still up in old-fashioned curlers. She looks nothing like Andrew, except for the glint in her gaze when she turns back to me. "I'm Hannah."

"Molly," I say.

She grins. "I know."

She bends down to scoop her toothbrush from the floor while Colleen joins us. "I have to put my contacts in," she says apologetically, holding up a little box. "Two seconds."

She leaves the door open as she heads back to the sink and I try not to stare at her reflection in the mirror.

Hannah.

She was only six when I first met Andrew, and over the years she's more or less stayed that way in my mind whenever he spoke about her. It's bizarre to see her now, to realize how much time has passed. Every Christmas I would get an update on her life and now here I stand before her.

About to wet myself.

Colleen clears her throat, drawing my attention back to her. "I've put the hot water on in case you wanted a shower. I'll leave the towels just inside the door."

"Hot water after ten a.m.?" Hannah teases. "Did we win the lottery?"

"It's Christmas and she's a guest."

"She's *Andrew's* guest." Hannah smirks.

I am seriously going to— "Do you mind if I use the bathroom?"

Hannah winces as she hears the urgency in my voice. "Sorry! Of course." She scurries past me, blinking her contacts in.

"Take your time, Molly," Colleen says as we trade places. "Hannah, get dressed. You're peeling potatoes."

"It's Christian's turn to peel potatoes."

"He's bad at it," she dismisses.

"He's bad at it purposefully so he doesn't have to do it!" Hannah's protests fade as they walk away and I close the door, barely taking the bathroom in before I run to the toilet. No one tries to come in in the minute I take to go through the motions, but I hear Christmas music coming from one of the closed doors on my way back to the bedroom, and Hannah singing along with a surprisingly good voice.

Andrew is lying on his back when I return, one arm flung over his face to protect him from the daylight.

"Was that my sister's dulcet tones I heard?" he asks.

I shut the door. "I scared her."

"You're very scary." He drops his arm to look at me and my heart does a little flip in my chest. "That was the best night's sleep I've had in weeks," he says. "Which is saying something considering it only lasted two hours."

"You were tired."

"Maybe." He watches me from the bed, his gaze warm and inviting. Still, I don't move.

"Are you coming back in?" he asks, noticing my hesitation.

I twist my hands in front of me. "I think everyone else is up, so..."

"So." He sighs, flipping the covers off.

"Your mother put the water on for a shower," I tell him.

"You go first. I'll guard the door."

"You don't have to—"

He barks a laugh. "I do. Trust me. The sock doesn't always work." He gets up and tosses me an old dressing robe I'd missed before. I shrug it on gratefully as I look around for my bag. And that's when it hits me.

"What?" Andrew asks when I don't follow him to the door.

"I don't have my stuff." I don't have *any* of my stuff.

He's momentarily confused before he realizes what I mean. In all the chaos of yesterday evening, of the journey home, of *everything*, I had completely forgotten the fact that not only did I not have my suitcase, but I hadn't brought anything to the hospital either. Nothing but the clothes on my back and the phone in my pocket.

He winces, running a hand through his hair. "Don't worry about it," he says. "We have plenty of clean clothes. Hannah will give you something. And Mam has a lot of... lipstick."

I try not to smile. "Lipstick?"

"Hairspray?"

"You need to get a girlfriend," I say without thinking, and immediately regret it at the look in his eye. "I'd settle for shampoo right now," I add, ducking past him into the hallway.

I follow him back to the bathroom where he shows me how to work the shower, jokes for five seconds about staying inside while I undress, and eventually takes guard in the hallway, just as he promised.

But even with him there, I take the quickest shower I can,

using the supermarket shower gel and shampoo sparingly before towel-drying my hair. When I look halfway decent, I pull the robe back on and gather my old clothes under one arm.

I step out to find Andrew still guarding the door. Only now he's not alone.

An almost unfairly attractive man stands beside him, a mug of tea in his hand.

Christian. The youngest brother.

He's a little taller than Andrew, with an expensive haircut and a fairer complexion that must come from his mother's side. He has that classical handsome look about him, dark eyes, a long nose, a hint of cheekbones. Whereas Andrew has always been a little scruffy, and even more so this morning, Christian looks like he belongs in a soap opera. Or, at the very least, a marketing campaign for men's razors.

He smirks when I appear, not exactly mean, but not exactly friendly either, and lacking the teasing warmth that I always get from Andrew.

"It's nice to finally meet you," he says, raising his mug in a mock toast.

"My brother," Andrew says needlessly. "Christian."

"Hi." I tighten the belt around my waist, pausing when both sets of eyes drop to my hands. Christian's immediately flick back up.

Andrew's take a second.

"Andrew was just telling me about your nephew," Christian says. "Congratulations. It sounds like the two of you have had quite the week."

"Something like that," Andrew scoffs. "Hannah's going to bring some stuff in for you," he adds to me.

"I can just wear my clothes from yesterday. She doesn't have to—"

"She wants to," he says, cutting me off. "And you have to be nice to her because it's Christmas." He nods to the shower before I can argue any further. "Water still warm?"

I nod and he smiles.

"My turn," he announces, pushing away from the wall. I step to the side to let him pass and he disappears behind the door, leaving me alone with his brother.

Christian studies me for a moment before bringing his finger to his lips in a shushing motion. With exaggerated slowness, he opens the door next to the bathroom, revealing a boiler similar to the one my parents have. With a wink, he flicks the switch, turning the hot water off.

"Happy Christmas," he says to me, and pads toward the stairs, sipping at his tea.

I wait until he's gone before turning the water back on and then I scurry back to the bedroom where I use Andrew's deodorant and get dressed in the same clothes I slept in. I'm barely covered for five seconds when Hannah calls through the door.

"Heard you needed supplies," she says when I open it. She tosses me an unopened packet of underwear as she steps into the room. "Don't worry," she says. "I've got hundreds. I'm making a dress out of them for school."

There's a lot to unpack in that sentence. I decide on the easiest option.

"You make clothes?"

"Yep," she says cheerfully. There's no hint of shyness or faux modesty about her and I love it. I wish I had been that confident at her age. "I thought you could wear this with your jeans," she adds, laying out a soft blue sweater with a subtle shimmer of silver thread throughout. "It's a little big but—"

"It's perfect," I say, touched by her kindness. "Thank you."

"No problem." She adds a pair of socks and a plain undershirt to the pile. "So are you dating my brother?"

"I—what?" I blink as she bounces onto the bed.

"He hasn't brought a girl home in *years*," she says innocently, stretching her long legs out before her.

Andrew brought someone home with him? A spike of jealousy runs through me as I think through his last couple of girlfriends and who was the most likely candidate. He definitely let *that* little detail slip by.

"Mam hated her," Hannah continues, smiling when I stare at her. "But she likes you. I can tell."

"You can?"

"She gave you the good towels."

The door opens before I can respond and Andrew thankfully appears. His eyes immediately find mine with a soft look that drops as soon as he notices Hannah.

"Get out of my room."

"This is Liam's room."

"Then get out of Liam's room."

"I was just talking to—"

"Out," he says, grabbing her arm.

"But I'm *helping*."

He pushes her into the hallway, shutting the door on her raised middle finger.

"Are you going to have sex?" she calls through the wood, and he bangs on the wall until her footsteps sound, moving toward the stairs.

"She's sweet," I say when he turns back to me.

"When she wants to be."

I pick up the sweater Hannah left me, wrapping it around

the packet of underwear that I'm suddenly ridiculously shy about. Andrew immediately notices something's up.

"She didn't say anything to you, did she?"

"No," I lie. I keep my eyes on the window, pretending to be captivated by the view of a field outside as I listen to him unzip the suitcase behind me. "What's the deal with your brother?"

Andrew sighs mournfully. "I knew you'd like him more. It's the dark, brooding thing he's got going on, isn't it?"

"I thought he was the prankster of the family."

"Many layers. I promise you he's not a jerk," Andrew continues. "No matter how much he seems like one." He pauses. "Though if you find yourself under some mistletoe, I'd rather you didn't—"

"Shut up." I scowl and he grins at me.

"So, what's the plan for today?" I ask, changing the subject.

He blows out a breath, his face scrunched like he's thinking hard. "Well, first is the five-K run, then a dip in the frozen lake, and then we'll—"

"Andrew."

"We're supposed to eat at six. Which means we'll probably eat at seven. It's eleven now so we've got a lot of time to kill. Watch movies, eat junk food." He shrugs. "It's Christmas."

It's Christmas. It's Christmas *Day*. Christmas Day and we made it. We're here.

"Do you want to call your sister?"

"Oh crap. Yes." I dive for my phone as Andrew grabs some clothes from his suitcase and shoots me a glance.

"I'll go change in Christian's room. He'll love that."

I smile at the offer of privacy and perch on the end of the

bed, hitting my sister's number. She picks up after the third ring.

"Christmas in the hospital," she says by way of greeting. "Can't wait to hold this over my firstborn for the rest of his life."

"How are you feeling?"

"My vagina is sore and they've stopped giving me drugs. Did you make it to Cork okay? How are the in-laws?"

"Okay so far." I tuck the phone under my ear as I undress and put on the fresh clothes Hannah left me. "They've been really nice but I still feel weird. I probably should have stayed in Dublin."

"Well, it's too late now," she says dryly. "Are you sleeping on the couch?"

"We're sharing a bed."

It takes a full twenty seconds for her to stop cackling.

"We haven't done anything," I protest in the middle of it. "We haven't even kissed."

"All right, Virgin Mary, I believe you. Stop putting so much pressure on yourself! Just enjoy the day. Offer to make your garlic bread." Her voice turns wistful. "I miss your garlic bread."

"I'll make it for you when you're home," I promise. "Do you have a name yet?"

"No," she huffs. "And do you know what could be great? If everyone could stop asking me. Maybe I'll be one of those trendy people who lets their kid pick their own name."

"I don't think the birth certificate people are going to wait that long."

"And that's bureaucracy for you."

"Can you at least send me some pictures of my nameless nephew?"

She can.

We hang up and five images come through just as Andrew returns, dressed in a fresh pair of jeans and a navy Christmas sweater with a reindeer on it.

"Look," I say, holding up my phone. "I'm an aunt."

"Hey now. How handsome is he? Is Zoe okay?"

"Just tired."

He frowns. "If you want to try and get back today, we can borrow Christian's car."

"No," I say quickly. "Don't be silly. I'll see her tomorrow." *And I want to stay here with you.* I don't say the words even though they're on the tip of the tongue, even though that's clearly what I mean.

I sit on the end of the bed, the covers still rumpled from when we slept, and run my hands up and down my thighs as Andrew starts unpacking his suitcase and hiding presents under the bed.

"You never told me you brought a girlfriend home before."

Confusion flashes across his face before he glances at the door. "Hannah."

"I'm learning all your secrets."

He smirks, not seeming the least bit worried by the question.

"Was it Alison?" I ask, thinking about his last long-term girlfriend before Marissa.

"Nope. Emily."

"*Emily?*" Quiet-voiced, teacher-of-children, sweet-as-can-be-until-she-ghosted-him-for-three-weeks-out-of-the-blue Emily? "Seriously?"

"I was young and in love. Or at least I thought I was."

"Was it a disaster?"

He laughs at the question, but I don't care if I'm showing my inner bitch right now. I'm determined to make a good impression on his family and knowing that someone else made a bad one will give me a lot more confidence.

"A huge disaster," he says, and I relax. "I shouldn't have asked her to come. We'd only been going out for a few months and I liked her a lot. I thought I was falling in love but it was too big a step. The jet lag hit her hard and she couldn't really eat, which upset Mam, and then we think she was allergic to the dogs, which *really* upset Mam, and..." He shrugs. "It felt like every little thing that could go wrong did go wrong. It's a miracle we didn't break up with each other there and then."

"And you didn't bring anyone else home after that?"

"You know I didn't," he says. But I don't. Not really. I didn't know about Emily, which only makes me think of all the other things I might not know about. That I *want* to know about. Want to and will. Because I have at my disposal an indulgent mother, a smirking brother, and a scheming sister. Not to mention the fact I haven't even met Liam yet.

Andrew's eyes narrow, guessing where my mind is headed. "If you want to know something about me, just ask me."

"But you're biased," I say pleasantly. "I want to know the shady things too."

We both pause as my stomach rumbles. "I guess I better feed you," he says, amused. "You ready to go downstairs?"

"As I'll ever be," I say, butterflies fluttering as I follow him into the hallway.

I hear them immediately. Hannah's defensive tone, Christian's quiet murmuring before her squeal of protest.

"*Mam!*"

The word echoes up the stairs as we climb down them and Andrew winces, pausing on the bottom step, just out of sight.

"Are you sure this is okay?" I ask, suddenly nervous.

"That I'm here, I mean? You guys take Christmas so seriously." *And I am bad at it.*

"It is more than okay, Molly. Trust me." His voice is firm and I try to believe him. I try even harder when he reaches out and squeezes my hand.

"You ready?" he asks, waiting until I nod. "Then let the day begin."

CHAPTER TWENTY-FOUR

The kitchen falls silent as soon as we appear and even Andrew seems a little freaked out by it, rocking back on his heels as he takes them all in.

"Don't be weird," he tells them, pushing me gently ahead of him. "Everyone, this is Molly. We have her to thank for getting me home this year."

"*Thank* is a pretty strong word," Christian says from where he lounges by the table. Hannah sits opposite, peeling a large mound of potatoes while their mother hovers behind them. At Christian's words, Colleen hits him on the back of his head before turning to the stove.

"How are you, Molly?" she asks. "Did you get any sleep?"

"A little," I say. "Thanks again for letting me join you."

"Not at all!" A timer dings and she moves a saucepan from one ring to another. The room is a mess of carefully controlled chaos with pots and pans and all manner of food in various stages of preparation. An old iPad showing a color-coded spreadsheet is propped against a stack of cookery books, and she examines it briefly before turning a knob on the oven.

"Do you need any help?" I ask, eager to be of use. Christian snorts as Colleen throws me a sympathetic smile over her shoulder.

"Mam's favorite thing to do at Christmas is to complain that no one helps her," Andrew explains.

"But then yells at you if you try," Hannah quips. "We're allowed to do basic food preparation and that's it."

"Did you or did you not burn your hand on the stove?" Colleen grumbles.

"I was *six*."

"I have everything under control," she says. "In fact, the greatest gift you could give me is to all be out of the house for as long as possible until dinner is ready. It's a beautiful day and you can go meet Liam and the kids in the village."

Christian grimaces. "I'm good."

"You're hungover," Hannah mutters, tossing a slice of potato skin at him.

"The dogs need a walk," Colleen continues as though they hadn't spoken. "And you can show Molly around."

"Around what?" Hannah scoffs. "The grass?"

"Hannah."

"I'm just saying."

"And *I'm* saying that I want you out that door in five minutes tops."

"But you said you needed me to—"

"I changed my mind."

Hannah huffs as she pushes her chair back but does as she's told, shooting me a quick grin before running up the stairs.

"You're the one who wanted a girl," Christian says mildly, which earns him another head whack.

"You're going too," she warns him.

"I can't." He lumbers to his feet to kiss her on the cheek.

"Promised I'd help Dad fix a fence or something. Think he wants to bond."

I raise my brows, glancing at Andrew. I can't imagine Christian out on a farm, though from the pained expression on his face, neither can he.

"Do you all help out?" I ask. Christian dumps his mug in the sink and tugs playfully on Colleen's apron string before he slips out the back door.

"A little bit," Andrew says. "Liam was the one who got into it. He has his own land a few miles over."

"Do you know anything about farms?" Colleen asks politely.

I shake my head. "City folk through and through."

"We'll give you the tour before you go."

Speaking of a tour... I step toward the fridge where a dozen family photos are pinned with fading magnets, the kind you used to find in old cereal boxes. Ruddy-faced children peer back at me, shots of the three boys on family vacations before later pictures of Hannah, first as a baby and then older, beaming as she's surrounded by her brothers. But it's one brother in particular who's caught my attention.

"I would really appreciate it if you could now move away from the fridge," Andrew says behind me.

"But you're so cute," I coo, peering at a photo of him as a toddler. "Though I have to ask..."

"Please don't."

"Why are you naked in every picture?"

"Because he refused to wear clothes," Colleen says by the sink.

"Mam," Andrew warns.

"Flat out refused until he was five," she continues, ignoring him. "I'd dress him, turn my back, and he'd have them whipped off in an instant. One time when he was three, he started stripping in the middle of the supermarket. I'll never forget chasing him around the frozen aisle. Screaming his head off, grabbing hold of his—"

"Hannah!" Andrew roars. "Hurry up!"

"I'm coming," she yells back. "Keep your pants on."

"Yeah, Andrew," I say. "Keep your pants on."

The look he gives me is one of huge betrayal.

"Two hours minimum," Colleen reminds us as he tugs me into the hallway. "And if anywhere is open, see if you can get some more bread!"

We emerge just as Hannah appears, running down the stairs in a green velvet dress and black Doc Martens. She skips the two bottom steps, landing with a thump that sends more family photos rattling.

"Did you make that?" Andrew asks as she hands us our coats she retrieved from upstairs.

She nods, complying with his gesture to spin around. The skirt balloons out when she does before falling gracefully around her legs.

"What did I tell you?" he asks, sounding genuinely proud. "The smart one."

Outside, Christian is sitting on the porch, shoving his feet into rubber boots as the dogs sniff around him. They immediately bound up to Hannah, who doesn't bother to put them on the lead as she corrals them toward the gate.

"I will give you one hundred euro to spend the day with Dad," Christian says to Andrew. Andrew only smirks, bringing me after Hannah, who's waiting for us at the top of the drive.

"He's been in a bad mood since he got back," Hannah says when we catch up with her. She's left her coat open to show off her dress and is shivering in the cold. "It's because he's the only single person this year."

Andrew's head whips toward her and, for a second, I think he's about to refute that, about us, but his eyes narrow. "You're dating someone?"

"Maybe," Hannah says.

"Since when?"

"None of your business."

"It is my business; you're sixteen."

"I can read and write too," she says, and takes off down the lane in a light jog that has the dogs running after her in excitement.

Andrew turns my way, looking for an ally, only to find me grinning instead. "What?"

"Nothing," I say innocently. "Just the big brother protective streak is kind of hot."

"I am not—"

"Oh my God, you are."

"She's sixteen!"

"Exactly." I laugh. "Sixteen. Not six. She's allowed to have a boyfriend."

"Girlfriend," Andrew corrects.

"Girlfriend." I nudge him with my elbow as we start to walk after her. "She's still a baby to you, isn't she?"

"Maybe," he admits. "It's weird, you know. She was only six when I left. And now she's—"

"Practically a woman," I say dramatically. His lips twitch as our eyes meet and when he doesn't look away I find it's my turn to ask, "What?"

"Nothing," he says. "Just glad you're here."

It takes twenty minutes to walk to the local village, which is just one stretch of road with a church, a pub, two mom-and-pop stores, and a garage. They are all predictably closed (besides the church), but there are plenty of people out, all getting their walk in before they spend the rest of the day eating. Or maybe that's just what I'm hoping will happen.

Hannah disappears off with a group of friends as soon as we arrive while Andrew is stopped by every second person we meet. It feels like everyone knows both him and the difficulty he had getting home, and a few even know me, or at least my name when Andrew goes to introduce me. Colleen has obviously been telling our adventures to anyone who would listen.

"You're so famous," I tease. "The prodigal son returned."

"Don't tell that to Christian," he mutters, but he seems pleased that I'm impressed, glancing at me every so often as I take in the village, even though I pretend not to notice.

Outside one of the houses is a small stall selling hot spiced apple juice and pastries and I immediately drag Andrew over to get my hard-earned breakfast. I'm tearing into a Danish when a girl of no more than five or six comes barreling toward us, a fairy wand in her hand.

Andrew scoops her up like a pro, planting messy kisses on her cheeks until she's squealing delightedly in protest.

"Yeah, that's what she needs," a man says from behind us. "To get even more hyper."

Liam. I meet my last Fitzpatrick child, the eldest brother, and finally get some real family resemblance. Whereas Christian and Hannah take after their mother, Liam definitely comes from the same side of the family as Andrew, with the same messy brown hair and hazel eyes. His are smaller though and gaze kindly at me from behind a pair of thin-rimmed glasses.

"You must be Molly," he says, reaching out to shake my hand. "Heard you were crashing the party today."

"Ah, don't worry," Andrew says. "She's staying in the barn. Another one!"

I turn at his call to see an older boy shuffle our way. Far too cool for the exuberant welcome his sister just gave, he gives his uncle a halfhearted hug, a shy but pleased grin on his face.

"Christ, Padraig, how big are you now?" Andrew asks.

"Don't," Liam sighs, buying his own cup of spiced apple. "I'm having to buy a new pair of trousers for him every week at this stage."

"Going to be as big as your dad, are you?"

Padraig shakes his head, though I notice he straightens his shoulders a little at the attention. Andrew introduces me to the children, who both greet me solemnly before turning immediately back to their uncle.

"Your dad said you were in the nativity play," Andrew says to Padraig as he hoists his niece, Elsie, into a more comfortable position. "One of the wise men. You sang a song?"

Padraig nods.

"A solo?"

He shrugs.

"What? Are you all shy now?" Andrew teases, ruffling his hair. "Are you too shy for presents too? What did Santa bring you?"

We stay chatting for another few minutes as Padraig finally starts opening up about the new LEGO set he got. Liam asks me questions about my sister and the baby while keeping an eye on his children and, specifically, what treats his brother buys them from the stall. When Andrew presents Elsie with an exceptionally large chocolate chip cookie that's about the size of her face, he excuses himself, taking them off to find Hannah and the dogs.

Andrew shows no inclination to join them, finishing the

last of my juice as he leads me toward the opposite side of the village, where only a few houses are dotted about. "Want to see the castle?"

"You have a castle?"

"Or maybe it was a monk's tower?" He doesn't wait for my answer, practically dragging me along as we leave the village behind. "I'll be honest, I didn't really pay attention."

He leads me to a bunch of old ruins five minutes away that might have been a castle, a monk's tower, or any number of things but is now overgrown with grass and wildflowers. It's quiet out here, away from the village, the peace broken only by the sound of the odd bleating sheep in the distance.

"Ta-da," Andrew says as we stand in the center of it.

I wait. "This is it?"

"This is it."

"I don't get a history lesson?"

He makes a face, turning in a small circle as though looking for a place of significance. "I had my first kiss over there," he says, pointing to an unremarkable patch of dirt glistening in the melting frost.

"I meant about the monks."

"I don't think the monks were really into kissing back then. Or now for that matter."

"Oh, he's so funny." I press a foot against the low wall and, finding it sturdy, step up, reaching out to Andrew so I can hold on to him for balance.

"Hannah thinks your mam likes me," I say as I walk along the perimeter. I feel like an overgrown child in my bulky winter clothing, but I kind of like it.

"She does. I bet you she even got you a present."

"She didn't," I groan.

"She always has spares in case some relative drops in unannounced. I hope you like mass-market scented candles."

"But I don't have anything for her!" Why didn't I think about that? I should have gotten something in the hospital gift shop.

"Just sign your name on my stuff. It can be from both of us."

"Uh, no."

"Why not?"

"Because a, that's not fair to you, and b . . . isn't that a little, I don't know, official?"

He laughs. "She has us sleeping in the same bed, Molly. I don't think a joint present is going to shock her that much. Just remind me when we get in. We tend to do presents before dinner."

I reach the end of the wall before it crumbles into nothing and jump down onto the grass. It's not as graceful as I envisioned and a shock jolts up my ankle, but I shake it off with a grimace as we move around a mostly intact part of the tower, stepping out of the shade and into the bright winter sunshine.

"So, is this it or are you— Hey!" My breath comes out in a huff as Andrew turns, stepping into me so I'm forced to move back. I hit the wall as I do and he follows, his arms going to either side of my head so I'm barricaded in.

Oh. "Hi."

"Hi." He smiles as I gaze up at him. "You know," he says, "I was really, *really* looking forward to seeing my family and being a good second son, and yet ever since I've come home, all I am is annoyed that I can't spend every second alone with you."

"Are you telling me I've ruined your Christmas and that I should have stayed in Dublin?"

"It was pretty selfish of you to come," he agrees. "And take up my precious time with thoughts of you."

"Thoughts of me?" I like the sound of that. "Indecent thoughts?"

"God no." He reaches for the zipper of my coat, flicking it once before pulling it down. "I'm a gentleman."

I smirk as his hands settle on my hips. "Castles get you all hot and bothered, huh?"

"There are about to be a lot of people in my house for the next few hours and it is going to be impossible to get a moment to ourselves. I think we should come up with a signal when we want to escape."

"I didn't go through the worst journey ever just so you could ignore your family," I remind him.

"Ah, it wasn't so bad."

"It was very bad! We were exhausted, and we spent a lot more money than we should have and it's only through sheer luck that we—"

He shuts me up with a kiss and I am so happy he does.

He tastes like spiced apples and smells like the winter air, crisp and clean and bright. I want to take a deep breath of him. I want to fill my lungs with him and only him and when he starts to move away, I cup the back of his head, keeping him right where he is.

"Now who's hot and bothered?" He smirks.

"I'm just not used to this yet," I admit. "I still feel sometimes like I'll wake up and we'll be on a plane. That none of it will have happened."

"It was always going to happen," he murmurs. "But trust you to choose the most stressful three days ever to do it."

"Hey!"

"It's true."

"At least I—" I break off, biting my lip as he shifts suddenly, fitting his thigh between my legs.

"At least you what?" he asks innocently, but I don't

respond, I *can't* respond, and he knows it, pressing up into me until my breath hitches in my throat. Andrews hears it and pulls back, but only so he can see my face when he does it again.

I grip his shoulders as heat pools low in my stomach, unable to take my eyes off his. I wish I could. He's got this cocky look about him that shouldn't be as hot as it is, but I'm too turned on to call him out on it.

"It's Christmas Day," I tell him instead, and he nods, distracted. "You said back in Chicago that I'd get the second part of my present at Christmas."

"Your what?"

"My present," I remind him. "You got me a two-part present."

"I did, didn't I?"

"So, where is it?"

"Where's what?"

"Andrew!"

He grins. "Two parts seems a little greedy now, doesn't it? Especially since we didn't actually go on the flight you claimed to have gotten me *and* since you gave away those chocolates—"

"I'm your present," I interrupt, and he laughs.

"Yes, you are."

Disappointment fills me as he moves his leg away and I'm about to protest when he suddenly grabs the back of my thighs, hoisting me up.

I panic, my ankles locking around his waist as I scramble to get a hold on him. "Andrew!"

"Much better," he says as we become eye level with each other.

"If you drop me, I'm going to kill you."

"I'm not going to drop you. I'm incredibly strong."

I huff, clutching him close as his hands move from my thighs to my ass. "Seriously?"

"I might have had some indecent thoughts," he admits, and when I don't protest, he leans in, pressing a hot kiss to my lips that the monks would *not* have approved of.

But they're not here right now, are they? There's only us, so I give in to it, kissing him back and tightening my hold around him until my body hums with pleasure. We stay like that for a perfect, blissful minute, cocooned in our own little world until a loud shout echoes around the walls, breaking us apart.

"Andrew!"

We both freeze, staring wide-eyed at each other as Hannah's annoyed voice calls from somewhere nearby. "Mam rang and told us to come home!"

"Whoever invented little sisters can burn in hell," Andrew mutters, resting his forehead briefly against mine before pulling away.

"Christmas with your family," I remind him as he lowers me carefully to my feet. "You love Christmas with your family."

"She also wants to know what kind of gravy Molly wants," Hannah continues, her voice drawing closer as he zips my coat back up. "Or if she should make another— Oh."

Hannah rounds the corner, stopping abruptly when she catches sight of us. Her sudden grin reminds me so much of Andrew that I'm a little spooked. "You guys smooching?" she asks, sounding delighted by the thought.

"Don't say smooching," Andrew grumbles, stepping away from me. He grabs my hand as he goes, tugging me once more into his side.

"Making out?" Hannah continues. "Swapping spit?"

"Would you shut up?"

"Tangling tongues?"

"Hannah—"

"Let me guess," she interrupts, rubbing her nose absently in the cold. "I'm too young to know what kissing is."

"You are."

"When did you have your first kiss?"

"That's none of your business," Andrew huffs, walking us back toward the village. Hannah latches on to my other side, not letting up.

"Didn't you have it in the castle? You did!" Her eyes light up at whatever expression she sees on his face. "Is that why you brought Molly here? That is so corny."

"Don't you have somewhere to be? Down the well, maybe?"

"Andrew can be very sentimental," she tells me, looping her arm through mine. "It's kind of cute."

"I'm not cute. I'm a grown man."

Hannah continues, undeterred. "For my seventh birthday I was *ridiculously* into Disney princesses," she says. "And he surprised me by coming home for the party. He had the full-on Prince Charming outfit from Cinderella and he brought me back the dress, you know the blue one? He waltzed with me in the living room and then had to do it with every single one of my friends."

"That *is* pretty cute," I confirm as Andrew shoots me a look, one that drops completely at Hannah's next words.

"It's why I got into fashion."

"It is?" he asks. His surprise is obvious. "You never told me that."

"It was definitely then. I was obsessed with that dress. I wore it every day after school for weeks until Mam threw it out and said it was an accident. I wouldn't stop crying and she told me if I loved something that much, I should learn how to make my own one. So, I did."

"When you were seven?" I ask.

"I didn't say it was any good. Mam helped me staple some crepe paper to one of her old skirts. But yeah. That's when it started."

Andrew's gazing at her with a look on his face that makes me want to kiss him again, but thankfully before I can and make Hannah go truly nuts, Liam's children come running around the bend, the dogs not far behind. Hannah uses the distraction to draw me away, letting the others bring up the rear as we stride down the path.

"You know," I say as we leave the village behind. "You make me feel very old."

She bursts out laughing. "Why?"

"Because the first time I heard about you, you were six."

"On the first flight?" she asks.

"That's it." I smile at her. "Andrew tells you about our flights?"

"He tells us everything about you. It's a tradition by this stage. Of course, you didn't come off in the best light the first two years," she continues slyly. "But he was always a bit of a drama queen. Then it was all Molly's doing this and Molly's doing that. She's got into law school, she's graduated law school, she's got a new boyfriend, she's got a new apartment, she's moved out of the apartment, she's got a new job. For the first few years, Christian was convinced he made you up, but honestly, that's why when you came, I was like, 'Hi!' It's like I already knew you."

"Well, I appreciate the warm welcome," I laugh. "He tells me about you too."

"Oh yeah?" she scoffs. "Like what? How annoying I am?"

"Like how impressed he is with you. Like he thinks you're the smartest out of all of them and how you're going to be famous one day."

She looks at me skeptically. "You're just trying to make him seem nice."

"I'm not. He tells me all the time."

She purses her lips, trying and failing to hide how pleased she is. "I guess he's not the *worst* brother," she says eventually, and we glance over our shoulders to where he's walking with the kids and Liam. Andrew frowns at the sudden attention, immediately suspicious, and Hannah collapses into giggles before giving me a friendly tug, quickening our steps up the lane.

CHAPTER TWENTY-FIVE

I meet my final member of the family when we get back to the house. Andrew's father, Sean, is a quiet, no-nonsense man who welcomes me with a warm, calloused handshake before thanking me for helping his son get home, just like the others. You'd swear I paddled the guy over on a dinghy.

Colleen continues to ignore my repeated offers to help, and instead grabs Andrew to do the dishes while Hannah uses the opportunity to shut me in her room so she can show me the outfits she's been working on. It wasn't just brotherly bias when Andrew said how talented she was. The pieces are gorgeous, even half-finished, and I dutifully act as a model for an hour as she talks me through her process.

Afterward, at Andrew's insistence, I sign my name on the various gifts he got for everyone. I still feel guilty, but relieved overall that he told me what his mother was planning or else I would have felt even more uncomfortable as I gathered around the enormous, picture-perfect tree with the rest of the family. As predicted, Colleen hands me a scented candle, beautifully wrapped with my name in neat calligraphy on the tag, but most of the attention is on Padraig and

Elsie, who unwrap their mound of toys and thank each person dutifully.

It's an odd sensation, joining in on these little rituals, the same ones I spent my entire adulthood avoiding, as if to prove to myself that I didn't care. And while it will always be awkward joining a group of people who know each other inside out, it's hard not to get caught up in the jokes and the teasing and the sheer unfiltered joy of it all. I don't think Andrew ever stops smiling. Not once.

But the highlight of the day is, of course, Christmas dinner. We're called to eat a little after seven p.m. to a small dining room that you can tell is used only on special occasions. I'm surprised at the amount of food, even though Liam's wife, Mairead, and the kids have joined us, but it makes sense when Andrew explains how his mother *slightly* freaked out about me coming and made double of everything, just in case. I know that half the fun of big holidays like this is the leftovers though, so I don't feel too bad about it.

We all manage to squeeze around their table, even though we're so close that I'm touching shoulders with Andrew on my left and Hannah on my right. But the kids eat quickly and grow bored, and it gets easier when they're excused and get up to run around the living room with the *Star Wars* lightsabers they got from Christian.

Despite the welcome I received, I'm low-key nervous at being the lone outsider at the table. As bizarre as it sounds, I'm worried they'll try to include me. Ask me polite questions about my life that I would politely answer but that no one cares about. Instead, to my relief, they practically ignore me. Bickering and talking over each other, including me only when someone tries to get me as an ally on their side. Usually Hannah. All the while Andrew is a constant presence beside me, explaining quietly when new names are mentioned and which household item Christian broke at any given time.

I'm so distracted trying to keep up with it all that I almost forget to be worried about the moment I've been secretly dreading.

No one batted an eyelid when Andrew declined a drink at the start of the meal, but as the hour goes on and more bottles are opened, it begins to get more noticeable.

Hannah's allowed a second glass of prosecco even though Christian has been sneaking her sips of his beer throughout the afternoon. He's on the red wine now. They all are, except me, and while Colleen seems to accept easily that I'm not drinking tonight ("I'm leaving early to get back to my sister"), I can tell she's starting to take it as a personal slight that Andrew refuses every bottle she offers him.

"I still have that headache," he says, his voice straining when she gets up for the third time to go hunting for something she thinks he might like. "Probably the jet lag."

I squeeze his knee under the table and his hand immediately covers mine, keeping me there.

"If that one is too heavy for you, we have a merlot in the—"

"Stop fussing," Christian says, spearing a carrot with his fork. "You'd swear he joined a cult."

"He traveled a long way to be here and I'm just making sure—"

"All you're making sure of is that your food is going cold and you're the one who spent all day cooking it." He grabs the glass she just placed in front of Andrew and tips it into his own. "There, problem solved."

Colleen throws her hands in the air in a fine-I-give-up movement and ignores Hannah's casual suggestion that she wouldn't mind trying some wine.

The brothers' eyes meet over the table, a silent discussion occurring that seems to relax Andrew as some of the tension in his shoulders loosens. The squeeze he gives my hand is the only warning I get.

"I actually wanted to talk to you guys about something," he says, and everyone's eyes swing our way. He hesitates at the attention and I'm not surprised, considering he told me he hadn't planned on telling them, but before he can continue Hannah lets out a small noise, her mouth dropping open as she stares at us.

"No way."

"What?" Andrew asks, confused.

"No *way*," she repeats. "You're engaged?"

"*What?*" Colleen shrieks as I almost die of mortification.

"We're not engaged," Andrew says quickly, but Hannah's not listening, already ecstatic.

"Oh my God, you definitely are!"

"No, we're—"

"Congratulations," Christian says loudly, smirking when Andrew glares at him. "Brilliant news."

"Christian—"

"Where's the ring?"

"There's no ring. We're not engage— *Mam*, stop it. We're not engaged. Hannah!"

Hannah drops my left hand where she'd been trying to look for a diamond. "Well, you should have said something."

"You want me to announce every time I'm not engaged to someone?"

"*No*, but—"

"What did you want to say, Andrew?" It's Liam who interrupts and thank God he does, because my heart is beating so fast, I'm starting to get dizzy. I calm down when the table falls quiet again and I give Andrew an encouraging nod when he glances at me.

"I just..." He takes a breath, dragging his gaze away from me to look at his family. "I've given up drinking," he says. "I'm sober. Not just for Christmas or for January... but forever, if I can."

Silence.

Christian is the only one who doesn't look stunned, as if he already suspected it, and, as a result, he's the first to speak. "That's great, Andrew," he says, unusually serious. "Well done."

Liam and Mairead quickly chime in with similar words of support, but Colleen just smiles at him, looking confused.

"But you don't have a drinking problem."

"I do, Mam," Andrew says. "Or at least I did."

"But you're not—"

"You don't have to explain yourself, son," Sean says quietly. "It's nobody's business except your own. I'm very proud of you."

"Thanks, Dad," Andrew murmurs as Hannah leans around me to smile encouragingly at him.

"Your skin is going to look *amazing*."

"What's wrong with my skin?"

"It's a bit dull," she says solemnly, and Andrew rolls his eyes.

Colleen, however, still seems upset, her gaze flitting around the table as though she doesn't know where to look, and Andrew's leg tenses beneath my hand as she stands.

"Well," she says abruptly and, before anyone can stop her, grabs two bottles of half-finished wine from the table.

"Hey," Christian complains as she takes the glass from his hand next.

"Support your brother," she snaps, bringing them to the sideboard before heading back for more.

"I am! I'm getting rid of his temptation!"

"That's not necessary," Andrew says as Sean hands her his own glass.

"Of course it is," she mutters. "You've been sitting there suffering while we're waving everything around in front of you. Molly, I don't know what you must think of us."

"I—"

"I can't even remember how much wine I put into the gravy." Her hand flies to her chest. "And there's brandy in the ice cream."

"Mam, it's okay."

"Did you join one of those clubs?" she asks suddenly. "Triple A?"

"It's just AA. And no, but I've joined another program that—"

"Your uncle Kevin has been told he has a gluten intolerance. Maybe you should talk with him."

"Mother of God," Christian mutters, dropping his head to the table.

"I know it's not the same," Colleen says. "But he's had to give up a lot. You know how that man likes his bread."

"There's gluten in beer too," Hannah pipes up, and Colleen gestures toward her with a *see* motion.

"I'm doing okay," Andrew says firmly. "I just didn't tell you guys until now because I didn't want you freaking out." At this Colleen harrumphs. "I don't want to be the guy that stops you having a glass of wine with dinner. It's a personal decision and I'm glad I made it. I've got plenty of support..." Another hand squeeze. "And I think I'm going to be able to do it," he finishes. "But I wanted to be honest and let you know."

Sean nods while Colleen sits back down, still looking flustered. "You didn't have any gravy, did you?" she asks.

"No."

"Good. That's good."

"You all right, Mam?" Christian asks as she starts folding her napkin into a tiny square.

"I'm fine."

"Want a glass of wine?"

"Yes, I think— *No*," she amends, horrified as Christian starts to laugh. Andrew grins as she glares at him and then Hannah starts listing all the sober celebrities she knows and Sean excuses himself from the table only to come back with a fresh bottle of sparkling water that Colleen quickly adds some sliced lemons to.

And they move on.

I don't know whether I've become more attuned to him these last few days or if he really is just that relieved, but it's like a weight has been lifted from Andrew's shoulders, and though he has to spend several minutes convincing his mother to pour more brandy over the pudding, it's worth it when they turn off all the lights and set it ablaze. That's accompanied by ice cream, and more dessert brought over by Liam, who says he saved a cake from their family holiday to Milan in November.

"It's panettone," he declares, starting to cut into it.

Andrew and I turn to each other at the same time and he smiles so wide that I burst out laughing, much to the confusion of everyone else.

After dinner, Liam and his family return home and the remaining Fitzpatricks (and me) move to the living room, where Andrew's father has a fire going in the hearth.

"Movie time," Andrew explains as we settle on the couch. It's the sinking kind, worn with age and impossible to get out of, and as soon as I sit beside him, I'm tipped into his side. Neither of us minds so much, Andrew quickly draping an arm around my shoulder like he's afraid I'm going to move away.

"What are we watching?" I ask.

"Dad always picks. It's the one time of the year he gets to be in charge of the television." Almost as soon as he's finished speaking, Hannah starts a drumroll on her lap as Sean stands, drawing all eyes toward him.

"No pressure," Christian drawls from where he's lounging on the floor with his back against the couch.

Everyone is wearing some sort of Christmas hat now, including me. And while a week ago, I wouldn't have been caught dead in it, I kind of love how ridiculous everyone looks.

Sean clears his throat, standing in front of the fireplace as he holds up a battered DVD case. "*Field of Dreams* is a—"

The family groans around me, cutting him off.

"We watched that last year," Hannah moans. "Mam!"

Colleen shrugs as she helps herself to more chocolate. Now that the dinner is out of the way, she's much more relaxed and looks ready to finally settle down for the night. Every few minutes I notice her watching us all and smiling like she can't believe all her children are home, as though nothing has ever made her happier.

Sean continues bravely on. "A classic film about family and—"

"At least it's not *Apocalypse Now*," Christian mutters.

"Why don't we watch *Sleepless in Seattle*?" Hannah suggests hopefully.

Andrew says nothing, observing the room with a small smile on his lips as he plays with a lock of my hair.

"Let Molly decide," Colleen says after another minute of arguing. "She's the guest."

"Um..." I try to straighten from Andrew's side as everyone turns to me, but he doesn't budge, his arm keeping me locked against him.

Hannah looks at me pleadingly.

"I kind of like *Field of Dreams*," I say.

Sean beams as Hannah boos me, but, despite the grumblings, the room goes quiet when the movie is on, even if Hannah spends half of it on her phone until Christian plucks it from her hands and slides it into his back pocket. A brief wrestling match occurs before Colleen tears them apart and then they have to put their phones in the kitchen drawer for the rest of the night.

When it's finished, Colleen switches over to catch the last half of *My Fair Lady* on television. By the time *that's* done, it's nearing midnight and Christmas Day is officially over. Andrew's parents excuse themselves first, and after another ten minutes, Christian stretches exaggeratedly as he catches Andrew's eye.

"Well," he yawns. "I'm wrecked. I'll see you guys in the morning." He gives Hannah a pointed look and pushes himself off the floor, heading to the stairs.

Hannah doesn't budge. Not until he comes back into the room and pinches the top of her ear, giving a sharp tug.

"*Ow*. Okay!" She bats him away as she follows him out, grumbling a goodnight.

And just like that we're alone again. I lift my head, finding Andrew watching me. He looks good like that, bathed in the glow from the Christmas lights, tired but sated as he curls a lock of my hair around his finger.

"You sleepy?" he asks.

"Not yet," I say truthfully. "Your family is really nice."

"I'm glad they got to meet you." He tugs my hair. "Want your Christmas present now?"

"Yes."

He laughs as he pushes me off him and drops to his knees by the tree. There are still a few presents wrapped underneath, which Andrew said were for the various wider family members who would drop in over the next few days. I don't think much of it until he returns to the couch with a round object, wrapped in purple tissue paper.

"Close your eyes," he says, and I do. A second later he drops something into my hands. The heavy weight of it catches me by surprise, and I make quick work unwrapping it as he sits back down beside me.

It's a snow globe.

But not the kind you see in airport gift shops, the cheap plastic things you're more likely to lose than keep. This one is big, like a paperweight, its base a heavy dark wood that takes up my whole hand. Inside there isn't a snowman or a miniature house, but a plane suspended in the night sky, its little windows a warm yellow.

"It's us?" I ask, not taking my eyes off it.

"It's us."

I turn it gently in my hands, running my fingers over the glass. "I don't have any Christmas decorations."

"I figured. I thought you wouldn't mind this one."

"Wouldn't mind?" I have to choke the words out. "I love it, Andrew."

He shrugs, watching me examine it.

"You're supposed to shake it," he reminds me, and I do, tilting it so the snowflakes flutter, until the plane is soaring through a winter's night. I lean forward so I can see it better in the light and Andrew's hand drops my hair in favor of rubbing slow circles into my back. It's like he can't stop touching me. And I don't want him to. In this moment, I don't think I've ever been as comfortable with another person as I am right now. The burnout I'd been experiencing the last few weeks, the anxiety and the nerves and the sleepless nights wondering what I should be doing with my life, it's all ebbed away, giving me a kind of clarity I haven't had before.

"Remember when I said I wanted to tell you everything?" I ask, not taking my eyes off the plane.

His fingers pause in their movements and I smile at whatever dramatic direction his mind just went. "Yeah," he says slowly.

"I don't have a secret love child somewhere."

"I was thinking CIA agent."

"I'm flattered." I place the snow globe carefully on the coffee table and sit up as best I can, twisting to face him. "I lied to you before. When I said I didn't know what I would do if I wasn't practicing law."

"I knew you were lying," he reminds me. "I said you were."

"Okay, well . . . I'm unlying to you now."

He just waits.

"I like food," I say, stating the obvious. I've always liked food. My greatest pleasure in life is eating and eating well. Finding new restaurants, trying new flavors. I introduced my friends to some of my favorite dishes the way a lot of people share their favorite movies, intently watching their faces to ensure they're reacting in all the appropriate ways. "I'm not good enough to cook professionally," I continue. "I know I'm not and I don't think I want to do that either. But . . ." I trail off as Andrew gently pulls my hand free from my hair. I hadn't even realized I'd been playing with it. "I did have one idea," I admit.

He smiles when I don't continue. "I'm dying of suspense here, Moll."

And it all suddenly seems so stupid. I don't know why I'm

talking it up so much or why I'm so scared to tell him. Maybe it's because I've never told anyone before. It's just one of those little dreams inside your head, like marrying a member of a boyband or winning the lottery. Only, as Andrew is about to find out, nowhere near as glamorous. "Did I ever tell you that I wanted to be a tour guide when I was little?"

He watches me for a beat, as though trying to weigh up if I'm joking or not. "No," he says eventually.

"Well, I did. I wanted to be one of those people who stands on top of the tour bus and leads a group of people down the street wearing a bright rain jacket and waving a matching umbrella over their head. My dad loves tours like that. He would take me and Zoe on them all the time. I always thought they were fun."

"And you want to be one now?" he asks curiously. "In Chicago?"

"Not exactly. I want to be a food guide. I want to take people around the city and show off all the restaurants and food stalls, not just the ones in the tour guides or the ones designed to be posted on Instagram. I want to show off the *real* places. Off the beaten track."

"So why don't you?"

"Because I don't live in a movie. Because I've got another eight months on the lease of an expensive apartment and student loans that I'm already spending a lifetime paying back. Because I live in America, which means I need health insurance. Because I spend several hundred dollars every year dyeing my hair."

"You dye your hair?"

"Of course I dye my hair. You think these highlights are natural?"

He looks very confused. "What, like the lighter bits? That's not your hair?"

"I dye my hair," I say. "I dye my hair and I pay a monthly subscription for my hot yoga classes, and I like getting massages when I want them. Which means I need enough money to pay for them."

"Or marry rich."

"Or steal."

"Or that," he agrees.

"It was just an idea. I don't know the first thing about how to get started. It would probably take years and might not even make me any money and..." I trail off, repeating the same things I've said to myself for weeks. In those moments in the dead of night when I can't sleep and I wake up so anxious and worried that sometimes it's like I can't breathe. I started a little bit of research, but never let myself think too much about it. The cons always outweighed the pros. The price of failure always much too high.

"Sounds like you're thinking a lot about what could go wrong and not about what could go right," Andrew says gently.

"I'm just trying to be realistic."

"I know you are, but I've had a lot of bad meals in my life, Molly, and not one of them has been from one of your recommendations. There's a reason everyone always asks you where to go when they want something to eat. And there's a reason you always have the answer. So, what if it doesn't fail? What if you're good at it and it takes off and you make enough money for everything you need and you live out the rest of your days doing what you love?"

"I..."

He frowns when I don't continue. "Have you really spent the last few weeks trying to figure out another career when you've had this idea in the back of your mind? Did you not think that maybe the reason your heart was so against every other path was that you knew exactly what you wanted all along?"

"No."

"Then what?" He meets my stare straight on, fully ready to argue with me. I hate when he gets all serious and reasonable about things.

"I've had too much ice cream to talk about this properly."

"That old excuse."

"It's true," I protest. "I'm tired."

"You're scared."

"So?" I ask. "There's nothing wrong with being scared."

"There's not," he agrees. "So long as you don't stay scared forever." He taps a finger under my chin when I look away, turning my gaze back to him. "You can get help," he adds. "It's not like you have to step outside one day and just start. There'll be people who can help you. *I* can help you. But you have to ask for it. You have to try. And I'd rather you tried than stay miserable, Molly. No matter how scared you are."

I don't know how to respond to that. Don't know how to do anything other than just stare at him. I don't understand how he always knows what to say to me. How he always knows how to cheer me up and calm me down like he understands me better than I do myself.

My fingers twitch with the now familiar urge to touch him, to be as close as I can to him, and I shift a little, drawing my legs onto the couch.

"There's a laptop in the other room," he continues, for once oblivious to where my mind has wandered. "Do you want to show me what you've been—"

"Let's talk about it in the morning."

"I'm not saying you need to make a decision; I just want to see what you've—"

"Andrew." I turn, swinging one leg over him so I'm straddling his thighs. His hands grip my waist, holding me steady as surprise and then heat flares in his eyes. "Let's talk about it in the morning," I repeat, each word slow and clear as I lean down and bring my lips to his.

CHAPTER TWENTY-SIX

I am officially obsessed with kissing Andrew Fitzpatrick.

Some people run. Some people bake. Some people paint miniature figurines or upcycle furniture to sell for five times the price. It's healthy to have hobbies. And now I have mine.

"That's it," he murmurs when I finally come up for air. "I'm bringing you home for Christmas every year."

I smile, tracing his nose with the tips of my fingers. I wonder how I resisted, staying away from him for all these years. My heart aches at the thought, at the time wasted, but I quickly disregard it. I'm glad we got to be friends first, that now I get to give myself to him fully without worrying which parts of me he might reject. He's already seen me at my worst. Tired and stressed, angry and crying. He's seen it all and still seems to want everything. To want me.

"Were you jealous of my exes?" I ask before I can stop myself.

Andrew just smirks. "Do you want me to be?"

"Maybe."

He doesn't reply immediately, seeming to think about his answer. "I wasn't so much jealous as I was happy when they made you happy," he says eventually. "And irrationally angry when they made you sad. I may have a protective streak when it comes to you."

I shrug, trying not to look as happy as I am by that statement. It doesn't fool him for an instant.

"You like that, don't you?"

"I don't know what you mean."

"No?"

"No, I'm emotionally very healthy and—" I yelp, laughing as he pushes me onto the couch.

"You're a terrible liar," he says, leaning down. I turn away at the last second, still laughing, but he doesn't seem to mind, his lips meeting my throat like that was his intended target all along.

He nuzzles into me, gentle at first and then hard enough that it sends my pulse fluttering.

I push at his shoulders, wanting a real kiss, but he doesn't budge, concentrating on the soft patch of skin where my neck meets my shoulder before drifting a trail to right below my ear. One hand pushes my hair back, the strands slipping through his fingers as he starts a delicious suction that leaves me reeling.

"Are you giving me a hickey?" I ask, only to squirm when he sucks harder before releasing me.

"No," he lies, sounding pleased with himself.

I scowl when he pulls back, but it's only halfhearted as I surge up to kiss him properly. He lets me this time, his mouth slanting over mine with a low groan that instantly becomes my favorite sound in the world, and when he pushes his hips into me, I gasp so loud I'm amazed I don't wake his whole family.

The thought of them has me breaking away, clambering off the couch on wobbly legs. Andrew blinks up at me, slightly dazed, and for a moment he looks disappointed, maybe even a little nervous, as if he thinks we've gone too far. But then I hold out my hand in a silent question, remembering what he said. That we'll take things as they come. That we'll do what feels right. And this, this right here, feels right. And when he puts his hand in mine and follows me out of the room, I know it with my whole soul.

I hold in a giggle as we attempt to make it up the stairs as silently as we can. It's a little after one a.m. and there are no lights on under any of the doors we pass. The house is fast asleep, but I've never been more awake.

I turn to Andrew as soon as we're in our room, but he moves away, striding to the radiator by the window with single-minded focus.

"Thank Christ," he says, pressing a hand to it. "Dad said he'd fix it this after—"

"Andrew."

"Right. Sorry."

He hops back over the bed, the movement a lot more graceful than it has any right to be as he comes to stand in front of me.

"Sorry," he whispers again. "You sure about this?"

"Yeah. You?"

"I'm sure. I am very, very sure." He steps closer, vanquishing the space between us. "Feels strange though," he muses. "To give in after all this time. I feel like I've been hiding it from both of us for so long. And now I'm just . . . not."

"Hiding what?" I ask, thoughts scattering as his fingers circle my wrists, clasping them gently.

"How much I've thought about this moment." I swallow

as his mouth drops to my ear, his words barely more than a whisper. "Do you want me to tell you?" he asks. "How much I want you right now?"

I shrug a little, or at least I think I do; my body no longer seems to understand what my brain is telling it.

"What do you want, Moll?" Andrew asks when I just stand there.

"I want..."

"Yes?"

Everything. The word gets stuck in my throat, choked down by the realization. I want everything with him. I want it so much I can barely stand it.

"A kiss," I say instead, trying to focus as his grip tightens ever so slightly.

He immediately acquiesces, capturing my lips with perfect aim, but it's not enough. It's nowhere *near* enough.

The kiss is soft. The kiss is sweet. The kiss... is a freaking tease.

I writhe against him, needing more, and when I pull away he loosens his hold on my hands so I can raise them to his chest, clutching him by his sweater.

"You," I say. "I want you. All of you."

Heat fills his gaze, as though charged by the same electricity I feel running through my own body. "You have me, Moll. You've had me for years."

"Then stop teasing," I mutter, and grab the back of his neck, pulling him down to me.

This kiss is stronger, surer, our lips moving against each other in seamless synchronization like we've done it a million times before. Andrew's hands drop to my waist, unbuttoning the front of my jeans before he slides them down my hips. I don't even break the kiss as they fall to my ankles, stepping out of them and kicking them to the side. My sweater comes next and I raise my arms as he grabs the hem and pulls it over my head. There's a slight edge to his movements now. Like with each piece of clothing, we grow more frantic and he follows me in our less-than-elegant striptease until we're both making out in our underwear, still rooted to our spot against the door.

He steers us toward the bed and my mind whirls, forgetting to be embarrassed by the noises I make and the cellulite on my thighs and the stretch marks on my hips. These are things I'd usually be thinking about the first time with someone new, but Andrew isn't new. And even if he were, I'd still be too distracted trying to get enough of him to care. Because no matter how much I try, I can't get enough. I want him to touch me everywhere; I want to feel him everywhere. I want ten hours of kissing and foreplay. I want him in me now.

And Andrew seems just as torn as I am, his hands moving up and down my body as if he doesn't know where to focus. When he's not kissing my lips, he's on my neck, my throat, licking down between my breasts and back up again before nipping me hard enough that it's just short of pain, a spiking pleasure that I know will leave another mark. I want it to leave a mark. I want proof of this night, of this moment, so that when I wake up in the morning, I'll remember exactly what happened.

"Bra," he mumbles in my ear, and I nod jerkily as I push up, reaching behind for the clasp.

"Do you have a—"

"Yes," he says, almost diving off me as he kneels beside his suitcase. I try not to stare at his ass in his black boxer shorts and then remember I can stare all I like now, and when he comes back to the bed with a victorious expression, I raise a brow at the row of foil packets in his hand.

"Do I want to know why you brought condoms home for Christmas?"

"It's called sexual health, Molly. And I have an old girlfriend in the village who—"

"Not funny," I snap, launching myself at him. He laughs as we fall to the bed and I straddle him, carefully tearing open a packet as his eyes skate over my bare chest before focusing on the pendant around my neck, the present he got me. He tugs it gently, positioning it in the hollow of my throat before sitting up to press the lightest kiss to it.

Our underwear are the last to go and they go quickly before I'm rolling the condom onto him and then suddenly our places are switched, his movements confident and sure as he pulls me under him.

"You good?" he asks, and I nod, grabbing his face to kiss him again. He lets me do so only briefly before he breaks away, skimming his nose along my jaw before he moves downward. It takes me a few seconds to realize he's not coming back up.

"Andrew?"

He only hums against my skin, his tongue tracing a circle around my belly button before he keeps going.

"You don't have to—" Shut *up*, Molly. My head hits the pillow, fingers digging into the bedsheets as he gently parts my legs.

The first touch of his tongue has me squeezing my eyes shut. The second has me squeezing my thighs, but Andrew doesn't seem to mind. If anything, it seems to spur him on as he grabs hold of my hips, keeping me as still as he can as I move against him. The man can take direction, I'll give him that, and he follows every movement of my body as I silently tell him where to go and what I need until he learns me better than I even know myself. Until he needs no direction at all.

And when one hand leaves my hip to join his efforts, I'm a goner. Pleasure ripples through me, almost unbearable in its sweetness.

I can only lie there, my breathing ragged as he waits for me to still before licking his way back up to my mouth.

"Okay, good job," I say, patting the side of his face. "Night night."

He smirks, taking me in before kissing me. My hands go to his back, exploring to my heart's content. The sudden freedom to do so makes me almost giddy and he encourages my enthusiasm by kissing me harder, by reacting to everything I do. He shudders when I run my fingers up the sides of his stomach; he grunts when I tug at his hair. I am fascinated by every one of his movements, every sound that comes from him, every muscle that contracts under my touch.

He feels warm and hard against me, and even though we're both sweating, I don't protest as he maneuvers us under the covers, the heavy drape of the quilt over our bodies only making me feel like we're closer together.

He settles more fully over me, testing his weight against mine, how our bodies fit together. So familiar yet new. And I know that whatever is happening, there's no turning back from this. This is not a one-night thing.

This is not a mistake.

How could I ever have thought this would be a mistake?

I'm so ready for him now that there's no hesitation when he moves into me, a moan escaping me as our eyes lock together. An almost pained expression comes over his face at the sound and he bends to kiss me with renewed determination, open, hot, and less skilled than before. The arms on either side of me tremble as though he's doing his best to keep himself in check and when he pulls back, the slow drag sends my nerve endings into overdrive.

He kisses me like I've never been kissed before. Like he's been waiting his whole life to do it.

Or maybe just ten years.

I grip him harder at the thought, pulling him into me until our bodies are pressed so flush together that there isn't an inch of space between us. And I don't want there to be.

I love this man. I love him I love him I love him and all I can think about is how he must love me too. He must. Because he wanted me here. He wanted me with him. Maybe long before I ever wanted him. And I'm so glad I stopped under that mistletoe. I'm so glad fate finally got fed up with waiting even if I don't have the bravery to tell him as much yet. But maybe I don't need to. My touch can tell him what my words can't and so I touch. I touch and I caress and I let my kisses speak for themselves. And as he brings my hands over my head, lacing his fingers with mine, I try to remember if I've ever felt this way before, if I've ever felt so *much* before, and then he pulls at my bottom lip and dips his head to press his mouth to the skin just above my heart and I can't remember anything at all.

CHAPTER TWENTY-SEVEN
ONE YEAR AGO

Flight Nine, Chicago

"I can't remember where I... No, I definitely left it on her desk. Well, if it's not there, then someone moved it. I don't know who! If I did, we wouldn't be in this mess."

"Molly."

I hold up a finger, reaching deep for my last shred of patience so I can make sure I still have a job in the morning. "Call Lauren and check with her," I say. "And don't tell Carlton... I don't care if she's gone home for Christmas, so have I!"

"*Molly.*"

"I'm on the phone," I hiss, glancing at Andrew. He glares at me from across the small plastic table, looking just as irritable and tired as I feel.

"Well, unless you want me to order you a glass of water, you need to get off it," he says.

It's only then that I notice the exhausted-looking server standing beside us.

Shit. Fine. "I'll call you back in five," I say, hanging up

with a pointed look at Andrew before I skim through the menu, already knowing what I want.

"Cheese fries," I say. "Thank you."

"I'm sorry, we're all out."

Of course they are. "The club sandwich is fine."

The waitress winces. There's a ketchup stain on the front of her blouse and her dark hair is falling out of its halfhearted bun. "We finished serving our sandwich menu at—"

"You choose then," I interrupt, handing the menu back to her. "Surprise me."

"Our soup of the day is—"

"Yes. Great. I'll have that."

She mumbles another apology and spins on her heel, going immediately to the party at the next table.

"Seriously?" Andrew asks when she's out of earshot. "She's barely more than a kid."

"I'll leave a good tip," I mutter, dropping my head into my hands. I massage my temples, trying to ease the migraine forming there. I know I'm being a bitch, but I don't know how not to be right now. Work is an endless nightmare that's only made worse by the holiday, our flight's been delayed for five hours, and now we've apparently waited thirty minutes to order food that they don't even have.

"It's not her fault," Andrew continues, and I have to fight back a scowl, keeping my head bent so he can't see my face. "What?" he asks when I don't respond. "You're not even going to talk to me now, is that it?"

Oh, for the love of—

"What do you want me to say?" I snap, sitting up so fast my head spins. "Because it feels like whatever I do, you're just going to take it the wrong way with the mood you're in."

"The mood *I'm* in? You're the one who's been on her phone for the past hour."

"Yes, because of *work*, Andrew. I have a job. One that doesn't just stop when I leave the office."

"How about one that stops for a few hours so we can talk to each other?"

"A few hours? We're going to be here all night at this rate!"

"Um... excuse me?"

"*What?*" We snap the word in unison, both of us turning to see the waitress standing terrified before us.

"I'm really, *really* sorry," she begins as my phone buzzes on the table. "But the soup..."

Andrew's still looking at me like I'm the worst person in the world and I'm starting to feel like it too, the pressure of work the last few weeks turning me into someone I barely recognize.

"We *definitely* have the chicken Caesar salad," the girl continues, and it's the earnest hopefulness in her voice that finally tips me over the edge.

The tears come instantly and once they start there's no way to stop them.

"I'm sorry," she gasps as Andrew mutters a curse word and slides out of his seat. "We have spaghetti? It will take longer but—"

"The salad's fine," I say, barely able to get the words out. "That sounds perfect, thank you."

She gives me a panicked nod as Andrew kneels beside me, placing a hesitant hand on my arm as everyone around us politely looks the other way.

"I'm sorry," I say, my voice wobbling. "I'm really tired."

"I know. Me too. I'm sorry for snapping."

"*I'm* sorry for snapping. Crap. My makeup."

"Don't worry about it."

"Don't be such a *boy*." I pluck a napkin from the dispenser, dabbing it under my eyes. My phone keeps ringing, but both of us ignore it. "I just wanted some cheese fries."

"I know. We can try somewhere else. Or I can steal them off that guy's table."

He says it so seriously that I snort, which is not a great thing to do while crying, but it does the job of shutting me up, the tears ending as quickly as they came.

"Ugh." I press the napkin to my nose, blowing lightly. "I'm sorry about work."

"You don't need to be. I know you—"

"No," I cut him off. "I'm being rude. They announced last month that they're making cuts, so everyone is turning on each other like it's a battle royale and I'm just..." I sigh, slumping in my chair. "I don't know when I last got a full night's sleep."

"Can I do something?"

My breath hitches at his words and I'm reminded again why I drop everything every year to fly home with this man. No "Maybe you shouldn't work so hard," no "Get yourself together, Molly." Just how he can help me. Even after I've spent the last two hours ignoring him, that's all he wants to know.

"Just pretend I've been nothing but great company," I say. "And tell me if my mascara's ruined."

"The bits all over your face or..."

I scowl at him, but he just smiles and then, to my surprise, rubs his thumb over my cheek, wiping away the stains. It's a strangely intimate gesture, his skin rough and warm against mine, and I still beneath the sensation, confused by my reaction to it. He swipes once more, slower this time as his smile fades into a frown.

"Molly..."

My phone rings and he jerks back, dropping his hand

like I've burned him. Before I can stop him, he gives me an encouraging nod, returning to his seat.

"You should get that," he says.

But to hell with that.

I silence the damn thing before shoving it into my purse.

"For all they know, I'm in the air," I say. "I'm all yours."

Something flickers in his gaze at my words, but whatever he's going to say is lost as the waitress returns, visibly sweating now.

"So, when I said a *chicken* Caesar salad . . ."

Now

I sleep in fits and starts. Either I wake or Andrew does and every time that happens one of us reaches for the other. At some point during the night, we come together a second time and it's slower and careful, but no less perfect, and when he brings me to that sweet spot, I have to turn my head into the pillow to muffle the sounds I can't help but make.

Only then does sleep come properly, and the next time I wake, the clock on my phone tells me it's a little before seven. Andrew is dead to the world beside me, his head turned toward mine, and for a few minutes I simply lie there, adjusting to the darkness, adjusting to, well, *this*.

I could get used to this.

Going to bed with him, waking up with him, repeating it over and over again until it stops being special. Until I can take him for granted.

Not in that bad way, but a comfortable one. Knowing that he'll be there. Just like he's always been.

I check the last few messages on the family group chat,

scrolling through endless photos of everyone holding the baby. Zoe's due home today and now so am I, and while I desperately want to see her and my parents, another part of me is miserable at the thought of spending just a few days away from Andrew. It makes me want to wake him so we can make the most of every minute we have left, though of course I don't, going down the normal route of staring at my phone in the dark for several minutes and liking everyone's Instagram Stories.

I've just finished sending a slightly-too-long update to Gabriela when nature calls and I use the excuse to slip out of bed. It takes some careful maneuvering, but it looks like the exhaustion has finally caught up with Andrew and he doesn't stir as I creep out of the room.

I go about my business quickly and am back outside the bedroom door when my stomach cramps with a familiar morning pang.

I shouldn't be surprised. I've always been a breakfast person (okay, I'm an every meal person) and despite stuffing my face for most of the day yesterday, habits are clearly hard to break. Tucking the dressing robe properly around me in case I run into a Fitzpatrick on my travels, I continue past Andrew's door and sneak down the same stairs we rushed up not hours before.

I feel my way through the dark house until I get to the kitchen where, after a bit of flailing, I manage to find the light switch. Taking Colleen at her word that I can help myself, I grab a slice of bread from a bread bin on the counter. I don't even bother to toast it, just lean against the counter as I tear off mouthfuls as fast as I can chew. I'd love a coffee but can't see a machine anywhere and it didn't escape my notice that everyone was drinking tea yesterday morning. I'm sure they must have a bit of the instant kind somewhere, but the thought of rooting around their cabinets is a step too far on the guest scale for me.

There has to be somewhere in the village I can get my caffeine fix. I haven't discussed timing with Andrew in regard to me going back to my parents, but we'll surely be able to—

I jump, startled as a cough sounds from somewhere nearby, and stuff the remaining bread into my mouth in case Andrew woke up and snuck down after me. But when I hear it again, I realize it's coming from outside and the porch that wraps around the back of the house.

Curious, I brush my crumbs into the sink and peek my head out the door.

Christian stands just outside, dressed in sweatpants and a hoodie. A lit cigarette is poised between his lips and there's a guilty, deer-in-the-headlights look on his face that vanishes as soon as he sees me.

"I thought you were Mam," he says, sounding more relieved than a grown man in his late twenties should be.

"Sorry."

"Couldn't sleep?"

I shake my head, wrapping my arms around myself as I glance about. Two robins hop around the frozen ground near us as though testing their bravery. It's cold, but not unbearable and I step out farther.

"Do you mind if I . . . ?"

He shrugs as I gesture lamely at the porch and I take a place against the wall on the other side of the door.

"You're up early," I say.

"I'm heading back to London in an hour or so. Boss is a dick, wants everyone in the office tomorrow."

That sounds familiar. "What do you do?"

"Real estate."

"Do you like it?"

"Nope." He smirks. "But it pays the bills. Well, kind of." He takes another drag, turning his head so he's not blowing smoke my way. An awkward silence descends, or at least one that's awkward on my part. Christian seems perfectly content to just stand there, watching me. Is this why people smoke? So they have something to do with their hands?

"So," he says, after thirty seconds of me desperately trying to think of another topic. "Are you and Andrew..."

"Engaged?"

He laughs at that. "Sorry about dinner," he says, not sounding sorry at all. "Hannah's a romantic."

"And you?"

"Just a younger brother." He tugs his hood up, burrowing into it against the cold. "But it's a thing now, is it?"

"It's new."

"New's not a bad way to end the year," he says, his tone kinder. "Even if he's always had terrible timing."

I only smile, a little confused.

"Do you know what you're going to do yet?" he asks.

"Like..."

"Stay in the States, back to Dublin?"

"Ah." The emigrant chat. "I have no plans to move back to Ireland. Chicago's felt like home for a while now."

"Good for you," he says. "Long-distance though. That's always looked hard."

"What do you mean?"

"Well, not that it can't work," he adds, and I freeze, my impromptu breakfast churning in my stomach. Christian hurries on, mistaking my silence for annoyance. "You'll be grand." A quick smile. "Has Andrew found an apartment yet? He never believes me when I tell him how Dublin is for renters. I think he has it in his head that he'll just come home and walk into a place."

I pull my hair into a halfhearted bun, my now clammy hands moving automatically as I tug the strands back again and again and again. "I'm sure he'll find something," I say. The words sound faint, as though spoken by someone else.

"Not in time though. When does the new job start? March?"

March? *March?* "I can't remember."

"Maybe you could get him to look at those places I sent on? He'll need to put his name down just to get a viewing. And tell him not to come crying to me when—"

Both of us flinch when the door flies open, Christian hiding the cigarette behind his back on instinct. Andrew steps out, taking in the scene before turning an accusing eye toward his brother.

"What are you doing out here?"

Christian shrugs. "Stealing your girl."

"Well, can you steal her inside? Preferably next to the radiator?" Andrew motions me back into the kitchen and I follow numbly. "And put that out before Mam catches you," he says to Christian. "What are you? Fifteen?"

Christian steps inside a second later, rubbing his hands together as Andrew turns on more lights. "They think it's going to snow today," he says, glancing out the window.

"They always say it's going to snow," Andrew says. "It will be on the mountains if there's anything." His eyes dart toward me and he frowns, shrugging the sweatshirt from his body and passing it to me. I put it on automatically, just so I have something to do other than look at him.

He's moving back to Ireland? He's moving back to Ireland and he didn't tell me?

"I'm going to finish packing," Christian says. "Take it easy, Molly." He doesn't wait for a response as he disappears back up the stairs.

"Are you okay?" Andrew asks when he's gone.

"I'm fine."

"Are you sure?"

"*Yes.*" I move around the counter, wishing he hadn't interrupted us and that I'd asked Christian what was going on.

Andrew just grins at me. "What am I supposed to think, waking up to an empty bed?"

"I'm sorry. I got up to pee and then I was hungry."

"You are? What do you want? Mam usually buys those little variety packets of cereal as a treat. I laugh, but I've never wanted anything more right now." He starts riffling through the cabinets, pulling out various breakfast items. As he does, an image comes to me, of him sitting at the airport bar, just before our flight was canceled.

Can I talk to you for a sec?

I'd been so caught up in what was happening I hadn't listened to him. Was that when he was going to tell me? Was that why he was so quick to suggest spending Christmas in Chicago even if it meant not seeing his family? Because it was the last time he'd get to do it?

"You want a coffee?" Andrew sets out two mugs on the counter and goes back to his rummaging. "No one drinks it but me, so I always bring home my own stash."

He glances over when I don't say anything, one hand holding a plastic-wrapped assortment of mini cereal boxes.

"You sure you're all right?"

I lean forward on the kitchen island, my arms dwarfed in the baggy sleeves of his sweatshirt, my feet sliding in the fuzzy slippers Hannah lent me.

"Christian said . . ."

Andrew's brows draw together when I don't continue, and he looks toward the stairs with a scowl. "Christian said what?"

"He thinks you're moving back here. That you're starting a new job. Looking for an apartment."

Silence.

I said it purposefully like we were sharing a joke, in an "isn't Christian funny, hah hah hah" way. But Andrew just places the cereal on the counter, his expression guarded as he removes a mini-packet of Rice Krispies.

Oh, hell no.

"Molly—"

"You can't be serious."

"It's not what it sounds like."

"It's not? Are you moving back here?"

"No."

Oh. Okay, now I'm confused. "But Christian said—"

"I know. He ... I had a plan. When Marissa and I broke up, I started re-evaluating things. My life over there. My sobriety. I thought that maybe I needed a fresh start."

"Back home?"

"I'm aware of the irony."

"But you're not moving home," I confirm, trying to wrap my head around what's happening.

"I changed my mind."

He changed his mind. And for the first time since we got here, I feel a prick of unease at his words.

"When?"

He hesitates, as if knowing in putting out one fire, he may have just started another.

"When did you change your mind?" I press.

"Does it matter?"

"*Yes*. Because from what you're implying, up until three

days ago, you'd planned for *months* to move home. And now you're just... not? Because of what? A kiss?"

"It's not just that and you know it."

"But if we hadn't kissed, that would still be the plan, right?" I start to feel a little sick. Back to his family, to his friends, back to a new life and he was going to throw it away for me? "You've got a new job?"

"I haven't accepted it. And I'm not going to." He's tense now, his good mood vanished. I'd feel guilty if I weren't so mad. I can't believe he didn't tell me. "Moll, come on, this isn't a—"

"*Don't* say this isn't a big deal," I warn. "I know you think it's not, but it is. You said so yourself how sad you were missing Hannah grow up. And your niece and nephew love you and your parents love you and you love Ireland, I know you do." The excitement on his face when we walked around Dublin, the calm that settled over him when we stood on the hilltop yesterday morning. I'd never seen him like that before. He said he needed a fresh start and now he was going to trade it all for something we've only just dipped our toes into? That we've barely begun to explore? Every long-term relationship I've ever had has ended with someone choosing something or someone else over me. So what happens when I give everything to this man and he turns around three months from now and realizes he chose wrong?

"We don't know what this is yet," I say, trying to get him to understand.

One look at his face and I know he doesn't. If anything, he looks pissed off. "I don't know what this is? Really?"

"We haven't even—"

"Flight one," he interrupts, placing the packet of Rice Krispies to the side as he moves on to the Coco Pops. "When you didn't even know me and you tried to protect me. You literally stole my phone to stop me from getting hurt. Flight two, I stared at the back of your head the entire time, waiting for you to turn around. I know you thought I was mad then, but I wasn't. I was embarrassed. I wanted to talk to you, but for the first time in my life I didn't know how. Flight three. Our first real flight. It was the quickest that journey has ever been for me. I was going to ask you out, but you said you had a boyfriend."

"Andrew—"

"Flight four." He moves on to the cornflakes. "When we got drunk on champagne and talked the whole way home. I don't think I've ever had so much fun in my life. Flight five, when you bought me that sweater. I didn't wash it for a week because it smelled of you. I carried that old food guide around with me for weeks, wondering if I should give it to you or not, and the look on your face when you opened it... I'd never been so happy to see someone smile. Flight six, when I saw you saying goodbye to your boyfriend. You wanted to know if I was jealous of your exes, Molly? I put it down at the time to not wanting you to date an asshole, but seeing you together felt like I was being ripped in two. I was with someone else at the time and just standing there looking at you felt like cheating."

He waits for me to interrupt again, but I don't. I just stare at him, feeling ridiculously close to crying.

"I lied when I said I wanted to kiss you once before," he continues. "Flight seven is the second time I wanted to. I don't know why. Nothing special happened. I just came up the escalator and you were sitting by the gate and I felt like I was home already. I hated parting that time. I hated it, but I didn't know why. Flight eight, you were basically dying from your period. You fell asleep on my shoulder and I could have pushed you to the side, but I didn't. My arm went dead, but I didn't move because I liked you touching me and I wanted to look after you. Sometimes I think it's what I was born to do. Flight nine is when we were delayed and you started crying because they were out of cheese fries. I'm pretty sure I would have sold all of my belongings just to get you some, and I was so close to telling you how I felt. So close to figuring this out, but you were exhausted and I didn't want to stress you out even more. By the time I got back after Christmas you'd already met Brandon and I was too late."

He moves then, rounding the table, and only stops when I take a step back, bumping into the stovetop.

"I was going to tell you about moving home. I swear to God I was. But not yet. Because more than anything, I wanted you to give me a reason to stay. I was going to flirt, test the waters, maybe ask you out on a proper date, but you were so busy with work and then the storm happened and..." He shakes his head, almost scowling at me now. "The storm happened and you dropped everything to get me home for Christmas because you knew that was what would make me happy. So, flight ten, Molly. Flight ten when you kissed me under the mistletoe and became the only girl I've ever truly wanted. Don't tell me I don't know what this is. Don't tell me I don't know what I want."

My heart is beating so hard in my chest, I swear that I can hear it. I can certainly feel it. An aching thump against my rib cage as though it's trying to leap out and join his. I want nothing more than to hold him, to touch him, but I stay where I am, the future repercussions of this scaring me more than anything ever has. Because it's easy to take the leap. To quit your job, to fall in love. Wanting is the easy part. It's the hard stuff that comes after. And the idea that Andrew might be making the biggest mistake of his life for me is enough to make my blood run cold.

"We both agreed that we would start at the *beginning*," I say when I can speak again. "This is not a decision someone makes at the beginning of a relationship."

"And if I move back here, we can't start at all. Is that what you want?"

"What I *want* is—"

We both tense as the staircase creaks. I fold my arms over my chest, half expecting Christian to return with some quip, but it's the youngest Fitzpatrick that appears in the doorway, barefoot in her flannel pajamas.

Andrew smiles, some of the intensity in his expression seeping away. "Hey, sleeping beauty," he says, his voice infused with lightness even though he doesn't take his eyes off me.

"What time is it?" Hannah asks, looking more ten than teen as she rubs her eyes, peering into the dim kitchen.

"Seven thirty."

"What?" She sounds horrified. "Why are you up?"

"Body clock is out of whack." He shakes the cereal. "Plus, variety pack."

Hannah doesn't look convinced, her eyes narrowing as she glances between us. "Are you guys fighting?"

"No."

"You look like you're fighting. You look like you're—"

"Go back to bed, Hannah," Andrew interrupts, but she just gives him a look as she goes to the sink.

"I'm getting water first," she mutters. "I'm allowed to get water. I live here."

Andrew gives her that quintessential I'm-going-to-murder-you sibling glare, but Hannah ignores him, her eyes flicking to me as she leaves.

I flash her a smile, but it must look as strained as I feel because her brow only furrows deeper as she leaves the room. There's a long pause where she's clearly trying to eavesdrop on the staircase before it creaks again when she gives up.

Andrew waits a moment before he turns back to me, planting his hands on the counter.

"I want to see my sister," I say when he goes to speak again.

"Molly—"

"We'll talk about it," I say. "We'll sit down like adults and talk about it. But I can't... I can't *think* right now."

I knew it. I knew as soon as Christmas was over something would happen. The magic would break. I just didn't think I'd be the one to break it.

Andrew presses his lips together, clearly unhappy. "I can borrow my mam's car and give you a ride back."

"I'll catch one with Christian."

"You're not even going to let me—"

"Not because of that." I sigh. "It makes sense, doesn't it? He's going there anyway. I just want you to think about it for a few days. Spend some time with your family, with your friends here. A lot has happened in a few days and it sounds like we both need space to just breathe."

"I don't need space."

"Well..." I stare at him, helpless. "I do."

There's a finality to my words that I didn't mean, but one he fully hears. He straightens, his throat moving as he swallows.

"Better make you that coffee then," he says, turning his back to me.

And I don't know what to say to that so I don't say anything at all, lingering for an awkward second before I slink back up the stairs. At the far end of the hall a door lies open, and it's there I find Christian, sitting on the edge of an unmade bed, his face creased in concentration as he tries to get a new pair of earbuds out of their plastic casing. He doesn't look up when I knock.

"Yeah?"

"Can you give me a ride back to Dublin?"

His fingers pause only briefly in their struggle as his eyes flick to me. "I think Andrew was planning on—"

"Makes more sense, doesn't it? Save on the gas?"

He frowns. "Is your sister okay?"

"She's fine," I say, trying to sound bright. "I just want to get back up and see her."

"It's not a problem," he says slowly. "I'm leaving in an hour though."

I shrug, backing out the door before he can change his mind. "Not like I have anything to pack."

I'm fully dressed by the time Andrew comes back up the stairs with my coffee. Neither of us speaks and before long the rest of the family is gathering to say goodbye. Colleen is upset to see her youngest son go even though she pretends she isn't, fussing over him before disappearing into the kitchen after their final goodbye. Sean and Hannah stay out at least, though Hannah is the most subdued I've seen her, eyeing Christian moodily as though he's leaving purely to ruin her day. I hang back until Colleen reemerges and presses three stacked containers of leftover food into my hands, along with another candle for my mother and a small, knitted toy lamb for Zoe.

"You'll come back and see us," she says, her words more an order than a request.

Andrew waits until the last possible second to hug me as he always does. For a moment I think he might kiss me, but he lets me go with a smile that I know is for the sake of the others.

"Call me when you get back," he says, and I nod, already feeling the distance between us.

Despite the cold weather, he remains outside as Christian drives us down the lane. I keep my head twisted back to look at him, watching until the very last second when he vanishes from view.

CHAPTER TWENTY-EIGHT

The drive back is strange. I'd been asleep for most of the journey down so was unaware of how deep in the countryside we were, and am amazed at how easily Christian navigates the winding, unmarked roads. It's a miracle he doesn't get lost, especially in the darkness. We're driving for more than thirty minutes before the sun begins to rise.

I also thought Christian would be the strong and silent type but, to my surprise, he's kind of... chatty. Not only that but the man won't sit still. As soon as we leave the farm, he switches the radio to some generic hits station and starts muttering about other drivers on the rare occasion we pass them. He fiddles with the heating, he pops a mint and offers me one. He taps his fingers against the steering wheel and grills me about life in Chicago just as Zoe had asked Andrew when she drove us home.

Once we're on the highway, he starts to calm down, and I wonder how much of what he said about his boss wanting him back in the office is true and if maybe, unlike Andrew, home for Christmas is more of a duty than a gift. One that he's happy to perform but glad when it's over.

It's only when we approach Dublin and the cars become busier with Christmas travelers that he brings up what happened this morning.

"Did he freak you out?"

"Huh?" I'd been distracted, busy staring at my phone, wondering if Andrew was going to message me.

"My brother," Christian says, giving the finger to someone cutting abruptly across us. "I never pegged him as the intense sort, but people change."

"Intense?" I ask. "Seriously?"

"What?"

"*You're* the intense one."

"Am I?" That seems to surprise him. And I suppose it's not hard to understand why. I think back to the first time I ever heard of him, on that very first flight with Andrew, when he'd pulled the birthday card trick just to embarrass him. "Is it the family?" he asks. "Couldn't handle a Fitzpatrick Christmas?"

"Your family is lovely."

"What then?" His tone is blunt, as if we didn't just meet yesterday. "Because don't think I didn't notice the awkward-as-hell hug you gave him back at the house. Or the fact that you keep pretending it's not a big deal that I'm the one driving you back."

"It's economical."

"It's suspicious as f— *Hey!*" He blares the horn as someone slows down too quickly in front of us, trying to make their exit. "A Kerry license plate. Typical."

I turn my attention back to my phone.

"It's just," Christian continues, and I sigh. "The way Andrew's spoken of you over the years, I know you guys are close. And I've never seen him be that touchy-feely with a girl before. I would have told him to snap out of it if he didn't keep smiling every time you walked into the room." His eyes slide to me, just in time to see me flush. "But I guess it's none of my business."

"It's not."

"Yeah." A pause. "Except it kind of is."

"Excuse me?"

"It kind of is my business," he says. "Because he's my brother and I love the idiot and I went to bed and he was happy and I woke up and he wasn't, so what? Why are you leaving so soon?"

"I'm not allowed to go back and see my newly mothering sister?"

"Andrew would have happily driven you back himself. What did you fight about?"

"We didn't fight. There was a misunderstanding and now we just need space to figure it out."

"What the hell could you have..." His eyes narrow as realization dawns. "He didn't tell you he was moving home, did he?"

"Not in as many words."

"So, I stood there freaking you out and you just lied and pretended you already knew?"

"I was trying to save face."

"You're good at it." He sighs. "Shit. I'm sorry. I thought he would have told you."

"Yeah, well, I thought he would have told me too."

Christian grimaces, eyes darting between me and the road. "All right," he says, and I can tell by his tone he's trying to lighten the mood. "So, how are you at long-distance?"

I clear my throat, covering my phone with my hand. I don't know if I should be the one to tell him this, but I feel like he's not going to let it drop. "It doesn't matter. Andrew said he's decided to stay in Chicago."

"What? Since when?"

I feel a little justified hearing the bewilderment in his voice. "Since now, I guess. Because of me."

"Huh. Okay." A myriad of expressions cross his face as he works through that little update. "And you don't like that?" he asks eventually.

"I don't not... It's a big thing," I say. "A big choice. For him to decide to stay just because it's where I am? That feels like a lot."

"And you think you're not worth it, huh?"

"I didn't say that."

"What, then?" There's a frown on his face like he's trying to figure me out. "Scared he's going to change his mind?"

"It's not a completely unrealistic outcome. This whole thing has happened way too quickly. Usually, you meet a guy, you hit it off, and you try each other on for a while. See if you fit. This feels like we were moving along at this snail's pace for ten years and suddenly, bam."

"Bam? Did someone step on the snail?"

"No, the snail... No, I meant now it's going too fast."

He gives me a confused look. "Okay."

I try again. "What I mean is, he's spent the last three days trying to get home to you guys. And watching you all together... He loves you. He loves this place. He's always said that. And now he's just going to throw that away for me?"

"See, now I think you're giving yourself *too* much credit," he says. "It's a difficult balance, I'll give you that."

"Christian—"

"He likes Chicago," he interrupts. "He's spent all his adult life there, just like you. And just like you, he moved there before he knew you even existed. I'm sure sitting next to you on an airplane once a year was thrilling, but I'm also going to take a wild guess that he didn't stay there because of that. He has a life over there. He has friends, he has memories, he has his roommate's dog that he won't stop sending pictures of to the family group chat. To be clear, the easiest option is for him to stay. And as to your weird snail analogy..." He stares out at the road, exasperated. "Yeah, fine, if you two just met three days ago, but you didn't. You've known the guy for ten years. And I think he's been a bit in love with you for ten years and he was just too stupid to see it. Why would you want to take it slow? I wouldn't take it slow."

"Being in a romantic relationship is not the same as being in a friendship. It could ruin a friendship."

"So what?" he exclaims. "Get a new friend! What else are you going to do? Pretend you don't know each other? Set him a series of tasks to prove himself?"

"No, I—"

"Because it sounds like you're so worried about losing him that you're not even going to try for something better with him, and if I'd known talking to you this morning would have sent you into this spiral, then I wouldn't have done it. I would have kept my mouth shut, flirted with you to piss him off, and stolen some money from his wallet on the way out."

I blink. "Flirted with me?"

"I've been threatening to flirt with you for years," he says with a smirk. "Because I knew it would rile him up. Because *you* rile him up. I'm telling you, Molly, you've been it for him for a very long time. And I think he's been the same for you."

Has he been? My hands grow clammy as my brain does what it's been doing ever since the mistletoe kiss and starts to filter through each and every moment when Andrew and I could have been more than friends.

"Okay," Christian continues when I stay silent. "That's a lie, I don't know if he's been the same for you. I barely know you. But Andrew's—"

"It is," I interrupt. "It is the same for me."

Christian starts to nod when he catches sight of my face. "Are you . . ." He trails off, horrified. "Are you crying?"

"No," I lie, pressing my hands to my cheeks.

"Ah here, Andrew's going to kill me if you tell him I made you cry."

"It's not you," I explain. "This happens a lot."

"That doesn't make it better."

"I'm just realizing I was an idiot." I wipe a tear and then two away, blinking to make sure no more will follow. "I suppose asking you to turn the car around would be too much?"

"We'd need some serious sobbing for me to do that." But he glances at me as though afraid I'm about to do just that.

"I think I'm in love with your brother," I tell him. "And I think I need to fix what happened this morning."

"Good for him and yes, you do, but I've got an airport pint with my name on it and I'm not turning this car around."

"I'm not above bribing you."

He laughs. "And I'm not above being bribed."

"I'm just saying, I've done it before. I'm very good at it."

"I'm dropping you home," he says. "And then I'm getting out of here. Just give yourselves both a break, see your nephew, see your family, and then give him a call. He'll know you'll need the space."

"Or—"

"Not happening," he says, and I slump back in my seat.

He's right though, I know he is. "You're pretty good at relationship chats," I say. "For a boy, anyway."

"Yeah, well. It's always easier when it's about other people, isn't it?" He tilts his head then, peering out the windshield at the thick gray clouds with an almost wistful expression.

"What do you know?" he mumbles. "And only a day late."

I follow his gaze, though it takes me a moment to see what he's talking about. The droplets on the window I first think are rain and then are most definitely not.

"It's snowing," I say, unable to hide my surprise.

"It will probably melt immediately," Christian says, echoing Andrew.

But it doesn't. It sticks.

It sticks and it keeps falling and by the time we get to Dublin, it's really coming down.

We crawl to a halt as we reach the city center, mainly because the flurry of snow has sent everyone haywire. It feels like everyone in Dublin is outside, kids and adults playing or simply standing about with big, delighted grins on their faces as the city gets its white Christmas. I start to worry I'm going to make Christian late, but he just shrugs me off.

I direct him back to my street and he drops me off, waiting for me to dump his mother's leftovers in the hall before driving off with a wave. As he does, the door two houses down opens and my sister appears, holding a baby carrier in her hands. She smiles as soon as she sees me, walking down the street before doing a double glance as Christian passes.

"Who's that tall glass of water?"

"Andrew's younger brother."

"You little—"

"Don't be gross," I complain, already knowing what she's going to say.

"How is that gross? I'm impressed."

"Shut up. Should you be on your feet right now?"

"Yes, *Mother*. If I can birth a human, I can walk the two doors down to the neighbor to show it off." She holds up the baby carrier and I peek inside.

My nephew is fast asleep, almost completely covered up by a variety of brightly colored blankets.

"How did Christmas in the countryside go?" she asks while I poke where I think his itty-bitty feet are.

"I'll tell you later," I insist, mustering up a smile for her. "Let's go inside. I want to spend what's left of Christmas with you guys."

"Since when?"

"Since now."

She pauses at the edge in my voice, looking distractedly at the scene behind me. "Did something happen?"

"No."

"Molly—"

"I'll fix it."

"What does that mean?"

"It means let's go inside. I need to call Andrew."

"I don't think you do." She nods at the street and I turn to see a vehicle approaching, its windshield wipers moving overtime.

I don't recognize the car but, as it draws closer, I recognize the man in the front seat.

So much for giving me space.

Andrew drives carefully down the street, his gaze focused on me as he pulls up to the house. It's only when he does that I realize he's not alone. Hannah bounds out of the passenger side, practically bouncing on the sidewalk as soon as he stops the car.

"She insisted on coming," Andrews explains as he shuts the door. "And now she needs to pee."

"I can help with that," Zoe calls, gesturing Hannah

toward the house. The girl shoots me an excited grin as she runs past.

"I like your hair," Zoe says to her.

"I like your baby."

"Thank you." Zoe shoots me a pointed glance as they step inside the house and I turn back to Andrew, who now stands stiffly by the car, his hands in his pockets.

"You followed me up here?" I ask even though it's obvious.

"I let you get a head start before I couldn't take it anymore. Hannah kept insisting I wait until New Year's Eve because it would be more romantic, but I figured you'd have gone by then."

I nod, folding my arms over my chest. "I was going to—"

"I wanted—" He breaks off his own interruption, running a hand over his head. Around us the snow continues to fall, blanketing the street. We're far from alone. A lot of front doors are open with people sticking their hands mistrustfully out or simply standing there, gazing at it. Bundled-up kids dart up and down the road, shrieking with delight every time one of them slips and falls. Someone's already started on a snowman next door.

"I know you don't want to put too much pressure on this," Andrew says, dragging my attention back to him. "I know you're scared that I'll flake out on you. But I'm not going to lie and say I'm not staying in Chicago for you. Because I am. For *you*, Molly. I don't want to do long-distance. And I don't want to just be friends. I thought I could do it once if that was how you felt, but not now. Not anymore. I don't want to not see you for months until we meet for a hasty lunch. I don't want to wonder how you are. I definitely don't want to meet your boyfriends. I want you, I want *us*, and I think we could make it work."

"Andrew—"

"I love you." He takes a breath once he's said the words, as though he had to race through everything else just so he could get to them. "I'm *in* love with you and I'm sorry it took me so long to figure it out. I'm sorry I wasted so many years trying to find someone else, when the only one I wanted was you."

I hear a faint *awwww* from Hannah behind me before the quiet hustling of my sister to get her back inside. I ignore them both. I ignore everything but the man in front of me.

"I don't think I could handle it if I lost you," I admit finally. "I think that's why it was easier to keep you as a friend all these years. Why I didn't even let myself think of you as anything more. Because if I did and you left—"

"I'm not going anywhere."

"I know," I say quickly. "I know that now. It's just... You're right when you said I keep thinking about failure. I don't know when I started doing that. I don't know when I started denying myself what I want, but I do. And I don't want to be that person anymore." I gaze up at him, laying my whole heart out like I never have before. "I want you to stay in Chicago with me. I want us to be together and I want to kiss you all the time. I don't want to wait or go slow or start at the beginning. I want you too. I want *us* too."

His eyes search my face, like he's looking for any hint that I don't mean what I say, but whatever he sees must satisfy him, because he takes a cautious step toward me. "All the time, huh?"

My laugh comes out like a hiccup. "We've got a lot of years to catch up on."

"Better start making up for them, then." And he does, dipping his head to press his lips against mine as softly as he did under the mistletoe.

"I'm in love with you," I say, because I need him to hear

this. I need him to understand what I suddenly, overwhelmingly do. "In an extremely non-platonic, never-leave-me way."

"I won't," he murmurs. His gaze softens as he wipes a snowflake from my cheek. "For as long you'll have me."

Forever.

Because I know in my soul there will only be him. There's only ever been him.

"You're cold," he murmurs after a moment of us just gazing at each other like two love-struck kids.

"I'm fine."

He grimaces. "Okay, that was just me being macho. I'm the one who's cold."

I smirk and go to hold his hand, but that's not enough for him. He draws me firmly into his side, arm wrapped around my waist, and I think about all the times he's done this before and how neither of us thought twice about it. It was always natural for us to touch, to be as close as we could to one another. Just another hint maybe that this was always supposed to be our fate.

We step inside and my nose tingles at the change in temperature. Andrew tugs my damp scarf and coat off, his eyes running over me when I shiver as though assessing for signs of damage.

I can hear Mam fussing over Hannah in the kitchen and catch a glimpse of my dad in the living room, rocking his sleeping grandchild with a look on his face I don't think I've ever seen on him before. Andrew hangs my coat up just as Zoe comes downstairs, dressed in a giant fluffy sweatshirt. She stops when she catches sight of us, eyes dropping to where we grip each other's hands like someone's trying to tear us apart.

Her lips twitch. "Oh, hey," she says casually. "Nice to see you again, Andrew."

"How are you doing?"

"Peachy," she says, though she's looking straight at me. "It's really coming down out there," she says after a beat. "We'll go from staring at it in wonder to complaining about it in less than twenty-four hours, I guarantee it. Are you sticking around?"

"For a while yet," he says, his tone just as light even as his fingers tighten around mine.

Zoe only nods. "I'll put the kettle on, then," is all she says, and turns without another word into the next room.

"Welcome home, Molly."

I look to my left to see Dad lingering in the doorway, still rocking his grandson.

"Hi, Dad."

"We didn't open the presents," he continues. "Well, except for your sister. She opened hers last week because your mother got her an air fryer and she wanted to try it."

"You waited for me?"

"Of course we did." Dad looks surprised. "It's not Christmas without you here, now, is it?" His eyes drift to Andrew. "Bet your mother was glad to have you back."

"She was," Andrew says. "Thanks to this one."

"Your arm will go dead," I add, but Dad only smiles faintly, his attention fixed firmly back on the grandchild in his arms as he turns toward the couch.

"Sure, he's only a small thing," he says, settling into the cushions. "Light as a feather. Come in here when you have a minute," he adds. "So I can say hello properly."

Andrew shares a smile with me before shrugging off his damp coat to hang it beside mine.

"Andrew?" Zoe calls from the kitchen. "Do you take milk in your tea?"

"Just a splash," he says like he's been here a thousand times before.

I hear Hannah ask for two sugars before politely accepting a second slice of cake from Mam.

"Okay?" he asks quietly, and I nod.

"Want to see me charm the hell out of your mother?"

"I'd like to see you try."

A familiar glint enters his eye. "Is that a challenge, Molly?"

"You talk big, is all."

"Always so competitive," he sighs, reaching in his coat pocket. "Luckily for me, I have a secret weapon."

I almost laugh. "Is that—"

"Homemade Christmas jam, direct from the heart of Ireland?" He holds it just out of my reach, tugging me forward. "You think I would show up to woo you unprepared? Mrs. Kinsella," he calls as we enter the warm kitchen. "I'm sorry to drop in unannounced. My mother insisted I bring something with me."

I take a seat at the table as Andrew does exactly as promised and immediately obliges my mother by writing down the family recipe.

Zoe sets a mug of tea in front of me with a look on her face that says I'm going to give her minute-by-minute details of everything that happened before she disappears to join Dad and the baby. Hannah takes another mouthful of cake as she slides her phone toward me, showing me the dress she's working on, and I try and pay attention, but it's hard when Mam is laughing and Andrew keeps glancing at me as though to make sure I'm still there. Hard when his hair is damp from the snow and his skin flushed from the heat of the house. Hard when, whenever he does catch my eye, he smiles that singular smile of his, as bright and as brilliant as I've ever seen it. And it's almost ridiculous how heart-burstingly glad I am that he's here. How grateful I am that we made it home. How wondrous it is to do something so simple as to sit in a warm kitchen at Christmas, surrounded by people I love as the snow swirls like a waltz outside.

EPILOGUE
TWELVE MONTHS LATER

Chicago, O'Hare Airport

"This is a mistake."

"The panettone?"

"*No*," I huff. Although... I glance at Andrew, suddenly nervous. "Why? Do you think we should have gone with the tiramisu? Because—"

"It was a joke," he interrupts calmly. "A cruel joke that I'll spend the rest of the day making up for."

"Andrew."

"That I'll pan-*atone* for."

"Don't," I warn, but he's already smiling, delighted with his pun.

"Stop stressing," he says. "You've planned this down to the minute. Everything's going to go fine."

"Planned it down to the minute and we're already running behind."

"Since when do you not factor in delays?" He nudges me and I tear my gaze back to him. "Stop glaring at the board."

"I'm not glaring at the board. I'm *looking* at the board. And—"

He pulls my beanie hat low over my eyes to shut me up and by the time I push it back he's already leaning down, kissing me through the stray strands of my hair now stuck to my face.

I let him because I'm nice like that.

And because I really, *really* like when he does it.

The bustle of the busy airport disappears around me as I relax into him, tugging on the end of his scarf to keep him right where I want him.

He's still smiling when he pulls back, looking down at me with an almost smug expression. "I don't think I'll get tired of that."

"Kissing your girlfriend?" I quip. "I hope not."

"More like getting to do it whenever I want."

I huff, while secretly agreeing with him. It was surprisingly easy coming together over the last year, blurring into each other's lives almost seamlessly. It makes me wonder if that was why neither of us had made the effort before. Because once we let ourselves have each other wholly, there was no going back.

My phone buzzes in my pocket and I mutter a "Finally" as I take it out. No one's been replying to my messages, which is *really* not helping my stress levels right now. But it's an email rather than a text that's come through.

"Is it Zoe?" Andrew asks.

"No," I say, still reading through it. I've gotten a lot better at not squealing when these things come through. "A new booking. My New Year's Eve tour is sold out."

"Look at that!" Andrew leans into me, dropping his head to mine as we read through it. "Congratulations."

"You still want to come on this one?" Andrew's joined my

tours dozens of times. At the start, I asked him to come to help boost numbers, but when he kept showing up even when we got busier, he eventually confessed that seeing me excited and doing what I loved got him all . . . well, you know.

"Of course," he says. "If you're not going to kick me out now."

"Never," I say, and I grin as he presses a kiss to my temple.

A month after our nearly disastrous trip home last year, Andrew moved in with me. I was the one to ask him, using the excuse that I would need help with the rent, which was true, but more that it was just the right time. We were seeing each other nearly every day anyway and it made sense, seeing as how he'd already told his roommates he'd be moving out and the fact that he'd been sleeping over most nights anyway.

A month after that, I handed in my notice. I was terrified, *more* than terrified. I was convinced I was making the worst mistake of my life and told Andrew as much more or less every minute of every day for about a week. But we'd taken it seriously. I had savings and a plan. I had help from Andrew and Gabriela, who more than came through on her promise to support me.

I went on a short course run by a local tour guide and got a job at the bottom of a big company. I spent my days in the cold rain, doing the early slots and the evening slots and the slots no one wanted, holding my bright yellow umbrella aloft as I took people around my adopted city. In my spare time, I spent a good chunk of my savings putting together my food places. Along with the help of Andrew and my friends, I designed chocolate tours and seafood tours, halal, kosher, vegan. Tours to suit every taste bud under the sun. And in early May, as tourist season started to peak, I took the plunge.

And Molly's Food Tours began.

The salary cut was... tough. Sometimes people didn't show and I was left waiting for hours and out of pocket for the week. Some days, it went perfectly. People tipped. Restaurants started contacting me, people started recommending me.

I was still learning, still growing. If next summer ended well, I'd maybe be earning enough to hire someone else. But I was trying not to think too far ahead, which I'd learned only made me stressed. I would get through the next six months and then maybe a year and then maybe two.

But first, I had to get through Christmas.

"I still think this is a mistake," I say, nerves fluttering again as I think about the next few days, even though the whole thing was my idea in the first place. "We're not going to last twenty-four hours before we all start killing each other."

"I wouldn't celebrate the holiday any other way." But he must see my panic isn't going anywhere because he sighs, reaching into his backpack. "All right. I was going to wait for an audience to give you this," he says, handing me a brown paper-wrapped rectangle. "But I think you need to be reminded of it now."

"Reminded of what? What's that?"

"It's your present, what does it look like?"

"Can I open it now?"

"No," he deadpans. "I gave it to you to hold awkwardly until—"

I ignore him, quickly undoing the string. We promised each other we'd only do small presents this year and my one is waiting at the bottom of the closet at home (a mini bottle of my favorite Tabasco sauce because he keeps stealing mine).

"I hope it's a letter explaining why you keep using my expensive shampoo when you have your own shampoo."

"It makes my hair shiny." He shrugs. "And it smells like you."

"That's creepy."

"Please. You love it."

I do my best to scowl as I slide the paper off, but I can't keep it up. Especially when I see what's inside.

It's a photo frame, which isn't exactly surprising. But what is surprising is the photo within it. Not one of Andrew's, but rather...

"It's my first review," I say, recognizing it instantly. It's hard not to. I already know the entire thing by heart, I've read it so many times. A polite and cheerful five stars from a Brazilian student visiting the city. I'd been doing my solo tours for a week and had spent every evening checking for updates with my heart in my mouth.

I still remember the moment I got it. It was the middle of the night and I'd woken up like I did a lot during that time, the nerves eating away at me. When I saw the alert on my phone, I almost threw up. When I started reading it, I woke Andrew so he could confirm it was real. There were some happy tears and then pancakes and then forwarding the review to every single person I knew. It had been a good morning.

"I love it, thank you." I rise up to peck his cheek.

"I am, as always, extremely proud of you, Moll. Even if you did pick a panettone over the tiramisu."

"Stop it."

"Probably should have told you that Mam *hates* panettone."

"She does not! She—"

"Molly!"

We both turn as my name rings across the arrivals hall.

The latest batch of passengers has started trickling through the doors and among them is Hannah. Her hair is dyed bright pink this year and is tied up in a high ponytail that bounces as she runs toward us.

My great, stupid Christmas plan is about to begin.

I half expected Andrew to laugh in my face when I suggested we invite both our families to join us in Chicago, but he got immediately excited about the idea. As nice as our little tradition was, neither of us wanted to spend the holiday apart and I think we were still experiencing PTSD from last year. To my even greater surprise, both the Fitzpatricks *and* the Kinsellas immediately said yes, though Andrew's brother Liam is going to stay at home with the kids and spend the holiday with his wife's family.

I really didn't know how everyone was going to fit. Both sets of parents had booked into a hotel, but Christian and Hannah *plus* Zoe and the baby are all staying in our apartment, where we'll be hosting Christmas dinner as well. My initial determination had turned into full-blown panic these last few days as Andrew and I got everything ready, but that starts to fade as Hannah throws her arms around me, the biggest grin on her face.

"It's so great to see you," she squeals, and I smile as I return her embrace.

"Also your brother," Andrew says beside us. "Who is also here."

"I like Molly more," Hannah says, squeezing me tight, but she lets me go to do the same to him as I turn back to the door just in time to see the rest of her family walk through. Hers and mine. Both my dad and Sean are in deep conversation, while Christian is wedged between our mothers, a look of waning patience on his face as they gossip around him.

Zoe appears a moment later, pushing an empty stroller with one hand and holding my nephew in the other.

Baby Tiernan looks about the airport with a kind of apathetic neutrality that morphs into grumpy confusion as my sister bends her head, pointing at me as she whispers in his ear.

"Auntie Molly!" I hear her say as she approaches us. "Remember your Auntie Molly? Auntie— Yeah, he doesn't care."

I smirk, kissing him on the head. "I'll win him over."

"I don't know. He only likes talking animals at the moment. Also spoons? Weirdly into holding spoons all day. I'm hoping it means he's a genius." She hands him over to Hannah, who doesn't bat an eyelid when he immediately starts playing with her hair, and Zoe turns back to give me a hug.

"You're regretting this idea already, aren't you?"

"Totally and completely."

"I've got you," she whispers into my ear, before pulling back to shove something into my hands. "Happy Christmas. Don't open it until you're alone," she adds as I gaze down at my present. "The smell is . . . not good."

"Is it cheese?"

"No," she says, smiling wickedly, and I wince as I slide it into my purse just before I look properly at my parents.

"Zoe?"

"Hmm?"

"What the hell is Mam wearing?"

"I thought I'd make an effort this year," Mam announces as she reaches us. She looks a little flustered, probably due to the oversized, bright red sweater she's wearing. *Granny Clause* is written in block letters across the front. "Your father and I wanted to mark the occasion."

"Then why isn't Dad wearing one?"

"Because he respects himself," Zoe mutters, ignoring the look our mother gives her.

"The girl at the shop said the whole point of a Christmas jumper is that it's ugly," Mam says worriedly, and I smile reassuringly.

"It's not ugly."

"It's a little ugly," Zoe says.

"I think you look brilliant," Andrew says to Mam as he joins us. "And it's the exact shade of the one I got for Molly and me, so you'll fit right in."

My head whips toward him. "Excuse me?"

"Two-part present," he says pleasantly. "Since you loved that so much last year."

"You're joking."

"Am I?"

"We should get this show on the road," Zoe says, extracting Hannah's hair from Tiernan's grasp as she lifts him back into her arms. "And then I need some sugar. If you're making us do Christmas, that means I get sugar."

"We're not wearing matching sweaters," I tell Andrew.

"We'll see."

"Molly!" Zoe calls. "Show. Road. Please."

I send one last warning look at the man I love before facing our party, who are all watching me expectantly.

Oh God.

I suddenly struggle to remember why I ever thought I could pull this off. Two vastly different families who expect two vastly different Christmases? And a *baby*? I mean, this is clearly a mistake. This is a large, expensive mistake that—

Andrew grabs my hand, squeezing tight. "Breathe," he says, his voice pitched so only I can hear him.

We've been working on the whole pessimism thing. Progress is slow.

"All people and bags accounted for," Colleen says kindly when I don't speak. "This was a marvelous idea, Molly."

"Though I suggest Tenerife next year," Christian says, eyeing the freezing Chicago weather outside.

"You ready?" Andrew asks, and I nod, summoning a smile as I take everyone in.

"Hats and scarves on," I announce, gesturing them toward the exit. "Keep together and no straying from the group. If you need the toilet, now is the time to use one and most important of all . . ." I glance up at Andrew. "Keep an eye out for mistletoe," I finish, ignoring his grin. I have to ignore it, or I'll just kiss him and then we'll never get out of here.

He snakes an arm around my waist as we trail our families out of the airport. "Mam's right," he says. "This was an excellent idea."

It was. It is.

And I just need to look at the man walking by my side to remember that even if it doesn't go exactly to plan, fate has a way of working things out in the end.

A LETTER FROM CATHERINE

Dear Reader,

Thank you so much for reading *Holiday Romance*! If you want to keep up-to-date with my latest releases, you can sign up for my newsletter at the following link. Your email address will never be shared and you can unsubscribe at any time. I also heard that very good things will happen to you? Worth a shot, isn't it?

https://catherinewalshbooks.com/newsletter

I love Christmas. I *love* it. When I was a child, it was because there was a magic around it that didn't exist at any other point of the year. Christmas meant food and presents and being shuttled around to various branches of my family so I could get said food and presents. As I got older, it meant days off work. It meant meeting friends in fairy-light-strewn pubs and wearing really nice boots.

Of course, most importantly, it meant spending time with people I love.

Like a lot of people, I moved away to work for a few years and, while I was gone, flying home for Christmas became very important to me. Some years, I could barely afford those flights but, like Andrew, it meant a lot to me to do it. Even though my family would be the first to insist we don't really "do" Christmas, the thought of not spending it with them was unthinkable. The days leading up to the journey would be filled with anticipation and, though I also faced my fair share of delays, I used to love getting to the airport and seeing everyone else excited to see their friends and family. The idea for *Holiday Romance* stems from this time in my life and the conversations I'd have with strangers as we flew home on those cold December nights.

I hope you loved *Holiday Romance* and if you did, I would be very grateful if you could write a review. I'd love to hear what you think, and it makes such a difference helping new readers to discover one of my books for the first time.

I also love hearing from my readers – you can get in touch via my website, or on Twitter or Instagram.

All my best,

Catherine xx

ACKNOWLEDGMENTS

Lots of people supported me in big and small ways while I was writing this book. I will definitely have forgotten some of them and I'm SORRY, but the ones I didn't forget are below.

My biggest thank you goes to all the book bloggers who championed *One Night Only* and *The Rebound*. Your support and love got these stories in front of so many new readers and I am eternally grateful for your reviews, posts, emails, and general awesomeness. You've kept me going through every late-night writing session and or-I-could-just-give-up moment. My greatest hope is that I get to meet you all in person one day to thank you. Preferably, this will happen on some sort of yacht with an elaborate tiered cake.

This book is dedicated to Áine O'Connell, who has been a lifeline for me since we first met and who, despite having no time of her own, always makes time for me. Dr. Siobhan Morissey helped me with all my airplane questions including but not limited to "What happens if there's a big storm?" and "How do planes work?" Poulomi Choudhury is always encouraging AND recommended a printer that actually works and thus will forever have my love. Donna MacKay bought me cake and then traveled an hour out of her way to post my purse back to me when I maybe accidentally sort of lost it in Edinburgh. Tilda McDonald is always on hand to offer career advice and has so far not asked for a commission. Bex Dash let me use her dog's name and gave my books both a

New York AND a Naples photoshoot. Jeanne-Claire Morley organized Molly's Paris itinerary via WhatsApp. Cornelia Conneff helped a clueless city girl with all my farm-related questions. Lucy Baxter responds to every message with unfailing support and Rachel Helsdown continues to be my first and most enthusiastic reader for every project.

Massive love to my editors, Celine Kelly and Isobel Akenhead, for helping to whip this book into shape. Isobel, thank you so much for your passion and belief in these stories. I'm so glad I found my way to you! Thank you as well to the entire team at Bookouture and everyone who worked so hard on getting this book out into the world.

As always, second biggest thank you to me, who once again wrote a whole book and didn't even have an emotional breakdown about it.

Yet.

ABOUT THE AUTHOR

Catherine Walsh was born and raised in Ireland. She lived in London for a few years before returning to Dublin, where she now lives between the mountains and the sea. When not writing, she is trying and failing to not kill her houseplants.

To find out more, visit:

catherinewalshbooks.com
@CatWalshWriter
@CatWalshWriter
@CatWalshWriter

RAISING READERS
Books Build Bright Futures

Thank you for reading this book and for being a reader of books in general. As an author, I am so grateful to share being part of a community of readers with you, and I hope you will join me in passing our love of books on to the next generation of readers.

Did you know that reading for enjoyment is the single biggest predictor of a child's future happiness and success?

More than family circumstances, parents' educational background, or income, reading impacts a child's future academic performance, emotional well-being, communication skills, economic security, ambition, and happiness.

Studies show that kids reading for enjoyment in the US is in rapid decline:

- In 2012, 53% of 9-year-olds read almost every day. Just 10 years later, in 2022, the number had fallen to 39%.
- In 2012, 27% of 13-year-olds read for fun daily. By 2023, that number was just 14%.

Together, we can commit to **Raising Readers** and change this trend. How?

- Read to children in your life daily.
- Model reading as a fun activity.
- Reduce screen time.
- Start a family, school, or community book club.
- Visit bookstores and libraries regularly.
- Listen to audiobooks.
- Read the book before you see the movie.
- Encourage your child to read aloud to a pet or stuffed animal.
- Give books as gifts.
- Donate books to families and communities in need.

Books build bright futures, and **Raising Readers** is our shared responsibility.

For more information, visit **JoinRaisingReaders.com**

Sources: National Endowment for the Arts, National Assessment of Educational Progress, WorldBookDay.org, Nielsen BookData's 2023 "Understanding the Children's Book Consumer"